Taslima Nasrin was born on 25 August 1962 in Mymensingh, Bangladesh. She took an MBBS degree from Mymensingh Medical College and practised as a government doctor for a few years. She began her literary career by publishing poetry and later started writing a syndicated newspaper column in Bangladesh, as well as novels and essays.

Taslima Nasrin was the recipient of the Ananda Puraskar, Calcutta, in 1992 and the Natosabha Puruskar, Dhaka, in 1993.

Taslima Nasrin lives in Dhaka.

*

Tutul Gupta (née Ray) was born in 1956. She went to Modern High School, Calcutta and later took an MA degree in English from the University of Delhi. She lived in Bangladesh from 1978–79 and taught in a leading school there. She has translated several children's classics and also directs plays for children.

Tutul Gupta is married with two children and lives in Calcutta.

Lajja

SHAME

Taslima Nasrin

Translated from the Bengali
by Tutul Gupta

PENGUIN BOOKS

Penguin Books India (P) Ltd., 210, Chiranjiv Tower, 43 Nehru Place, New Delhi 110 019, India
Penguin Books Ltd., 27 Wrights Lane, London W8 5TZ, UK
Penguin Books USA Inc., 375 Hudson Street, New York, NY 10014, USA
Penguin Books Australia Ltd., Ringwood, Victoria, Australia
Penguin Books Canada Ltd., 10 Alcorn Avenue, Suite 300, Toronto, Ontario M4V 3B2, Canada
Penguin Books (NZ) Ltd., 182-190 Wairau Road, Auckland 10, New Zealand

First Bengali edition published in Bangladesh 1993
Revised and updated edition published by Ananda Publishers Pvt. Ltd. 1993
Copyright © Taslima Nasrin 1993

This translation first published by Penguin Books India 1994
Copyright © Penguin Books India 1994

10 9 8

Typeset in Palatino by Digital Technologies and Printing Solutions, New Delhi

To the people of the Indian subcontinent

Let Another Name for Religion be Humanism

Contents

Contents

Preface

I detest fundamentalism and communalism. This was the reason I wrote *Lajja* soon after the demolition of the Babri Masjid in Ayodhya on 6 December 1992. The book, which took me seven days to write, deals with the persecution of Hindus, a religious minority in Bangladesh, by the Muslims who are in the majority. It is disgraceful that the Hindus in my country were hunted by the Muslims after the destruction of the Babri Masjid. All of us who love Bangladesh should feel ashamed that such a terrible thing could happen in our beautiful country. The riots that took place in 1992 in Bangladesh are the responsibility of us all, and we are all to blame. *Lajja* is a document of our collective defeat.

Lajja was published in February 1993 in Bangladesh and sold over 60,000 copies before it was banned by the government five months later—their excuse was that it was disturbing the communal peace. In September that year a fatwa was issued against me by a fundamentalist organization and a reward was offered for my death. There have been marches on the streets of Dhaka by communalists clamouring for my life. But none of these things have shaken my determination to continue the battle against religious persecution, genocide and communalism. Bangladesh is my motherland. We gained our independence from Pakistan at the cost of three million lives. That sacrifice will be betrayed if we allow ourselves to be ruled by religious extremism. The mullahs who would murder me will kill everything progressive in Bangladesh if they are allowed to prevail. It is my duty to try to protect my beautiful country from them and I call on all those who share my values to help me defend my rights.

The disease of religious fundamentalism is not restricted to Bangladesh alone and it must be fought at every turn. For myself, I am not afraid of any challenge or threat to my life. I will continue to write and protest persecution and discrimination. I am convinced that the only way the fundamentalist forces can be stopped is if all of us who are secular and humanistic join together and fight their malignant influence. I, for one, will not be silenced.

*

While this is a novel and all the characters in the narrative are the product of my own imagination, and any resemblance they bear to actual people, living or dead, is entirely coincidental, I have also included in the text numerous incidents, actual historical events, facts and statistics. I have verified these to the best of my ability; my sources of information include *Ekota, Azker Kagoz, Bhorer Kagoz, Glani* (The disgrace), "Communal Persecution and Repression in Bangladesh", "Communal Discrimination in Bangladesh: Facts and Documents", and "Parishad Barta".

Dhaka   *Taslima Nasrin*
March 1994

Chronology of Events

- 1947—The subcontinent was divided into India and Pakistan on 15 August 1947, the day the British left India. Bengal was partitioned as well, as a result of which East Bengal became a part of Pakistan.
- 1952—In East Bengal (then known as East Pakistan) a Language Movement was launched to declare Bengali as the national language.
- 1966—A six-point charter of demands was presented in order to attain self-rule.
- 1969—The people of East Pakistan revolted against the dictatorial regime of Pakistan.
- 1971—On 26 March 1971, East Pakistan attained independence and became the sovereign state of Bangladesh. However, the struggle continued for a further nine months, culminating in the complete ouster of Pakistani troops on 16 December 1971, which is celebrated as Bijoya Dibas or Victory Day.
- 1975—The government of Sheikh Mujibur Rahman was toppled in a military coup.
- 1978—The Constitution of Bangladesh, which had enshrined secularism as one of its main principles, was modified to make Islam the State religion.
- 1990—As a result of the Babri Masjid dispute in Ayodhya, Uttar Pradesh, large-scale communal disturbances took place in Bangladesh.
- 1992—In the aftermath of the demolition of Babri Masjid on 6 December 1992, communal riots began in Bangladesh and the minority community in the country was severely persecuted.

Day One

Suranjan lay on his bed. Every now and again his sister Nilanjana, whom they all called Maya, would come into the room and say, 'Dada, aren't you going to wake up and do something before it is too late?' Suranjan knew that Maya wanted him to look for a place where they could go into temporary hiding from the danger that threatened them. But Suranjan was in a rebellious mood. Why should he flee his home simply because his name was Suranjan Dutta? Was it necessary for his family—Sudhamoy, his father, Kironmoyee, his mother and Nilanjana, his sister—to run away like fugitives just because of their names? Would they have to take refuge in the homes of Kamal, Belal or Haider just as they had done two years back? He remembered that day—30 October 1990—clearly. Kamal, who lived in Eskaton, had feared that something would happen to them and had come all the way to their house and urged them to leave with him. There had been no lack of hospitality in Kamal's house. They had had eggs and toast for breakfast, fish and rice for lunch and spent long, lazy evenings on the lawns. They had slept peacefully and comfortably on thick dunlopillo mattresses and had altogether had a glorious time! But no matter how pleasant their stay at their friend's house, it had provided no answers to the basic question: Why had it at all been necessary to take refuge in Kamal's house? It was true that Kamal was an old friend of Suranjan's and friends did visit each other but not in such circumstances. Why did he have to seek refuge in Kamal's home? Why did he have to run away from his own home? Kamal had never had reason to do so. And wasn't this country as much his as it was Kamal's? Then why was he seemingly deprived of his rights, and why was his motherland turning her back on him? Why could he not say to her, I am a son of this soil, please see that no harm comes to me!

Suranjan stayed in bed, thinking these thoughts, and ignoring

1

his sister. She paced up and down the room, and then began wandering aimlessly around the house. She was thinking that no one seemed to realize that something had to be done before something awful happened to all of them. On television, CNN had shown in vivid detail the demolition of the Babri Masjid on 6 December 1992. Scenes from the incident were still being shown and Sudhamoy and Kironmoyee sat riveted to their seats in front of the TV. As they watched the destruction unfold before their eyes, they too were hoping that Suranjan would take them to a Muslim friend's house. But Suranjan had decided he would do nothing. And should Kamal or some other Muslim friend come to take them away, he would say: 'I won't leave my home whatever the circumstances.'

These scenes in the Dutta household were taking place on the 7th of December. The previous afternoon, a sinister darkness had come pelting down on the banks of the Saryu river in the city of Ayodhya. On that fateful day, a mob of so-called kar sevaks had demolished a mosque which was more than four hundred and fifty years old. According to the Vishwa Hindu Parishad (VHP), the mosque was the birthplace of Rama and therefore the religious property of Hindus. Sectarian volunteers had decided to initiate a programme of kar seva (or cleaning up) of the area in and around the Babri Masjid in order to sanctify the surroundings. Barely twenty-five minutes before the so-called act of kar seva could commence, disaster had struck. The kar sevaks had begun to ruthlessly demolish the mosque. The entire drama had unfolded in the presence of high ranking officers and ministers of the Vishwa Hindu Parishad, the Bharatiya Janata Party (BJP), the Rashtriya Swayamsevak Sangh (RSS) and the Bajrang Dal. The officers and men of the Central Reserve Police Force (CRPF), Provincial Armed Constabulary (PAC) and the Uttar Pradesh police had stood by without moving a muscle as the destruction of the mosque had continued. At two forty-five in the afternoon one of the domes was destroyed. At four, the second was smashed and by four forty-five the third dome was also broken to pieces by the fanatical kar sevaks. In the process of demolishing the massive structure, four kar sevaks were buried under the debris and many hundreds were seriously injured. All this and more was reported in minute detail in the newspaper Suranjan was browsing through. A banner headline screamed: BABRI MASJID DEMOLISHED.

Suranjan had never been to Ayodhya, nor had he seen the Babri Masjid. How could he have when he had not even stepped out of Bangladesh? Whether the demolished structure was the birthplace of Rama or a sacred mosque was a matter of little significance to Suranjan. But it was evident to him that the demolition of the sixteenth-century edifice had struck a savage blow to the sentiments of Muslims in India and elsewhere. The act of destruction had damaged the Hindu community as well for it had been nothing less than an attack on 'international harmony and the collective conscience of the people' in the words of the newspaper. The report continued in this vein:

> Needless to say, in Bangladesh too, the reaction to this event is bound to create frantic waves of religious hysteria. Temples will be smashed and levelled to the ground, Hindu homes will be burnt and their shops will be looted. At the instigation of the BJP, the kar sevaks broke down the Babri Masjid only to strengthen the Muslim clerics of Bangladesh. Did the BJP, VHP and their associates, harbour the notion that their insane actions in Ayodhya would cause a reaction only within the geographical boundaries of India? In India the entire ordeal has already given birth to widespread communal riots. Five hundred people have died. Six hundred, maybe even a thousand. The number of deaths increases by the hour. Did the devout Hindus, who were intending to look after the interests of their religion and their community, realize that there were almost twenty-five million Hindus living in Bangladesh too? Not only in Bangladesh, in almost every country in West Asia, there is a fair scattering of Hindus. Did the Hindu fanatics ever consider what severe adversities they might have to face? As a political party, the BJP should have been responsible enough to realize that India cannot be isolated from the rest of the world. If a malignant situation has taken form in India, the pain caused by it will be felt all over the world and most certainly by her immediate neighbours.

Suranjan shut his eyes, then opened them again for Maya was shaking him and saying, 'Aren't you going to do something? I hope you realize that our parents are depending on you to keep us safe.'

Suranjan yawned, stretched lazily and said, 'You go if you want to. I am not moving one step out of this house.'

'And what about them?'

'I don't know.'

'What if something should happen?'

'What can happen?!'

'What if they raid our house? Burn it down?'

'Let them.'

'You mean you'll sit and watch all this happening?'

'No, I won't sit, I'll lie down.'

Suranjan lit a cigarette on an empty stomach and longed for a cup of tea. Kironmoyee normally brought him tea in the morning but she hadn't done so today. It was pointless asking Maya. All that the girl could think about was escape to some safe place. She would scream the house down if he asked her for some tea. He could have got up and made a cup of tea himself, but he felt too lazy. In the other room, the television blared on. He was not in the least inclined to sit and stare at the CNN coverage. Suddenly he heard Maya yell again and again from the other room: 'Dada just lies down and reads the papers. He does not seem to have a care in the world.'

It was not as though Suranjan did not understand how critical the situation was. A crowd of people could enter the house at any moment to loot and plunder and even raze it to the ground. In the circumstances, neither Kamal nor Haider would refuse them shelter. But he felt ashamed to go running to them. Maya continued to protest loudly. 'If none of you have any intentions of moving out, I may as well leave on my own. I'll go to Parul's house and stay there till the situation improves. I don't suppose Dada has plans to take us anywhere. He may not have the will to live, but I certainly do.' This last despairing outburst seemed to indicate that Maya had finally realized that her brother wasn't going to do anything to find them shelter and that if she wanted to find a temporary refuge she would have to do it herself.

On his part, Suranjan still lay in bed thinking. Even if they moved, would they be safe. They had been lucky in October 1990, for they had escaped the terror and destruction of that time. He reviewed in his mind the events of that month.

- A mob had set fire to the Dhakeshwari temple. The police had not made the slightest attempt to stop them. The main temple where prayers were offered was burnt to ashes and the dance hall of the temple had been damaged as well.
- The Shiva temple, the guest rooms and the ancestral home of

Shridham Ghosh were all razed to the ground.

- The main temple of the Gouriya monastery, the temple for devotional dance as well as its guest rooms were demolished. Valuables inside the temple were looted.
- The main temple inside the Madhav Gouriya monastery was destroyed.
- The Jaikali temple was smashed to smithereens.
- A room situated on the boundary wall of the Brahmo Samaj was blown up. Inside the Ram-Sita temple an exquisitely carved throne was totally destroyed. Needless to say, the temple's sanctum sanctorum itself was badly damaged.
- The monastery at Naya Bazaar was demolished, so too was the temple at Bongraam with crowbars.
- At the very entrance of Shankhari Bazaar a number of Hindu shops were looted and burnt. Sheila Bitaan, Surma Traders, saloons, tyre shops, laundries, Mita Marble, Saha Cabinet, restaurants . . . nothing Hindu was spared. As a matter of fact, from the entrance of the Shankhari Bazaar there were ruins as far as the eye could see.
- At Dhamrai, the Shoni temple, a part of the gymnasium complex, was plundered.
- The homes of at least twenty-five families were incinerated by two to three hundred communal thugs. At Lakshmi Bazaar, the walls of the Bir Bhadra temple were broken down and everything inside was destroyed.
- The shops selling gold and umbrellas on Islampur Road were also put to the torch.
- The famous Maran Chand sweetshop on Nawabpur Road was completely destroyed. Maran Chand's shop in Purana Paltan also suffered the same fate.
- The image of the goddess Kali in Rai Bazaar was damaged beyond recognition.
- In Sutrapur, Hindu shops were not only looted but had to suffer the added indignity of having their signboards replaced by Muslim ones.
- Similarly, Ghose and Sons, a sweetshop in Nawabpur, was initially looted—later a banner of the Nawabpur Youth Union Club was hung up on the shop front.
- The Botthali temple in Thathari Bazaar was destroyed.
- Also in Nawabpur, an old shop called Raamdhon Poshari was gutted.
- Just a few yards away from the Babu Bazaar police outpost, another sweetshop called Shuklaal Mishthana Bhandar was plundered.

- The showroom and factory of Jatin and Company were destroyed.
- The ancient Shamp mandir was partially damaged.
- At the crossing of Sadar Ghat, Ratan Sarkar's market was looted and later destroyed.

Suranjan's mind ticked off one by one the places that had been ravaged in the 1990 carnage. Was this what was known as rioting? Was it possible to refer to the events of 1990 as riots? And did the word riot mean one community's ruthless victimization of another? No, such a phenomenon could not be dismissed as rioting. What had actually happened was that one community had invaded the sanctity and privacy of another community in a cold-blooded, remorseless way. This was nothing short of tyranny and oppression. Sunlight filtered through the window and bathed Suranjan's forehead but it was the mild winter sun and he felt no discomfort. Suranjan continued to lie in bed and hope for tea.

*

In the other room, his father Sudhamoy also thought about the past. When he was a young man all his aunts and uncles had begun to leave Bangladesh one by one. As the steam trains pulled out from Mymensingh on their way to Phulbaria, the guard's whistle would invariably be accompanied by the heartbroken wails of people leaving the only country they knew. As their neighbours left, they would call out to Sudhamoy's father: 'Sukumar, come, let us go away. This is the homeland of the Muslims. Life is uncertain in this country.' But Sukumar Dutta was determined not to betray the values he had always upheld. He would say, 'If there is no security in your own country, where in this world can we go looking for it? I cannot run away from my homeland. You go if you want to. I am not leaving the property of my forefathers. Coconut and betel nut plantations, yards and yards of rich paddy fields, a house that stands on over two bighas of land . . . . I cannot leave all this to become a refugee on the platforms of Sealdah station.' At that time Sudhamoy was about nineteen years old. Most of his college friends were migrating to India, and to a man they warned him, 'Your father is going to regret this decision sooner or later.'

Sudhamoy, however, had learnt to say like his father, 'Why should I leave my homeland and go somewhere else? If I live it will be on this soil, and if I die it will be in the very same place.' But the inexorable migration continued to take place and the number of students in the colleges gradually dwindled. Those who had not left in 1947 were now making preparations to leave. And so it was that Sudhamoy studied with only a handful of Muslim boys and few poor Hindu students at Lytton Medical College from which in course of time he earned a medical degree.

In 1952, Sudhamoy was an energetic young man of twenty-four. On the streets of Dhaka at the time, there was a great deal of nervous excitement as the Bengalis agitated for the use of Bengali as the national language. Mohammed Ali Jinnah, the Pakistani head of state, however refused to accept the demand and declared that Urdu would be the sole national language of Pakistan. The young, brave and politically conscious Bengalis of East Pakistan (as Bangladesh was then known) were not deterred, however, and rose in protest against Jinnah's decision. The city roads were awash with their blood but no one backed down. Bengali, they maintained, must be the national language. Sudhamoy, too, was charged by the spirit of revolt. He participated in and often headed the processions demanding 'We want Bengali . . . .' He was present the day Rafiq Salaam Barkat Jabbar was shot by the police. And as the protests swelled there was every likelihood that he too would be shot and declared a martyr.

He participated in the 1969 National Movement as well. The Pakistani strongman Ayub Khan's police forces had standing instructions to fire at processions. Refusing to be cowed down by the threat the Bengalis carried on their crusade for the implementation of an eleven-point Charter of Demands. Alamgir Mansur Mintu was shot dead by the police and Sudhamoy carried his dead body on the streets of Mymensingh. Hundreds of grief-stricken Bengali-speaking Pakistanis followed him, silently gearing themselves for the inevitable imposition of martial law . . .

The Language Movement of 1952, the United Front elections of 1954, the Education Movement of 1962, the Six Clause Movement of 1966, the movement protesting against the Agartala Conspiracy case, the General Elections of 1970 and the Freedom Movement of 1971 . . . were all rallying points for the politically conscious Bengali youth of the country; every new agitation only underlined the fact that division of the country on the basis of the two-nation theory was an incorrect move. Maulana Abul Kalam Azad had said:

> It is one of the greatest frauds on the people to suggest that religious affinity can unite areas which are geographically, economically, linguistically and culturally different. It is true that Islam sought to establish a society which transcends racial, linguistic, economic and political frontiers. History has however proved that after the first few decades or at the most after the first century, Islam was not able to unite all the Muslim countries on the basis of Islam alone.

Jinnah was also aware of the fact that the implementation of the two-nation theory was actually an exercise in futility. When Mountbatten was planning the divisions of Punjab and Bengal, he had himself said, 'A man is Punjabi or Bengali before he is Hindu or Muslim. They share a common history, language, culture and economy. You will cause endless bloodshed and trouble.'

Starting from 1947 and stretching upto 1971, the Bengalis witnessed wave upon wave of bloodshed and trouble, all of which culminated in the Freedom Movement of 1971. An independence that was earned at the cost of three million Bengali lives, proved that religion could not be the basis of a national identity. Language, culture, and history on the other hand were able to create the foundation on which to build a sense of nationality. Pakistan was initially able to begin forging a common bond between the Muslims in Punjab and the Muslims in Bengal. But both Hindu and Muslim Bengalis soon showed up the fallacy of the two-nation distinction when they began balking at the prospect of making major compromises with the Muslims of Pakistan.

In 1971, Sudhamoy was a doctor on the staff of the S. K. Hospital in Mymensingh. He was a busy man, both at home and at work. In the evenings he practised in a shop in Swadeshi Bazaar. At this time, Kironmoyee was preoccupied with their second child, a baby of six months. Suranjan, their son, was then twelve years old. Sudhamoy had to shoulder a lot of responsibility, both in terms of caring for his young family as well as running his hospital virtually single-handedly. Occasionally, when he had the time, he would go to Shariff's place to meet his friends. Around the 8th or 9th of March, his friends, Shariff, Faizul, Bablu and Nemai, had gone to the racecourse grounds to listen to the speech made by Sheikh Mujibur Rahman. At about midnight, on their way back, they knocked on Sudhamoy's door in Brahmapalli. Apparently, Mujib had said, 'If even one more gun shot is fired, and if one more of my men is killed, then my request to all of you is to convert each of your homes into forts. Accumulate all that you have to confront the enemy whenever the need arises. This time it is a struggle for freedom, a struggle for independence.' Shaking with excitement, his friends had said, 'Sudha-da, it's time we did something!' Sudhamoy knew that nothing could be achieved by sitting and waiting for events to take their course, but he had a family and a job to think about, so he did nothing. Then, on the 25th of March, when Pakistani soldiers pounced upon the Bengalis totally unawares, his friends had come back and knocked on his door a second time. 'We must go to war,' they had whispered, 'there is no other way out.' Sudhamoy found himself in a dilemma. His family was his main concern now; also he was too old to go to war. But his friends' request kept nagging at him. He was unable to concentrate on his work at the hospital. Finally, he spoke to Kironmoyee, asking her if she could manage on her own, should he have to go away somewhere. Terrified, Kironmoyee had said, 'Let's go away to India. All our neighbours are leaving one by one.' This was a fact, for Sudhamoy had himself seen Sukanto Chattopadhyaya, Sudhanshu Haldar, Nirmalendu Bhowmick and Ranjan Chakraborty leave. The exodus of 1947 was being repeated, and Sudhamoy was furious. He cursed all these people and called them cowards. Some days after this, Nemai said to him, 'Sudha-da, the army is out on the streets. They are catching Hindus and killing them. Come, let us run away.' In 1947 his father, Sukumar Dutta, had been firm in his decision not to leave the country. Sudhamoy assumed the same stance and told Nemai, 'You go if you want to . . . . I am not running away from my home. We'll kill those Pakistani dogs and get our freedom. Come back if you can, at that time.'

Eventually, it was decided that Kironmoyee and their children would stay in Faijlu's village home in Phulpur, while Sudhamoy would accompany Shariff, Bablu and Faizul to Nalitabari. But before he could put this plan into action he was caught by the army. He had gone out to buy a lock even though he knew he was on a dangerous mission. The army was out on the streets and no Bengali was safe. Tense and excited, he crept through the deserted city. Only a few shops were half open. Suddenly, three men appeared in front of him and shouted at him to halt. One of them caught him by the scruff of the neck and asked him in Urdu, 'What is your name?'

Sudhamoy did not know what name would be appropriate for him to take. He remembered that Kironmoyee's friends had warned her that if she wanted to live she must change her name to something like Fatema Akhtar. Sudhamoy realized his Hindu name would not go down well with his tormentors and he forced himself to forget his own name, his father Sukumar's name and his grandfather Jyotirmoy's name. Despite this he was shocked to hear his own voice uttering the name, Shirajuddin Hussain. One of the men said gruffly, 'Open your lungi.' Before Sudhamoy could do anything about it, they yanked his lungi off themselves. With blinding clarity he saw at that moment just why Nemai, Sudhanshu and Ranjan had run away . . . .

Ever since India had been divided into two Pakistans and one India, many Hindus had deserted their homes in East Pakistan for India. They had been able to do this because the division of the subcontinent on communal lines had left the borders open for Hindus to escape to India. The rich and the educated middle class left in droves. According to the 1981 census, the Hindus in Bangladesh amounted to 10.57 million or 12.1 per cent of the total population. In the twelve years since then, this number had expanded to roughly twenty or twenty-five million Hindus. Officially, the number of Hindus in the country was deliberately understated. By Sudhamoy's own estimation, at the present time, in the early 1990s, Hindus constituted around twenty per cent of the population.

In 1901, 33.1 per cent of the population of East Bengal was Hindu. In 1911, this figure went down to 31.5 per cent. In 1921, it was 30.6 per cent. In 1931, it had further decreased to 29.4 per cent and in 1941 it was only twenty-eight per cent. It was to decrease further. Within ten years after the division of India in 1947, the percentage of Hindus went down from twenty-eight per cent to only twenty-two per cent. In ten years there had been a greater reduction in the number of Hindus than there had been in the previous forty years. During the Pakistani regime, Hindus kept migrating to India. According to the 1961 records, the percentage of Hindus had gone down to 18.5 per cent, and in 1974 it was only 13.5 per cent. However, after Bangladesh achieved independence, the haemorrhaging of the Hindus from the country was somewhat stanched. By 1981, Hindus constituted 12.1 per cent of the country and it was logical to conclude that the number of Hindus leaving their ancestral homes had grown less in number. But for how long could this be expected to continue, especially after the troubles in the years leading up to the 1990 riots and now this in 1992! Were the Hindus now expected to leave the country?

A pain had started up on the left side of Sudhamoy's chest. It was an old, recurring ache. His head hurt too. Perhaps his blood pressure had increased. On the television, CNN continued its coverage of the 6 December disaster. However, the Babri Masjid was no longer shown, every time mention was made of it. Sudhamoy guessed this was being done at the instance of the government which was obviously trying to protect the Hindus from the anger of the majority community. But people who were used to reacting violently at the slightest provocation surely didn't need to wait for CNN's TV reportage to begin rioting. He felt a sharp twinge in his chest; he rubbed it to ease the pain and lay down on his bed. Maya still paced the veranda restlessly. Sudhamoy knew his daughter wanted to flee somewhere, anywhere, but how would that be possible as long as Suranjan refused to get up? Sudhamoy stared helplessly at the sun-bathed veranda outside on which Maya's shadow had lengthened. Kironmoyee sat still, her eyes filled with plaintive entreaty, 'Let us live, let us go away,' they seemed to say. Where could Sudhamoy go if he decided to leave his home? At this age would he be able to run around as he had done earlier? In the past he had never spared himself. He was always in the thick of everything and invariably headed local groups protesting against the Pakistani rulers. The bonds of hearth

11

and home had not been able to keep him from such involvement. Where was he to get that kind of strength today? He had hoped that in the independent and secular State of Bangladesh, Hindus would enjoy the same political, economic, cultural and religious privileges that the Muslims enjoyed. Unfortunately, the principle of religious impartiality had slowly lost its place in the country's scheme of things. Today, the national religion of Bangladesh was Islam. And, the fundamentalists who had once opposed the Freedom Movement in 1971 and had maintained a low profile during the struggle, now ruled the roost, organizing processions and meetings. It was the same group of people who were behind the ruthless crusade against Hindus in 1990, these were the hooligans who had broken Hindu temples and burnt down Hindu shops and homes. Sudhamoy shut his eyes. He did not know what would happen this time around. The one thing that was certain was this: As the Babri Masjid had been destroyed by Hindu fanatics it would be the Hindus in Bangladesh who would have to suffer. Hindus like Sudhamoy had not been spared by the Muslim fundamentalists in 1990, so why should they be spared in 1992? And so they would have to flee like rats! Just because they were Hindu? Just because the Hindus in India had broken the Babri Masjid? Why should he be held responsible for all this? Once again he turned to look at Maya's shadow on the veranda. It never seemed to keep still. It suddenly disappeared as Maya entered the room. Her enchanting, dark face was full of anxiety and beaded with sweat. She said loudly, 'You people can stay and rot in this place, I am leaving.'

Kironmoyee said sternly, 'Where do you think you are going?'

Maya, dismissing the threat in her mother's voice, combed out her hair in brisk strokes. 'I am going to Parul's house . . . I can't help it if you don't want to survive. I don't think Dada intends to leave this place either.'

'And what are you going to do with your name? Nilanjana is a dead giveaway.' Sudhamoy said remembering, even as he spoke, the time he had called himself Shirajuddin.

Maya remained unmoved. '*La Ilaha illalahu Muhammadun Rasulullah* is all that you need to say to become a Muslim. That's just what I'll do, and I'll call myself Feroza Begum.'

'Maya!' Kironmoyee said in anguish.

Maya glared at her mother, as if to say there was nothing wrong about her proposed course of action. She seemed unmoved by the sadness in Kironmoyee's face. Sudhamoy sighed helplessly and looked from Maya to Kironmoyee and back again. He could understand Maya's restlessness. Only twenty-one, she had not witnessed the division of the country in 1947, nor had she seen the riots of 1950 or 1964. She had not seen the country attain freedom in 1971. All she had known from the time she was very young was that the national religion was Islam and that she and her family belonged to the Hindu minority which often had to make compromises with the system. And all she had really faced was the trauma of the riots of 1990 and this had been enough for her to take the decision that she did not want to throw away her life . . . . Sudhamoy's eyes glazed over as the pain in his chest increased and pushed all thoughts of Maya from his mind.

*

Suranjan's thirst for tea remained unquenched. He got up and went to the bathroom. He would have preferred to have had his first cup of tea before he brushed his teeth but it was not to be. There was no sound or sign of Maya. Had the girl really gone away? Suranjan took his time to brush his teeth. The whole house seemed ominously tense, almost as if someone was about to die. It seemed as though a thunderbolt would explode at any moment— symbolizing as it were the death that each one of them appeared to be waiting for. Still thirsting for his tea, Suranjan walked into Sudhamoy's room. Propping himself comfortably on the bed, he asked, 'Where is Maya?' No one answered Suranjan's question. Kironmoyee, who was sitting abstractedly by the window, got up and went to the kitchen. Sudhamoy, who had been staring listlessly at the ceiling, shut his eyes and turned over in his bed. Nobody seemed to want to pay the slightest attention to Suranjan. It began to dawn on Suranjan that perhaps he had failed in his responsibility towards his parents and sister. He had been expected to find a refuge for his family, but he had been unable to do so, or more appropriately, had chosen not to do so.

Suranjan knew that Maya was in love with a young man called Jahangir and was sure she would go out with him if she had the opportunity. And now that she had left the house, who was there to stop her? Among the more liberal Muslims, it was fashionable to enquire after the Hindus every time a riot broke out in the city. Jahangir would almost certainly check to see if Maya was all right. In the event that this happened, Maya would probably consider herself very fortunate and might even decide to marry him out of a sense of gratitude! The boy was two classes her senior and Suranjan had the nagging apprehension that he would not, in the end, marry Maya. Judging from his own experience, this sort of inter-religious marriage in Bangladesh was near impossible. He had been set to marry Parveen, but the marriage had not taken place when he had refused to comply with Parveen's demand to convert to Islam. He had said it was not necessary for either of them to convert. In addition to this hurdle, Parveen's family had not approved of her Hindu suitor; they had finally married their daughter off to a Muslim businessman. She had cried her heart out in protest, but had eventually acquiesced in her family's wishes.

Suranjan stared regretfully out at their small veranda. Theirs was a rented house: no courtyard, no place at all to wander around barefoot. Kironmoyee came in with a cup of tea. As he took the tea from his mother, Suranjan said casually, 'It is already the month of December, but it's hardly cold enough. I remember how I used to love drinking date fruit juice on winter mornings.'

Kironmoyee sighed and said, 'This is a rented house. Where will you get fresh fruit juice? The house in which I had planted all kinds of saplings was sold for a pittance.'

Suranjan sipped his tea, and thought wistfully about the fresh juice that the gardener would bring down from the date palms. Standing beneath the trees, Maya and he would watch him excitedly, as they shivered in the winter cold. Every time they spoke, a white vapour would escape from their mouths. All those lush green fields in which they used to run about, the orchards full of mangoes, jamun, jack-fruit, guavas, betel nuts and coconuts . . . . And now it was all gone. And to think of the times without number Sudhamoy had told them, 'This is the homestead of your forefathers. Never leave this place and go away.'

Unfortunately, Sudhamoy had been compelled to sell the property. One day when Maya was only six years old, she had got lost on her way home from school. They couldn't find her anywhere in town. She had not gone to any of their relatives' homes, nor was she visiting with friends and acquaintances. Needless to say, there was tremendous tension and anxiety in the house. Perhaps the loafers who hung around the gates of Edward School gossiping and idling away their time, had kidnapped her. Two days later Maya had come back home all by herself. She had been unable to provide any clues as to where she had been or who had kidnapped her. For two whole months after the incident she had behaved in a strange manner. She slept fitfully and would wake up abruptly in the middle of the night. She was afraid to meet people. At times, at night, people would stone their house. They began to receive anonymous letters that threatened to kidnap Maya again unless a ransom was paid. Sudhamoy had gone to the police. The men on duty at the police station had made a routine record of the complaint and had taken no further action. There were other sorts of aggravation. The local boys would invade their orchard, pluck the fruit from the trees, trample the vegetable garden, strip the flowers from the bushes and there was nothing they could do. Realizing the futility of protesting to officialdom, Sudhamoy would complain to his neighbours. The usual reply was: 'What can we do? This is how it has always been. There won't be any improvement.' Suranjan had tried to round up some friends to deal with the rowdies, but Sudhamoy would not have any of it. Instead, he decided to leave Mymensingh altogether. He would sell his house. There was, in fact, another reason to sell. For a long time now, all sorts of litigation had been going on in regard to the house. His neighbour, Shaukat Ali, had tried to fake documents and occupy a sizeable part of the property and Sudhamoy was getting tired of battling him in court. Suranjan, however, disagreed with his father. He did not feel the house should be sold. At that time he was a student in college, bright and full of ideas. He had been elected a member of the college governing body on behalf of the Students Union. If he had so wished he could have bashed up the hooligans who were bothering them. Sudhamoy, however, restrained his son, for he was by now determined to sell his property and move to Dhaka. He explained to his family that his medical practice was suffering as patients hardly came any more to Swadeshi Bazaar where he had his practice. The few who came were Hindus and very poor, so poor that he felt ashamed to ask them for fees. Understanding his father's sorry state of mind, Suranjan had not forced the issue.

But he still remembered the vast property he had grown up on, the two bighas of land on which their home had stood. He still remembered the day on which their huge house, which was worth at least one million takas, had been sold off to Raisuddin Sahib for a mere two hundred thousand takas.

On the day they were to leave, when Sudhamoy had said to Kironmoyee, 'Come, come let's get our things together, we have to leave,' his wife had fallen to the ground and cried pitifully. Suranjan had found it hard to believe that they were actually leaving their ancestral home. The place of his birth, the place where he had spent his childhood playing in the fields, the place by which the Brahmaputra flowed, the place where all his friends were . . . . He had not wanted to leave all this and go away. Even Maya, who had been the most compelling reason for Sudhamoy to make the decision, was unwilling to go. She had shaken her head vigorously and said, 'I don't want to leave Sufia and go away . . .' Sufia was her school friend and lived in the neighbourhood. The two would play for hours every evening with their dolls, pots and pans. They were extremely close to each another . . . . And what of Sudhamoy himself? Although he had not wavered in his decision to leave the house, he felt very sorry for he had a great deal of affection for his place of birth. But he had said, 'This life is short. I want to live peacefully with my children for the rest of my life.' But was it possible to exist peacefully anywhere at all? Probably not, Suranjan had thought.

Sudhamoy had heaved a sigh of relief on reaching Dhaka, despite the fact that it was in independent Dhaka, that he had had to finally forgo his dhuti and wear pajamas instead. After a while Suranjan had begun to understand his father's predicament. Circumstances had driven him to this situation and there was no way in which he or his son could break through the one insurmountable barrier that stood between them and a peaceful life.

Deep in these thoughts, Suranjan lounged on the bed staring at the sun that flooded the veranda. All of a sudden his repose was interrupted by the noise of a fast approaching procession. As it drew closer, Suranjan strained to decipher the slogans that were being shouted. Sudhamoy and Kironmoyee were also tensely alert as they tried to interpret the agitated shouts. Suranjan noticed Kironmoyee get up and shut the windows. Even so, as the procession passed by their house, they could clearly hear the voices say, 'Let us catch a Hindu or two, eat them in the mornings and evenings too . . .' Suranjan saw his father shiver. His mother stood with her back to the window that she had just shut. Suranjan remembered that they had used the same slogan in 1990. Who were *they*? Ironically, they were boys from the neighbourhood! Jabbar, Ramjan, Aalamgir, Kabir and Abedin! They were all friends who lived in the same area, met frequently, discussed matters of mutual interest without rancour, and even took joint decisions on issues of significance. And it was the same people who wanted to make a snack of Suranjan!

*

When Sudhamoy had first come to Dhaka, Asit Ranjan had hired a house for him in Tantibazaar and had said, 'Sudhamoy, you are a rich man's son. Will you be able to stay in a rented house?'

Sudhamoy had answered, 'Why not? Aren't other people living the same way?'

'Yes, they are. But you have never felt the pinch of need or scarcity from the time you were born. Whatever made you sell your own house? Maya, after all, is just a little girl. It's not as if she faces the dangers that plague our young women. In fact we had to send our daughter Utpala away to Calcutta because she could not even attend college without being teased and threatened. The local boys would often bully her and say they would abduct her. Now she is staying with her maternal uncle at Tiljala. You know, Dada, it is quite a strain to have a grown up daughter.'

Sudhamoy had known that there was a lot of good sense in what Asit Ranjan had said to him. Even as he listened to his friend, he was reminded of an incident in which a young girl student of his had had her sari stripped off her in the middle of the street by a gang of boys. She was a Muslim, as were the boys who had shown her so much disrespect. Therefore, Sudhamoy would console himself that when it came to young women it was not a matter of Hindus and Muslims but a question of the weak always being

17

bullied by the strong. Women were the weaker sex, and as such were oppressed by men who were the stronger sex. Asit Ranjan had not taken any risks, and had finally sent both his daughters to Calcutta. He earned a fair amount of money, ran a jewellery shop in Islampur and owned an old two storey house. He had not remodelled his house nor did he appear to want to buy a new one. One day he had said to Sudhamoy, 'Dada, don't spend all your money, save it. If you can, you should send the money you got for your property to my relatives, who are there, to buy a plot of land for yourself.'

'What do you mean, there?' Sudhamoy had asked.

'In Calcutta,' Asit Ranjan had answered in a small voice. 'I mean, I have bought some too.'

Sudhamoy had grown very angry. 'You mean, you want to earn the money here and spend it in that country? You know, you should be condemned as a traitor.'

Asit Ranjan had been surprised by Sudhamoy's outburst. He had never heard a Hindu talking in this manner. Almost everyone was keen to use their savings to buy land in India as their future in Bangladesh was so uncertain. Settle down in this country, and one fine day your very being was uprooted and you were left high and dry. So why take chances?

Every now and again Sudhamoy would wonder why he had ever left Mymensingh. Why hadn't his love for his ancestral home prevented him from taking such a drastic step? There had been problems regarding Maya's well-being, of course, but there would always be such problems, no matter where they lived. And, in any case, where cases of kidnapping were concerned, there didn't appear to be any distinction in the choice of victims, for both Hindus and Muslims were kidnapped. The suffering the victims and their families felt was also the same, no matter what their religion. And so it all came down to the same old question: Was he afraid, by virtue of being a Hindu, of being an insecure, fearful human in his own home? Sudhamoy was afraid to ask himself this question aloud. Sitting in the cramped little house at Tantibazaar, he would wonder time and again at his reasons for fleeing his ancestral home to come to this alien place. Was he running away from himself? Why did he feel like a refugee despite having been the owner of a vast property? Did he feel so useless because he had been afraid of losing the case against Shaukat Ali who had armed himself with false documents. How galling it was, he thought, to lose a case that had to do with one's own home? But if he were to look at the whole thing positively, it was obviously wise to have left the place with his self-respect intact instead of fleeing after losing the case. A cousin of his had lost his house despite valiant efforts to save it. He had lived in the Akur Takur area in Tangail and a Muslim neighbour called Jamir Munshi had claimed a yard of his land. The matter had been taken to court. Five years later, the suit had been decided in favour of the neighbour. Sudhamoy's uncle, Tarapada Ghoshal, was compelled to leave Bangladesh and migrate to India. Was it the fear of suffering Tarapada's fate that had prompted Sudhamoy to sell his ancestral property? Perhaps that was it. Also, it had become evident to him that his importance in the area had been declining. Besides, he had lost many friends to emigration and death. Those who were alive and continued to remain in the area, seemed to have lost all hope . . . it was almost as though they felt life was not worth living. Whenever he spoke to them, Sudhamoy had the sense that they feared the approach of a monster in the middle of the night which would crush them. The country of everyone's dreams was India, and most of them secretly plotted to cross the border at the first opportunity. Sudhamoy had often said, 'When there was a war in the country, you ran away like cowards. After we won our independence, you came back to assert your heroism, and now, at the slightest provocation, you plan to go back to India. Honestly, what a bunch of cowards you are!' In the face of his anger and scorn, friends like Jatin Debnath, Tushar Kar, and Khagesh Kiran had begun to keep their distance. If they met by chance, they were not at ease in his presence. Slowly, Sudhamoy had become a stranger in his own hometown. Ironically, his Muslim friends too—people like Sakur, Faisal, Majid and Ghaffar—had begun to melt away, though it was quite apparent that their reasons were different. Often, if he went to a Muslim friend's house, he would be met with statements like, 'Sudhamoy, please sit in the other room while I finish with my namaaz.' Or 'Oh, you've come today! But we have Milad at home . . . .'

As his leftist friends grew older, they had begun to turn to religion and Sudhamoy who had never had much time for such things, found himself increasingly friendless. The gradual disappearance of logic, sensibility and humanity from his beloved hometown had inflicted a severe wound on Sudhamoy's psyche and in the end he had wanted to run away not so much from Bangladesh but from what his cherished Mymensingh had become. He had wanted to run away before it was too late and his dreams were finally swallowed by death.

Initially, Suranjan had found it very hard to adjust to the tiny rented house they had moved to and he had protested vigorously. But he had gradually got used to his new lifestyle. He had enrolled in the university, made new friends and had learned to love his surroundings. After a while, he got involved in politics and was asked to attend meetings and participate in processions . . . .

Kironmoyee, too, had found it hard to adjust to her new surroundings and would often wake up crying at night as she remembered the beloved home she had left behind. She would wonder if the little scaffold she had made for the bean plant was still there. She would remember how the guavas in their garden were always the best in town, and she hoped that the green coconut trees were still being taken care of . . . . Sudhamoy had felt no less anguished . . .

In Dhaka, Sudhamoy had applied for a senior government job, one that would be a promotion on the official position he had had in Mymensingh. But whenever he went to the Ministry to check on the fate of his application, they would keep him waiting in a small room, among the clerical staff. Sometimes, he was allowed to sit and wait in the Assistant Private Secretary's room. 'Please, could you tell me if they'll look at the file?'he would ask often but was never given a proper reply.

Once in a while the people at the Ministry would respond in monosyllables, and that was about all. Some of them would say, 'Doctor, my daughter has an upset stomach. She has also been complaining about a pain in the left chest. Why don't you prescribe something for her?' And Sudhamoy would dutifully open his briefcase, take out his prescription pad and write down the name of the medicine in big bold letters. Later he would ask, 'My job will be done, won't it, Farid-babu?' Farid-babu would flash a big smile and say, 'Do you really suppose all this is in our hands?'

Later he had discovered that officers junior to him had got their promotion. In his very presence, Sudhamoy had seen his file being slipped under those of Dr Karimuddin and Dr Yaqub Molla. These doctors had even started working as Associate Professors. As for himself, Sudhamoy had only succeeded in wearing out the soles of his shoes. Every time he turned up at the Ministry, he would get the same answers, 'Maybe tomorrow, not today. Your file has been sent to the Secretary.' Or, 'Not today, come the day after tomorrow, the Secretary is busy at a meeting.' Or 'The Minister has gone out of the country, so could you come back after a month.' Sudhamoy had patiently listened to these explanations until he realized that nothing was going to come of all this watching and waiting. After almost two years of striving to get a promotion, Sudhamoy realized that only those who were destined to get it managed to cross the eligibility line, even if they did not deserve it. But he was nearing the age of retirement, and at this stage he should have at least been an Associate Professor although he had never been the demanding sort at least where his job was concerned . . . .

He had finally retired as an Assistant Professor. One of his colleagues was a man called Madhav Chandra Pal. On the day of Sudhamoy's retirement, he had put a garland of marigolds around his neck and whispered into his ear, 'It is not right to expect too many benefits in a Muslim country. What we are getting is more than enough for us.' So saying, he had laughed mirthlessly. Madhav Chandra was also an Assistant Professor and had been passed over for promotion a couple of times. There had been many charges against him including an objection to the fact that he had travelled abroad to the Soviet Union. In time, Sudhamoy had realized that Madhav Chandra was right. While the country did not blatantly discriminate against the Hindus and despite the fact that the Constitution of Bangladesh did not have a clause prohibiting the employment as well as the upgradation of Hindus in the government, the police force, or the army it was a fact that no Hindu occupied the post of Secretary or Additional Secretary in the administration. There were about three Joint Secretaries, and just a handful of Deputy Secretaries. Sudhamoy was certain that none of these officials expected a promotion. Where the police force was concerned there were only six Hindu DCs in the entire country and in the High Court there was only one Hindu judge. Because it was allowed, there were indeed a few Hindu police officers, low down in the ranks, but it was absolutely impossible to find a Hindu Superintendent of Police. Although he took a long time to accept it, Sudhamoy realized that he was not made Associate Professor simply because he was a Hindu called Sudhamoy Dutta. Had he been Muhammad Ali or Salimullah Chowdhury there would hardly have been any obstacles in his way. And this sort of discrimination wasn't limited to government jobs alone. Even where business and trading were concerned, no Hindu could hope to achieve anything on his own. It was essential for him to have a Muslim partner, because no establishment with a purely Hindu name was given a licence to operate. Even more crucial was the fact that no nationalized bank or bank aiding industrial concerns was willing to help a purely Hindu establishment.

Weathering all these disappointments, Sudhamoy Dutta had managed to settle down, after a fashion, at Tantibazaar. He had made his home habitable enough. And although he had forsaken his hometown, he found he could not forsake his country. As he used to say every so often, 'Mymensingh alone is not my country, the whole of Bangladesh is.'

The other members of his family did not exactly share his feelings. Kironmoyee would sigh and say, 'I should have been breeding fish in the pond and planting new vegetables. The children should have been eating fresh fruits from the trees. And now, all our money goes in paying rent every month for this house.' Or she would wake up Sudhamoy late at night and say, 'The money that we have from selling the house and from your retirement benefits is quite a big sum. Let us cross over . . . many of our relatives are already there!'

Sudhamoy had a stock reply to her suggestions, 'Do you suppose your relatives are going to feed you even once a day? You might think of staying with them, but they will probably feel you're a casual visitor and will say soon enough—"Where are you staying? Would you like to have some tea?"'

'If we have our own money, why should we beg from others?' Kironmoyee would persist.

It was at this point that Sudhamoy's stubborn nature would assert itself. 'I will not go. You go if you want to. Yes, I've left our ancestral home, but it does not mean that we are also leaving our country.'

They lived for a while in Tantibazaar. After that they shifted to Armanitola, lived there for six years, and finally moved to Tikatuli, where they had lived for the last seven years. In the meantime, Sudhamoy had discovered he had a heart condition. After his retirement he had run a small private practice out of a shop at Gopibagh in the evenings, but he'd been unable to go there regularly. Patients came for consultation to his house instead. A table was kept in the drawing-room for Sudhamoy to examine his patients. The room also had a divan and a cane settee and chairs in a corner. The bookcase in the room had all kinds of books in it—medical journals, literature, books on sociology, politics . . . Sudhamoy spent most of his time in that room. In the evening people like Nishit-babu, Akhtarujjaman, Shaihdul Islam and Haripada often came to see him. They would discuss the political situation in the country, and Kironmoyee would make tea for them. Most drank their tea without sugar because of the various ailments that accompanied advancing age. None of them was young, and the same could be said of Sudhamoy as well.

Sudhamoy jumped up with a start as the sound of another approaching procession filled the room. On his part, Suranjan grit his teeth and seethed with anger. Kironmoyee showed fear but Sudhamoy appeared curiously placid after his initial nervousness. Why wasn't he reacting? Should he not also show some signs of fear, apprehension, rage?

Day Two

Most of Suranjan's friends were Muslim. None of them were overly religious and they accepted Suranjan as a close friend even though he was Hindu. For instance, last year, Kamal had invited the whole family to his house. Suranjan did have Hindu friends like Kajal, Ashim and Jaideb but he was closer to Pulok, Kamal, Haider, Belal and Rabiul. And, in fact, whenever Suranjan had been in trouble, it was Haider, Kamal and Belal who had helped more readily than his Hindu friends. Once Sudhamoy had to be admitted to the Suhrawardy Hospital at 1.30 in the morning. Dr Haripada had diagnosed myocardial infarction and it was necessary to take him to the hospital immediately. When Suranjan had informed Kajal, he had yawned and said, 'How can we shift him so late in the night? Let's wait till the morning, and we'll do something about it.' But the moment Belal was told, he had rushed over in his car. He had made all the arrangements, had admitted Sudhamoy to the hospital and had been around to help out. On that occasion he had reassured Sudhamoy time and again, 'Uncle, don't worry. Everything will be all right. You can think of me as your own son.' Suranjan had been overwhelmed by his friend's concern. And for as long as Sudhamoy was in the hospital, Belal had come to visit him. He did not stop at merely enquiring after Sudhamoy's health, and organizing transport to go to the hospital, but also spoke to the doctors attending on him to take extra special care. How many people took so much interest in their friends? Kajal also had money, but was he as large-hearted? Almost all the expenses for Sudhamoy's treatment were paid by Rabiul. He suddenly appeared at their Tikatuli house one day and asked Suranjan, 'Is your father in the hospital?' Before Suranjan could reply, he had put a sealed envelope on a nearby table and said, 'Don't think of your friends as strangers.' And with that he was gone, as swiftly

24

as he had come. Suranjan had opened the envelope and found five thousand takas. But it wasn't only because of their financial and material support that he was close to his Muslim friends—he found he was closer to them than his Hindu friends in thought and in sentiment. In sum, the friendship he shared with Haider, Kamal and Rabiul was far deeper than his relationship with Kajal, Ashim and Jaideb. In matters of the heart, too, he had loved Parveen more meaningfully and passionately than he would any Archana, Dipti, Geeta or Sunanda.

Suranjan had never learned to differentiate amongst his friends on a communal basis. When he was a child he had known that he was a Hindu but hadn't quite known what it meant. While studying at the village school in Mymensingh in Class III or IV he had had a massive argument with a boy named Khaled. When this argument had reached its peak the boys had abused each other with the worst obscenities they could summon up. It was then that Khaled had angrily referred to him as a Hindu. Suranjan was sure that the word Hindu was as derogatory as swine or dog. It was only after he had grown up somewhat that he had learned that Hindu was a noun describing the religious community to which he belonged. When he was old enough to make up his mind on the matter he declared that he was above all, first, a human being and then a Bengali by race. No religion had created this race and he wanted his people to know no communal barriers, and live together in perfect harmony. He would say to his friends and his family that Bengalis as a race must not subject themselves to any communal distinctions whatsoever, so that the term 'Bengali' would always be considered indivisible in character. Unfortunately, however, Suranjan's idealistic views did not find many takers in Bangladesh. Rather unity was being sought not between people of the same nation, but between people of the same religion, even if they lived in two different countries. As a result, simply because of a difference in religion a certain section of the people were considered outsiders, perhaps even outcasts in their own country. It was this view, which was gaining acceptance everywhere in the country, which had resulted in the division between the Hindus and Muslims.

*

Today is the 8th of December. The entire nation is on strike, a strike which has been called by the fundamentalists. A spokesman for one of the powerful parties, the Jamaat-i-Islami, had earlier announced, that the strike was being called to protest the Babri Masjid demolition. Suranjan had lazed about in bed for two days, mulling over the strike, before he decided to bestir himself and see what was happening in Dhaka, his favourite city. In the adjacent room, his mother too lay in bed, terrified of what might happen to them. Suranjan was not sure if Sudhamoy felt any fear. The only thing he had made clear was that he would not go into hiding this time. If this should result in their death, so be it. If the Muslims came and hacked them to pieces, it was entirely up to them. Suranjan was not sure how wise his father's stand was, but he was almost as determined as Sudhamoy was to remain in the house and not flee. Maya had left on her own, so he could do nothing about her. She had gone to live in a Muslim house to seek shelter with Parul Riffat. Poor Maya, he hoped she would survive.

As he prepared to go out, Kironmoyee got up with a start and asked, 'Where are you going?'

'I want to go and take a look at the state of the city. Wonder what the hartal has done to it.'

'Don't go out, Suro. You can't tell what might happen outside.'

'What will be, will be. One day we'll all have to die in any case. And for heaven's sake, don't panic so much. It really annoys me to see you people panic.' Suranjan said disgustedly as he carefully combed his hair.

Shuddering with fear she ran up to Suranjan and took the comb away from him. 'Listen to me, Suranjan,' she said. 'It is dangerous to go out. Even though there's a hartal, they are attacking shops and temples. Stay at home. There is absolutely no need for you to go out and see what's happening in the city.'

But Suranjan had always been a disobedient child. Why should he listen to Kironmoyee now? He brushed aside her objections and walked out. Sudhamoy who was sitting by himself looked up in surprise as his son went out but made no move to stop him.

The evening air was bracing but it was overlaid by a sullen and ghostly silence. Suranjan had seemed unafraid inside the house but now that he had left its shelter he was a little afraid. Even so, as he had decided to wander around the city, that was just what he would do. As he set forth, he felt a further unease when he realized that this time around none of his close friends had enquired after them, nor had they offered shelter. Not Belal, not Kamal . . . nobody. Even if they had come, Suranjan thought to himself, he would not have gone with them. Why should he anyway? Would they have to pick up their bags and flee every time there was a riot in the city? It was a real shame. Indeed, he thought, he had been a fool to accept Kamal's hospitality the last time there had been trouble. If they had come to him this time he would have definitely said, 'How can you kill us and take pity on us at the same time? It would be better if you gathered together all the Hindus living in this country, made them stand in a row in front of a firing squad and killed them. All your problems would be over then. You wouldn't have to kill them in batches, nor would you have to make a show of saving them surreptitiously.' Just as Suranjan entered a bigger street, a group of boys shouted out,'Catch him, he's a Hindu.' The boys were his neighbours. For the last seven years he had been meeting them at least once a day. Suranjan knew a couple of them personally. One of them, a boy called Aalam, often came to their house to ask for subscriptions for the club the local boys belonged to. Suranjan had sung in some of the cultural functions organized by their club, and had even thought he would teach some of the boys the songs of D.L.Roy and Hemanga Biswas. They were often in his house asking for all sorts of help; and because they were neighbours Sudhamoy often gave them free medical treatment. And it was these very same people who were threatening to beat him up today because he was a Hindu! Suranjan walked briskly in the opposite direction, not out of fear, but out of shame. He was truly ashamed and anguished by the thought of these boys beating him up. And his sense of shame and sadness was not directed towards himself, but was aimed at those who would be beating him up. Shame most affected those who inflicted torture, not those who were tortured!

Suranjan walked up to Shapla Square. There was a tense silence in the area. A few small groups of people stood around. Bits of brick were strewn across the street along with burnt wood and broken glass. It was clear that rioting had broken out in this place a little while ago. Some young men ran off on some mission and in another direction some stray dogs ran around aimlessly. A few rickshaws went past, the rickshaw men ringing their bells. Suranjan did not quite know what had happened. Only the dogs which had no fear of bigotry and communalism, seemed to be running about for the sheer joy of it. Perhaps they were also pleased that they could go where they liked on the empty streets. Suranjan felt like doing so too. The usually busy Motijheel Commercial Area was now bare and silent and it tempted Suranjan to relive his childhood; it would be wonderful to play football with a jambura fruit, or fix stumps and play a game of cricket. While he was musing over these pleasant possibilities, he looked over to his left and saw a building that had been burned down. He realized that it was the Indian Airlines office. Nothing remained of its signboard, its doors and windows. Some people stood around looking at the charred ruin, gesticulating and laughing. As he stood watching he suddenly had the strong feeling that he was being watched. He walked away quickly from the burnt office. Why did he have to care about the number of houses that were burnt? As he walked on, he saw many more houses on fire. Was he enjoying the smell of burnt wood and clay as he normally enjoyed the smell of burning petrol? Maybe he was! Outside the Communist Party of Bangladesh or CPB office, he noticed a crowd. Stones lay scattered on the road. There was a bookshop nearby from which Suranjan had often bought books. That hadn't been spared either; a partially burnt book brushed against Suranjan's feet. It was Maxim Gorky's *Ma (Mother)*. For a moment, he thought he was Pavelvolasov, and he imagined himself setting fire to his mother and later crushing her beneath his feet. He shivered involuntarily at the thought, the charred book at his feet. More people had gathered; they talked in loud whispers and the whole place was charged with tension and excitement. What had happened? What was about to happen? Nobody quite seemed to know, though rumours filled the air. The only thing that was obvious was that the CPB office had been burnt. But why? Some said the communists had changed their strategy but in spite of this, they were unable to escape the rage of the Muslim fanatics. Comrade Farhad had apparently died and a grand funeral was being organized, a Milad had been called which had been attended by all. And despite this, to imagine that communalism had burned up the Communist Party office!

Suranjan stared helplessly at the ruined office of the CPB. All of a sudden Suranjan saw Kaiser approach him. He had not shaved or combed his hair and his eyes were bloodshot; there was a strange anxiety in his voice as he demanded, 'Why have you come out?'

'Am I not to come out?' Suranjan retorted.

'No, it's not that. But you know these swine . . . all this talk about religion. Tell me, do they really believe in religion? Terrorists from the Jamaat Shibeer Youth Command have done all this. They burnt the party office, the bookshop and the Indian Airlines office. These people who were against independence now lie in wait for any opportunity that they can make use of to create trouble. As though everyone is waiting to hear them screaming.'

They walked away from the damage together. Suranjan asked, 'Which other places have they torched?'

'Chittagong's temples at Tulsidhaam, Panchanandhaam and Kaibolyadhaam were broken to pieces. All the temples in Malipara, Samshan mandir, Korbanigunj, Kalibari, Chatteswari, Bishnu mandir, Hajari lane and Fakirpara were set ablaze. Ironically, there were processions at the same time pleading for communal harmony.'

Suranjan sighed deeply. Kaiser pushed back his untidy hair and said, 'It wasn't only temples yesterday. They had even set fire to the fishermen's colony in Majhirghat. At least fifty homes were totally destroyed.'

'What else?' Suranjan asked, suddenly indifferent to everything.

'They raided the Madhav mandir and Durga mandir in Jaidebpur. At Sherpur, the Annapurna mandir at the Krishi Centre and the Kali mandir at the Sherighat Ashram were completely destroyed. In Faridpur, the temples in the Ramakrishna Mission were looted. The guru and his students were seriously injured.'

'And?' Suranjan continued to be unconcerned.

'At Narshindi, the temples and houses at Chalakchor and Monohordir were destroyed. In Narayangunj, the temple at the Morapara Bazaar in the Rupgunj station was demolished. At Comilla, the old Abhaya Ashram was burnt. At Noakhali also all kinds of atrocities were perpetrated.'

'Like what?'

'The Adhor Chand Ashram at the Sudharam police station and seven Hindu homes have been destroyed. All the Hindu homes in Gangapur were first looted and then set ablaze. The Sivakali temple at Shonapur and the gymnasium at Binodpur were destroyed. The Kali mandir at Choumuhini, Durgabari mandir at Durgapur and the temples at Qutabpur and Gopalpur were razed to the ground. Dr P. K. Singha's medicine factory, Akhanda Ashram, and the temples in the Choyani area were all demolished. In Choumuhuni, Babupur, Tetuia, Mehdipur, Rajgunj Bazaar, Tongirpar, Kazirhaat, Rasulpur, Jameendarhaat and Porabari ten temples and eighteen Hindu homes were looted and set on fire. A shop, a car and even a lady were set alight. Of the seventeen homes in Bhabordi, thirteen were torched and all of them looted and the ladies were tortured. Biplab Bhowmick was stabbed. Yesterday all the houses and temples in Birahimpur were damaged. The Jagannath mandir, three shops in the Charhazaari village, as well as clubs were looted and plundered. Two houses in the Charparbaati village, one house in Daasherhaat, two temples at Charkukri and Muchhapur and the Jaikali temple were burned. All the people living in Sirajpur were beaten up and all the homes were at first looted and later set ablaze.'

At the end of this long litany of destruction, all Suranjan said was 'Oh.' He did not intend to say anything more. All he wanted to do now was kick the stones in his path as he used to do in his childhood. Kaiser kept telling him about more and more cases of burning and looting but Suranjan had stopped listening, he was not even interested. The two of them stopped in front of the press club. There was a group of journalists standing outside the building, deep in animated discussion. Suranjan stared at them, vaguely interested. He tried to listen in on what they were saying. Some said that in India at least two hundred people had been killed in riots and police firing. The number of people injured amounted to many thousands. The activities of the RSS, Shiv Sena and other fundamentalist groups had been restricted. In the Lok Sabha, Advani was resigning from his post as leader of the Opposition. Some were saying that in Chittagong, Dipak Ghosh, a disciple of the Nandankanan Tulsidhaam, was caught by the Jamaatis as he was trying to escape. They had meant to set him on fire but there had been some durwans close by, who had said that Dipak was a

Muslim and he was allowed to go after being beaten up by the Jamaatis.

All those who knew Suranjan were shocked to see him there. They asked why had he left his house and told him he should go home immediately as more violence was expected.

Suranjan did not say anything. He was confused and disoriented. Did he have to stay at home just because his name was Suranjan Dutta while Kaiser, Latif, Belal and Shahin could not only be out of their houses but could also discuss the events that were taking place and join processions denouncing communalism. Surely this was not fair. Wasn't Suranjan as conscientious, logical and as independent a thinker as the rest of them? He leaned against a wall, a vacant look on his face as he lit a Bangla Five that he had picked up from a nearby cigarette shop. He felt very lost and isolated. Many of the people around him were his acquaintances, indeed he was quite close to some of them, and yet he was so alone! He felt depressed that he could not join the people around him as they excitedly discussed the demolition of the Babri Masjid and the destruction of the temples in this country. Even if he wanted to merge and mingle with them, he could not, for there was a line he could not cross. He understood why people tried to avoid him and excluded him from their groups, even pitied him but it wasn't easy to accept. He inhaled deeply on his cigarette and puffed out a number of smoke rings. And then in the middle of the frenzied activity around him, he let his body go limp and slumped against a nearby wall.

The number of people throwing sidelong glances at Suranjan increased. Most of them were surprised to see him, because there was not a single Hindu out of doors. They were huddled in their homes out of fear. Little wonder, then, that people were shocked at Suranjan's audacity.

Kaiser had joined a group of people, who were preparing to take out a procession. Journalists converged on the scene with bags and cameras. Among them was Lutfor. Suranjan knew Lutfor but refused to call out to him. A little later Lutfor himself came up to him and expressed shock at seeing him there.

'Why are you here, Dada?'

'Why shouldn't I be?'

Lutfor was genuinely concerned and worried. 'I hope there has been no trouble at home?'

Suranjan was interested to see that Lutfor's tone and manner were protective. Normally the boy was shy and reticent and never looked anyone directly in the eye. He was a decent young man and it was Suranjan who had spoken to the editor of the *Ekata* magazine, and managed to get him a job. Lutfor now lit a Benson, and continued to quiz Suranjan, 'Suranjan-da, sure there has been no problem?'

Suranjan laughed and said, 'What problem?'

Lutfor was a little embarrassed.

He said, 'You know how it is, Dada. I mean the state of the country.'

Suranjan dropped his cigarette butt and stubbed it out. He was somewhat surprised for Lutfor had never raised his voice to him as he had now begun doing. Suranjan could not help feeling that Lutfor was being a bit impertinent. Lutfor exhaled cigarette smoke, frowned and said, 'Dada, I think you should stay elsewhere today. It's not safe to stay in your house. Don't you think you can stay in a neighbouring Muslim home for at least two nights?'

Suranjan looked blankly at a burning length of string that hung outside the cigarette shop and answered with studied indifference, 'No.'

'No?' Lutfor was alarmed by Suranjan's attitude. Suranjan could sense the concern in Lutfor's voice. But what the young man was saying to him was not new; everyone who had had the urge to give him advice recently had said more or less the same thing. 'It is not right to stay in your house, better go into hiding. Don't go out of doors, don't disclose your identity. Go out only when the situation has eased somewhat . . .' Suranjan wanted to light another cigarette, but Lutfor's grave demeanour and incessant warnings dissuaded him. He folded his arms on his chest and looked around him. The trees were all clothed in dark green leaves, their garb for the winter. He had always loved this season and the things that went with it: steamed pancakes in the mornings, sun-drenched quilts to snuggle into in the nights, ghost stories told by his mother . . . .

He was jerked back to the present by a bearded man with a

bag slung across a shoulder. The man stood next to Lutfor and loudly listed the atrocities that had taken place this far:

Dhakeshwari mandir, Siddheswari Kali mandir, Ramakrishna Mission, Mahaprakash Math, Narinda Gouriya Math, Bholagiri Ashram have all been stoned, looted and plundered. Swamibagh Ashram has also been looted. Twenty-five homes near Shoni's gym have been burnt down. The Shoni mandir and the Durga mandir have both been destroyed and burnt. Narinda's Rishipara and the Dayagunj Jelepara have not been spared either. Farmgate, Paltan, the Nawabpur Maran Chand sweetshop and the Deshbandhu sweetshop at Tikatuli have also been demolished and set ablaze. The temple at Thathari Bazaar has also been torched.

Lutfor sighed deeply and said 'Oh!' Suranjan wondered whether he should leave now, because he did not want to be in the other's company for much longer. At the same time he did not quite know what it was he wanted to do or where he wanted to go. Should he keep standing there, join the procession or go away to some distant place? Perhaps he should go to some wilderness where there were no friends or relatives .... The bearded man with the bag slung on his shoulder melted into another crowd to repeat his announcements. Lutfor began making preparations to leave because Suranjan's indifference had begun to bother him.

There was still a lot of tension in the air. Suranjan's mood again swung towards a desire to participate in all that was happening. He wanted to blend with the crowd, he wanted to make a survey of the temples that were destroyed and burnt, he wanted to enquire about the homes and shops that were looted and plundered. He wanted to protest against the recent events. 'These fanatics should be whipped. These fake religionists are imposters who provoke in the name of religion.' But he could not bring himself to do any of these things; and his desire to be a part of everything that was going on around him was further dampened by the pitying looks that those around him gave him. Voicelessly, these people seemed to say to him that he was not fit to participate in the excitement. And to think that until now he had been so adept at making speeches on a wide variety of subjects and taking the lead in all sorts of activity! Today it was as though some strange force had left him speechless, and no one around him appeared to want to encourage him to say something, do something, stand up and fight.

Kaiser broke through the crowd and came up to him. He whispered, 'They are planning to hold a meeting at Baitul Mokarram to discuss the Babri Masjid issue. People are gathering; it will be safer for you to go home.'

'Aren't you going?' Suranjan asked.

'Oh, no,' said Kaiser, 'I would rather attend a meeting on communal harmony.'

Standing behind Kaiser were two boys named Lytton and Mahatab. They too said, 'It's for your own good. They've even torched Jalkhabar. It's happening all around us. Can you imagine what they'd do if you were recognized? They are running around openly with knives, lathis and choppers.'

Kaiser called a rickshaw with the intention of sending Suranjan home in it. Lutfor appeared and, catching hold of Suranjan's hand, said forcefully, 'Come on, Dada, go straight home. I really don't understand what made you come out today!'

Everyone around him began insisting that he go home. Some people who did not know him, came running up to find out what the matter was. His friends explained that Suranjan was a Hindu and that it was not safe for him to stay here. The others nodded in agreement. 'Yes', they said, 'he must go home.' But Suranjan had not left home only to be forced back there. His friends nudged him gently towards the rickshaw; Lutfor still held his hand. Suddenly feeling rebellious, Suranjan jerked his hand away.

*

Sudhamoy was tired. All he wanted to do was lie back in bed and relax. But he found himself tossing restlessly. On top of all this, Suranjan had gone out. Soon after Suranjan had left there had been a knock on the door. Sudhamoy had jumped up from bed, hoping it was Suranjan back already. But it was not his son, only Akhtarujjaman, a retired sixty-year-old professor who lived in the neighbourhood. The old man stepped inside, and bolted the front door almost instantly. 'Has there been any trouble?' he asked in a subdued voice. Sudhamoy looked at the stacks of books lying on the table in the room and answered listlessly, 'No, what could have happened?' Akhtarujjaman drew up a chair and sat down. He was suffering from cervical spondilitis. Keeping his head unnaturally straight because of his ailment, he said, 'I am sure you've heard all about the Babri Masjid? Nothing is left of it. It's a shame!'

Sudhamoy murmured noncommittally in reply.

'You don't have anything to say? Are you supporting them?'

'Why should I support them?'

'Then why don't you say something?'

'Evil people have done evil work. All I can do is feel very sorry about the whole thing.'

'I can hardly believe that this sort of thing could have happened in a secular State! What a shame! The entire national ethos, all those political announcements, their Supreme Court, the Lok Sabha, their political parties, the democratic tradition, everything they profess is actually nothing but a lot of noise and hot air. Whatever you say, Sudha-babu, compared to India, there has hardly been any rioting in this country.'

'Well, what about 1964, then 1990, and now . . . '

'Not 1964. It would be better to say 1950. After 1950, the thing that stood out about the 1964 riot was the spontaneous protests against communalism. The day the riots began, under the leadership of Manik Mia, Jahur Hussain Chowdhury and Abdus Salaam, all the newspapers printed banner headings that read, "East Pakistan stand up for your rights!" In his effort to save a Hindu family, a fifty-five-year-old man by the name of Amir Hussain Chowdhury lost his life. Oh how touching that was!'

The pain in Sudhamoy's chest had increased. He reclined more comfortably on his bed. Perhaps a cup of hot tea would have revived him somewhat but who would give him the tea? Kironmoyee was so distressed by Suranjan's actions that she could hardly be expected to make the tea. Why did Suro have to go out on his own? And if he had to go out why couldn't he have taken Haider with him? But then Suranjan had always been the impulsive sort, and it would have been impossible to keep him at home if he had wanted to go out. Sudhamoy knew all this, but distress and anxiety were aspects of human nature that understood no logic. Now he masked his fear and anxiety and turned his attention once more to Akhtarujjaman. Sudhamoy said, 'Ironically, all religions point towards one goal—peace. Yet it is in the name of religion that there has been so much unrest and lack of peace. So much blood has been shed and so many people have suffered. It is indeed a pity that even at the close of the twentieth century we've had to witness such atrocities, all in the name of religion. Flying the flag of religion has always proved the easiest way to crush to nothingness human beings, as well as the spirit of humanity.'

It was Akhtarujjaman's turn to make a noncommittal reply.

Kironmoyee came into the room with two cups of tea. 'Is your chest pain any worse?' she asked her husband, 'Why don't you take your pills?' She put the cups on the table and sat down on the bed.

Akhtarujjaman said to her, 'Boudi, you don't wear sankha and sindur, do you?'

Kironmoyee looked down and answered, 'Not since 1975.'

'Thank God! At least you can be sure of your safety. It's better to be safe than sorry.'

Kironmoyee smiled a wan smile. Simultaneously, a similar smile appeared on Sudhamoy's lips.

Akhtarujjaman drank his tea in quick gulps. Sudhamoy's chest pain was certainly not improving. He said, 'I have given up my dhuti too, quite some time back. For the sake of my dear life, my friend.'

Akhtarujjaman put down his cup and said, 'I'll be off now. I think I will check up on Binod-babu before I get back.'

After the old professor had gone, Sudhamoy lay back on his bed. His tea, that he had not touched, cooled on the table.

Kironmoyee shut the door and sat down. Her back was to the light and her face was covered in shadow. There was a time when Kironmoyee sang kirtans beautifully. She was the daughter of a famous advocate in Brahmanbaria and had been married at sixteen. After they were married, Sudhamoy had encouraged her to learn Rabindra Sangeet. And she had, in fact, taken lessons for a while, from Mithun Dey. Soon she had become such a good singer that she was often requested to sing in public, in Mymensingh, for there were only a handful of talented singers in town. Sudhamoy recalled one incident, when she was to sing at the Town Hall. At that time, Suranjan was only three or four years old. Sudhamoy had begun to sweat with nervousness as Kironmoyee's turn to take the stage came after a famous singer called Sameer Chandra Dey.

She had sung the song, '*Ananda loke . . . Mangala loke . . . Birajo, Satyasundaro . . .*' (In this world of peace and happiness, let us live together to perpetuate its beauty . . .) The audience had gone into raptures and screamed for an encore. She had obliged and had sung at least three more songs. She had sung them all with such feeling and with such beauty that even an atheist like Sudhamoy had been touched so deeply that he had wept.

After independence, Kironmoyee had been reluctant to sing in public. Suranjan had once pleaded with his mother to sing at a local function that featured stars like Sumita Naha and Mitali Mukherjee but she had laughed and told him, 'I don't practise anymore nor is my voice in perfect tune, so I'd rather not sing.'

Sudhamoy had said to her, 'Don't be modest. You used to sing so well, people know you. There was a time when people cheered you and asked you for more.'

'Yes, I know. But those who clapped their hands and applauded me also said, "It is only because Hindu women are shameless that they learn how to sing; that is why they sit in public in front of unknown men and sing for everyone."'

'You mean Muslim women don't sing?' Sudhamoy had asked.

'Yes, they do now. But earlier, when they hadn't attained much prominence, we had to put up with all sorts of unkind remarks. Minati-di was such an excellent singer. But one day she was really discouraged when a group of boys confronted her and accused her of trying to teach Muslim girls how to sing.'

'But it is a good thing to teach singing, isn't it?' Sudhamoy had said.

'That wasn't what everyone thought. A lot of men used to say it is not for women to learn singing. They believed it would spoil their character.'

'Oh I see.'

Gradually Kironmoyee had lost all interest in her singing. Her ustad, Mithun Dey, would try to encourage her but Kironmoyee would sigh sadly and say, 'No, Dada, I don't like to sing anymore. What is the point, when people say it is indecent to sing and dance?'

Sudhamoy had respected her wishes to stop singing in public but he would complain occasionally about her refusal to even sing at home. But where was the atmosphere to sing in the house!

Often, in the middle of the night, when sleep eluded them, they would get up restlessly and seek refuge on the rooftop. There, as they stared silently at the stars in the distant sky, their hearts would long for their house on the banks of the great river, Brahmaputra. On such occasions, now and again, Kironmoyee would hum the tune of a Tagore song, which talked of sweet memories that could never be forgotten. Listening to her, Sudhamoy's stern heart would soften and he would be filled with a sense of longing for the good things of the past. He would yearn for the fields that he had bounded across in his childhood and in his youth; the school courtyard; the brimming river and the path on the river bank that led through deep forests.

Intrinsically a stern man, in his later years Sudhamoy was a man whose spirit had been broken by the sorrows that had been heaped upon him. He would often wake up weeping in the middle of the night; at such times he would enfold his wife in a tight embrace to allay his sadness. 1971 had been a particularly bad year for it was then that his friends Jaganmoy Ghoshal, Prafulla Sarkar and Netai Sen were murdered virtually in front of him. They were taken to an internment camp and shot to death. Later, their bodies were taken in trucks and thrown into the wilderness.

Whenever they found Hindus, the Pakistanis would capture them, kick them with their boots, attack them with bayonets, gouge out their eyes and then break their backs. If they survived this sort of brutality, they were then killed. Sudhamoy had seen many Muslims being beaten up but their lives would usually be spared but this never happened with the Hindus. During the war of independence, the corpses of many Hindus and Muslims who fought for their country were piled into a well in the local sweepers' colony. In a poignant moment, even as the country rejoiced in its new-found independence, the relatives of people he had known like Majid, Rahim and Idris had come and cried over the bones of both Hindus and Muslims that were stacked in the well of Mathurpatti. Their tears had fallen even more copiously when they had realized that they had no way of distinguishing between the bones of the Majids and the Anils. In time, the injuries Sudhamoy had received from his captors—a broken leg, three broken bones in his rib cage—had healed as had the wounds on his brutally mutilated penis, but the scars on his heart would always remain. Sudhamoy had never really recovered from his incarceration during the country's war of independence. He had returned alive from the camp but only just, and ever since he had never felt truly alive. The life of deception and fear he had lived since then had not improved his mental state either. For seven years he had lived in a small bamboo hut under the assumed name of Abdus Salaam in the village of Arjunkhila in Phulpur. Suranjan was called Saber and people called Kironmoyee Fatema. When he recalled that time, he would feel that the broken ribs that had almost pierced his heart, had hurt him less than the shame of his beloved wife hiding under the name of Fatema. In December when the freedom fighters had come down to Phulpur and the whole village had reverberated with cries of 'Joi Bangla', Sudhamoy had finally been able to repeat the name that he loved so much . . . 'Kiron . . . Kiron . . . Kironmoyee . . .' The flaming pain that had been burning in his heart, was now quenched. That he now had the independence to call Kironmoyee by her own name in the midst of so many people, was Sudhamoy's own idea of having achieved Joi Bangla.

Sudhamoy's reminiscing was suddenly cut short by harsh knocking on the door. The visitor was Haripada Bhattacharya. The Nificard tablet that he had kept under his tongue had helped to ease Sudhamoy's chest pain to some extent so he was able to greet his friend.

'Are you ill?' Haripada asked. 'You look very pale.'

'Yes, Haripada. For quite sometime now, I have not been keeping well. I have not had my blood pressure checked either.'

'Had I known earlier, I would have brought my B.P. instrument.'

'Suranjan has chosen to go out in the midst of all this. Can you imagine how worried we all are? And how did you manage to get here?'

'Took a short cut. I avoided the main road.'

For a long time, no one said anything. Then Haripada took off his shawl and said, 'Today in Dhaka, people are protesting against the demolition of the Babri Masjid. At the same time, peace marches are also being taken out. Political parties and various other organizations have asked everyone to maintain communal harmony. From parliament too, a message was sent to the people asking them to keep calm. Sheikh Hasina has also broadcast a message saying communal harmony must be maintained at any cost. Two hundred and thirty-six people were killed in rioting in India, curfew was imposed in forty towns and communal parties have been banned. Also, Prime Minister Rao has promised to rebuild the Babri Masjid.'

Haripada now sat down looking grave. He asked, 'Have you decided what to do? Are you going to stay on in this place? I don't think it is advisable to stay here any longer. I was thinking of going to my in-law's home in Manikgunj. But this evening, my brother-in-law came and told me that in Manikgunj city and in the police station area, more than a hundred homes had been looted and burned. Twenty-five temples were torched. In a village called Bokjhuri, all the Hindu homes were burnt down. Also, in the middle of the night they barged into Deben Shore's house, dragged out his daughter Saraswati and raped her.'

'What do you mean? Is what you're saying true?' Sudhamoy exclaimed loudly in shock and fear.

'Where is your daughter?'

'Maya has gone to a friend's house.'

'A Muslim home, I hope?'

'Yes.'

'In that case it is all right.' Haripada said, heaving a sigh of relief.

Kironmoyee who had been as alarmed as her husband by the news Haripada brought, was reassured by their friend's opinion of Maya's course of action. Sudhamoy removed his glasses, wiped them and put them back on. He said, 'Actually this is a riot prone area. We did not see so much rioting in Mymensingh. By the way, Haripada, have you heard anything about riots in Mymensingh?'

'Yes, I heard that in the Bathuadi village of Phulpur, two temples, and a small prayer room and in Trishal, one Kali temple were destroyed.'

'But in the town? Surely nothing could have happened in the town? Actually all this rioting is scarce in the northern part of the country. In Mymensingh, what do you say Kironmoyee, did they ever burn temples?'

Before Kironmoyee could reply, Haripada said: 'The puja

office on North Brook Hall Road, the idol of Kali in the zamindar's house as well as the temple were all destroyed completely. Today, in Shantinagar, the sweetshop called Jalkhabar and Satarupa Store were looted and then burnt down. In Kushtia, six temples were attacked at midnight by the Jamaat Shibeer people. Apart from this, when I hear of the happenings in Chittagong, Sylhet, Bhola, Sherpur, Cox's Bazaar and Noakhali, I am a little afraid.'

'Afraid of what?' Sudhamoy asked.

'An exodus . . .'

'No, no. I don't think there'll be any large scale rioting in this country, nor do I think there will be mass migrations . . . '

'Dada, have you forgotten what happened in 1990? Or were you not affected at all?'

'Oh, all that was staged by the Ershad government.'

'Come on, Dada. Why don't you take a look at the records of the Bangladesh Government Statistical Bureau? This year's exodus will be massive. People don't leave their homeland because of a staged crisis. After all, the soil of one's own country is not like the soil in a flower pot, which can be watered every day and changed occasionally. No, Dada, I really feel quite nervous and scared. One of my sons is in Calcutta, studying. But both my grown up daughters are here, and I spend sleepless nights worrying about them. I think I will go away . . .'

Suddenly incensed, Sudhamoy pulled off his glasses and shouted at his friend. 'Have you gone mad, Haripada? Don't say such things ever again.'

'I know what you'll say. You'll tell me that I am doing well in this country, getting enough money, that I have my own home . . . .Isn't that so?'

'No, Haripada. That is not the reason. It has got nothing to do with the amount of money or the opportunities that you have. Even if you were not earning enough it would be unfair to go away. Isn't this your country? Look at me. I am a retired man, and I don't earn very much anymore. My son does not earn either. I manage with the little that I get from my meagre medical practice. I hardly have any patients coming to me these days, but does that mean I will leave the country and go away? Those who desert their country are inhuman. Whatever be the condition of this country at the moment,

Bengalis as a race are not uncivil. Yes, there is some amount of rioting now, but surely all that will subside. When there are two countries side by side, and one of them is on fire, some of the flames are bound to overflow on to the neighbouring one . . . . And, mind you, Haripada, in 1964, the riots were not started by Bengali Muslims, but by the Biharis.'

Haripada wrapped himself up in his shawl and said, 'You know why I hide under the cover of this shawl, Dada? It is not for fear of the Biharis. It is your Muslim brothers that I am afraid of.'

Having said this, he stealthily crept out of the house and into the darkness. Kironmoyee left the door slightly ajar to see if there was any sign of Suranjan. She was becoming more and more tense with every passing minute, but there was no sign of their wayward son. Every now and then a procession would go past, shouting slogans in the name of Allah. One demand that was repeated over and over again was that the Indian government should rebuild the Babri Masjid, failing which they would not be spared.

Late at night, Suranjan finally returned. He was so exhausted, he was unsteady on his feet. He told his mother that he would not have any dinner.

*

Suranjan turned off the lights in his room and lay down but he just could not sleep. As he tossed and turned in his bed, his mind turned to the past. Some years previously, he had worked for *Ekata* magazine as a reporter and his journalistic training had instilled in him the ability to order his thoughts quite well. It had also given him access to a lot of information on what was actually happening in the country.

The State of Bangladesh was founded on the basis of four major principles: nationalism, secularism, democracy and socialism. The country had worked long and hard for its independence. Beginning with the Language Movement in 1952, the struggle had been long and arduous but independence had finally been achieved. In the process, the evils of communalism and religious fanaticism were defeated. After independence, the reactionaries who had been against the very spirit of independence had gained power, changed the face of the constitution and revived the evils of communalism and unbending fundamentalism that had been rejected during the war of independence. Religion was used as a political weapon and a large number of people were forced to follow the dictates of Islam. Thus, unlawfully and unconstitutionally, Islam became the national religion of Bangladesh. As a result, communalism and religious fanaticism exploded out of control. Suranjan began to mentally catalogue the heavy toll communalism and religious fundamentalism had taken on his country:

- In the Daoudkandhi subdistrict of Comilla district, village Sabahaw, on 8 February 1979, at least four hundred people from neighbouring villages attacked a group of Hindu sages who were living there. They had yelled as they swept down on the sages, 'The government has declared Islam as the national religion. So, if you wish to stay in an Islamic State you must become Muslims, and if you don't then it will be best for you to leave this country.' The holy men had looked on helplessly as their homes were looted and their temples were destroyed. Many of them were captured and taken away and some hadn't returned to this day. The women were brutally raped and tortured, and some of the people who were attacked had never recovered completely.

- In the Abirdia village of Shibpur subdistrict, in Narshindi district, Nripendra Kumar Sengupta and his wife, Anima Sengupta were locked up in an advocate's house, while they were cheated of 8.75 bighas of land. The property was registered in someone else's name. On 27 March 1979, Anima made a written complaint to the Narshindi Police Superintendent that she was being harassed by some people; the neighbours were too scared to say anything against the accused. Anima was taken into police custody and was tortured for four days before she was released.

- In the same year on 27 May, in Baulakandha village of Kaukhali subdistrict in Pirozepur district, about ten or twelve armed people attacked the home of the Haldars. They demolished the house, destroyed the temple and chanted that all Hindus should be killed and all temples should be broken up and converted into mosques. They left with the warning that all Hindus should leave the country immediately.

- In the Goschi village of Raujan, in Chittagong, on 9 May at least a hundred and fifty Muslims forced their way into the home of the Baidyas, bombed it and set it on fire for good measure.
- On 16 June in Atghar village of Swarupkathi, Pirozepur district, about ten or twelve policemen, captured Gouranga Mondol, Nagendra Mondol, Amulya Mondol, Subodh Mondol, Sudhir Mondol, Hirendranath Mondol, Jahar Deuri—a total of sixteen Hindus. Later they were all dragged into Gouranga Mondol's home where they were beaten up in the courtyard. When Gouranga Mondol's wife, Benu, had tried to stop them the policemen took her into the house and took turns raping her. The other women in the house who tried to come to her aid were all harassed and insulted. Sanatan Mondol's daughter, Rina, was also forcefully raped, and later abducted. Rina had still not been found.
- On 18 June, at around 11 p.m., in Chandkathi village of Nazirpur in Pirozepur district, three policemen accompanied by local watchmen and other armed rowdies, searched the whole area for Hindus who were warned to leave the country as soon as possible. The members of a certain club including Dulal Krishna Mondol and five other Hindus, were taken into police custody and harassed. After all this, these innocents were released on bail, the amount of which ranged from eight to ten thousand takas. Subsequently, a number of Hindus left the area. In twelve villages of the Ghazirhaat union of Dighlia in Khulna district, Hindus were consistently persecuted. Having lost the elections, the candidate for chairmanship, Mulla Jamaluddin's people prevented the Hindus from farming, stole their crops, took their cattle, and looted their shops.
- In Durgapur village of Barisal district, on 10 December, Abdus Sobahan Bhuiya and Gholam Hussain armed themselves and walked into the house of Rajendranath Das. The intruders had fallen out with Das over property. At first they threatened murder; later they had taken all the gold and jewellery and had finally set the house on fire. When the people in the house had tried to prevent the intruders from taking away a statue of Radha-Krishna, made from an alloy of eight precious metals, they were mercilessly beaten. Before they left, the murderous duo threatened Rajendranath with dire consequences if his family and he did not leave the country.
- On 26 August, in Talbunia village of Rampal in Bagerhaat district, some policemen acting under the influence of local fundamentalists walked into the house of an octogenarian called Lakshman Chandra Pal and beat up his grandson, Bikash Chandra Pal. They had also thrashed his sons, Pulin Bihari Pal

and Rabindranath Pal. When Pulin's wife had tried to intervene, they beat her as well. After that they had dragged Pulin, Rabindranath and Bikash to the police station, accused them falsely of various crimes and jailed them. No bail was set for them. It had transpired that sometime before independence, Abdul Hakim Mulla from Sholakura village had molested Lakshman Chandra's niece, and had assaulted the rest of the family. The accused had been arrested, tried and sentenced to imprisonment. Once out of prison, accompanied by three men, he had gone to Lakshman Chandra's house and taken their revenge on each member of his household, aided and abetted by the local police. These attacks on Lakshman Chandra showed up the abject lack of security in the area and many Hindus left.

- Hindu homes in Gopalgunj, Kotalipara, Maksadpur and other parts of the Gopalgunj district were victims of theft, dacoity, looting, forcible occupation, illegal lawsuits, forgery, rape, and general all round mayhem. Temples in the area were destroyed and the police forces actively helped in the persecution of the Hindus.

- The chairman of the Kotalipara subdistrict, set his henchmen loose on Hindu women in Mandra Lakhinpar village of Kushala Lakhinpar in broad daylight. These thugs extorted money and valuables from the Hindu residents of Motherbari, Lakhirpar, Ghagharbazaar, Khejurbari and forced their terrorized victims to sign documents that made over all their goods to their assailants. Hindus began leaving these areas and the trickle became a flood after Mrs Bhoumick of Kotalipara's Sonali Bank was assaulted and Mamata and Madhu of Kandigraam were raped.

- Late in the night of 3 July, some policemen entered the house of Anilchandra of Garibpur village in the subdivision of Chitalmari of Bagerhaat. Anilchandra was not at home so the policemen beat up his wife and child.

- On the same night, the policemen looted the house of the village schoolmaster, Amulya-babu. On the 4th, the police attacked the house of Kshitish Mondol of Surigati. None of the men of the house were around so they raped Mondol's wife and daughter.

- In the same village, policemen raided the house of Shyamal Biswas on the 5th. Unable to find Shyamal-babu at his home, they raped his daughter and then made off with all the valuables.

- A few days after these incidents, a local hooligan forcibly took possession of Nirod Bihari Roy's house in Chitalmari village. Roy's complaints to the local administration had no effect.

- A Hindu of Kalashira village was evicted from his house by Mansur Mallik.

- The Chief of the Education Department of Gopalgunj was notorious for enticing Hindu women with the promise of jobs, and when they took the bait, raping them. Two women of the Biswas household in Demakoyir village were raped in this manner. The same person, by threatening to transfer Hindu schoolmasters and teachers, managed to amass a fair amount of money from them in the form of bribes.

- Jagdish Haldar's house in Alti village of Gopalgunj was raided by the police as well as young armed hooligans. In this joint effort, the members of the house were beaten up and all their possessions looted. Before leaving, the raiders threatened to murder every member of the house.

- In the same year, on 12 August, in many more Hindu homes, similar atrocities were perpetrated by the police and young Muslim hooligans. Some temples were also destroyed in the process. Ashutosh Roy, Sukumar Roy, Monoranjan Roy, Anjali Roy, Suniti Roy, Bela Biswas were tortured. The marauders said before they left that no temple would be left standing in this country.

- Fundamentalists as well as the police made an issue out of the death of the Chairman of Maksadpur subdistrict (in Gopalpur district). In reprisal for the death, the area's Hindus were threatened with torture. The wife of Shibu from Basudebpur village and Kumari Anjali of Mahatali village were raped by the police.

- On 20 June, at Bastukathi village of the Swarupkathi subdistrict (in Pirozepur district), the police suddenly attacked the Hindu community. The standing crops of the Hindus on the banks of the Bastukathi river were destroyed by the police. The farmers were rounded up and released only after payment of huge ransom.

- In the same village on 11 June, subdistrict health worker, Minati Rani, her sister-in-law and her brother were accosted on the road and confined to a temporary police camp where they were subjected to various threats. They were later released after a fine of one thousand takas was paid. Sudhangsu Kumar Haldar's fourteen-year-old daughter, Shiuly, of Purbajala Bari village of Swarupkathi, was abducted by a hooligan, while she was on her way to her uncle's house. Shiuly lay unconscious on the road. In reply to Sudhangsu Haldar's plea for justice to the local elders, he was told, 'If you cannot bear these, then you will have to leave the country.'

- On 7 April 1979, at Burigunj Bazaar of Shibgunj subdistrict (in Bagura district), members of the Masjid committee attacked the house of Dr Sachindra Kumar Saha in an apparent reaction to a fight over the construction of a mosque. They broke open the doors and windows of the house, looted it and set it on fire. The adjacent temple was razed to the ground. Then the mob went on a rampage for more than two hours and looted property worth over 1.1 million takas. In the mêleé, Dr Saha's son somehow managed to escape and reached the local police station. When the police arrived, they were attacked by a convict and his accomplices with sticks, iron rods and bricks. A number of police officers were injured. Later, Shibgunj subdistrict's acting chief official filed criminal charges against the main accused and sixty-five of his accomplices and had them arrested. However, upon the intervention of higher officials they were all released. After the incident, Dr Saha and his family went in fear of their lives as did the Hindu community in the area.

- The Hindus of Tikrapara village of Alfadanga subdistrict (in Faridpur district) were so brutally assaulted on 3 and 4 May 1979 that they left their ancestral homes en masse to seek shelter elsewhere.

- The wife, minor daughter and daughter-in-law of Haren Biswas of Rahatpur village of Raipur union of Mohammadpur subdistrict (in Magura district) were assaulted by one of the influential people of the area. When a case was filed against him, he and his friends started to harass Haren Biswas ultimately forcing them to leave the country.

- On 19 and 20 May, the police arrested Anil Kumar Bagchi, Sushil Kumar Pandey and Makhan Lal Ganguly of Debagraam village of Kotalipara subdistrict (under Gopalgunj), and accused them of being involved in the Bangabhumi agitation; they were only released after a large sum of money was paid to the police. An unwilling Ramesh Chandra Ojha of Mirakathi village of Jhalkathi district was forcibly converted to Islam. Pressure was then brought to bear on Ramesh Chandra's wife and his elder brother to become Muslim. When his wife's complaints to the village elders fell on deaf ears and the threats became too insistent to bear she left the village fearing for her life.

- Sudhir Baidya's wife of Jobai village of Kochua subdistrict (under Gopalgunj) was raped by a policeman dismissed from the force. Sudhir Baidya, shamed and fearful, went into hiding and his wife's life was threatened.

- In the same village, Upendra Malo's cow was slaughtered and eaten; Upendra was humiliated when he went to the administration for justice.

- Kartick Roy of Boultoli village of Boultoli union (in Gopalgunj) was killed defending his paddy from marauding Muslims. His wife, Renuka, was forced to tell everyone that he had died a natural death.

- Manju Rani Seal, a student in the ninth standard and the daughter of Premanand Seal of Dakshin Chandpur village (in Laksam subdistrict in the Comilla district), was abducted at 8 p.m., on the evening of 4 December 1988, by Abdur Rahim and his goons. A case was registered the next day at the Laksam police station by her distraught family. There is still no trace of Manju Rani. Her abductors threatened Premanand Seal and his family but the police took no action when informed. Hindu families in the area are now terrified of sending their daughters to school.

- On 25 April, the police of Gutia village of Uzirpur subdistrict (in Barisal district) arrested sixteen Hindus while they were singing kirtans. They were all daily labourers from the nearby betel leaf farm.

- Hindus from Siddhirpasha village of Abhoynagar subdistrict (in Jessore district) were selling land worth twenty thousand takas per bigha at eight thousand takas and fleeing to India. This was after the passing of the National Religion Bill; there was a rumour in the village that Hindus would not be able to sell their land and property. Madhab Nandi told his fellow Hindu villagers to ignore the rumour. A few days later, around a dozen armed people raided his house in the middle of the night and raped his young daughter and daughter-in-law who was seven months pregnant.

- Deben Biswas of Khoksa subdistrict of Kushtia district was gunned down on 15 May. Even though a case was registered, no one was arrested.

- On 12 and 16 August 1988, some policemen accompanied by a gang of armed thugs raided the village of Garibpur in Chitalmari subdistrict (of Bagerhaat). They disfigured the idols of the local temple and raped the girls of the village. When they left they took around twenty-five of the village youth captive. The young men were thrashed mercilessly and released only after a ransom was paid. Narayan Bairagi, Sushanto Dhali, Anukul Baroyee, Ranjan Dhali, and Jagdish Bairagi were kept in custody for a long time.

- The same story was enacted in Charbaliari village. Fifteen to sixteen people were detained and then released on payment of ransom.

- Similar incidents took place in Hijla and Barbaria villages. Eight or nine locals were detained, harassed and then released on the payment of bribes.

- In Parkumira village of Tala subdistrict in Satkhira, Rabindranath Ghosh's young daughter, Chhanda, a third standard student, was raped by her schoolteacher on 16 May 1979. On that night, Chhanda was asleep in the veranda of her house along with the rest of the family. In the middle of the night, her schoolteacher abducted her with the help of some young hooligans. They took the terrified little girl to a garden nearby and raped her. The next morning, Chhanda was found unconscious in a pool of blood and was rushed to the Satkhira Hospital. Although a case was filed against the perpetrators in the Tala police station, no one was arrested.

- In Muksudpur subdistrict of Gopalgunj district in Gohala village, Ujjala Rani was raped by five people who had taken over her father's property. When the local police were told about the rape, they refused to register a case.

- In Jhalkathi, Nolchhiti, Swarupkathi, Banaripara, Agailjhora, Uzirpur, Nazirpur, and Gournodi of Barisal district, several members of the minority community were arrested for ostensibly belonging to the Sarbahara Party. They were tortured for a considerable period of time before being released on the payment of adequate bribes. For fear of police torture many Hindus in these areas were going under cover.

- In the Agailjhora subdistrict, Kashinath Haldar was so badly tortured by the police that it was feared that he would succumb to his injuries.

- In the Digha union of Naotana village of Nazirpur subdistrict (of Pirozepur district), the police falsely accused Kesav Sadhu's only son of being a member of the Sarbahara Party, and beat him up so viciously that Kesav Sadhu took one look at his battered son, suffered a heart attack and died.

- In the Charamdhua union at Charamdhua village of Raipur subdistrict (in Narshindi district), seventy or eighty hooligans led by a duo raided Hindu homes. After the attack twenty families comprising at least 150 people left the village as refugees.

- In the Jahangirpur village of Madan subdivision (in the Netrakona district), on 16 May, a group of fundamentalists raided the house of Binoy Baishya, a minority leader. Binoy-babu's family members were detained for thirty-six hours to make it easier for them to loot and plunder. When the police were informed, they arrested the two sons of Binoy-babu. However, they were later released.

- In Bankergunj, Chandpur union, of the Durgapur village, on 10 December, under the supervision of Gholam Hussain Pintu, more than a hundred men, raided the home of Rajendra Chandra Das. The family members who argued with them were not only beaten up but set alight as well. When Rajendra Das complained to the police, the rogues set fire to his place and threatened the lives of his family. Later, when he filed a suit in the subdistrict court, no notice was taken of his complaint by the authorities.

- Dinesh Chandra Das of Mirwarispur village in the Begumgunj subdivision of Noakhali village was forced by a group of people to give up all his property.

With this endless list of calamities running through his mind, sleep continued to elude Suranjan. He remembered his two-year stint in 1988–1989 as a reporter with *Ekata* and recalled how at that time his notepad was always full of such tales of suffering and woe. Some of it was printed in the magazine and others were left out. And his editor would say to him: 'Do you understand, Suranjan, all these are cases of the strong oppressing the weak, the rich oppressing the poor. If you are rich, it doesn't matter much if you are Hindu or Muslim. Unfortunately that is the rule of a capitalist society. If you go and look for yourself you'll find that poor Muslims also are being persecuted. This is because the rich always torture the poor—they don't care whether their victims are Hindu or Muslim.'

Day Three

The winter chill wasn't as penetrating as it usually was and Suranjan shoved aside his quilt. He didn't feel like getting out of bed, especially as he hadn't slept all night, so he lolled about thinking of the events of the previous night. He had roamed all over town, though he had not felt like visiting anyone or talking to anybody. Although he had disobeyed his parents and left the house, he had felt very concerned for them, even though his concern hadn't been enough to make him want to return home. The problem was that Kironmoyee's fear communicated itself to him and his father's listlessness was no help at all. And his sister! He had felt like drinking just so he could drown the fear he had seen in Maya's eyes as she had pleaded with him to help the family. He thought fondly about his sister. It seemed like just the other day when she had been a little girl who had held on to his finger as they walked beside the river. He remembered that every year before the pujas, she would throw little tantrums and ask for new clothes. Suranjan would tell her, 'Forget the pujas! They'll be dancing those indecent dances in front of stuffed clay images, and you want to wear new clothes on such an occasion? Honestly I wish you would grow up.'

At this Maya, who was darkly beautiful even as a child, would plead sweetly, 'Dada, take me around to see the pujas . . . please?' And Suranjan would scold her, 'Why can't you just be a normal human being? You must stop behaving like a Hindu.'

Maya would giggle and ask, 'Why? Aren't Hindus human?'

In 1971, Maya had had to take on the name 'Farida'. Suranjan often made the mistake of calling her by her pseudonym a year after it was no longer necessary and Maya would protest and scowl angrily at him. To make amends, Suranjan would buy her a chocolate and Maya, all anger forgotten, would beam with joy! As she stuffed the chocolate into her mouth, her soft eyes would dance with happiness. There were other good memories of her. Every year, during Id, when she saw her friends playing with gaily coloured balloons, she would demand some for herself. She would also ask for crackers and sparklers. At other times, she would tug at Kironmoyee's sari and plead with her mother for the sort of food her Muslim friends ate. 'They are going to cook pulao and meat at Nadira's house. I want to have pulao too . . . ,' she would say. And Kironmoyee would cook some for her.

And now Maya had left the house. She had been gone since the day before yesterday but there was still no news from her. His parents were not all that worried, presumably because she was taking refuge in a Muslim home. Besides, Maya was the responsible one in the family. Already, despite her youth, Maya was making money from two tuitions. She was a student at the Eden College, and she rarely, if ever, asked for any financial help for her education.

It was Suranjan who always needed money. He had no job, and was making no use of his Master's Degree in Physics. Soon after he had passed out of college he had been very keen on finding employment and was interviewed for a few jobs. He had been one of the sharpest students in the University, but ironically the students whom he had helped with their studies, got more marks than him in the final examinations. The same story repeated itself when he went looking for work. Those who had scored less than him, got good jobs as teachers. It wasn't as though he hadn't done well in his interviews. And yet, surprisingly enough, those candidates who had clicked their tongues in disappointment at not having fared well, would be the first to get appointment letters. Meanwhile, Suranjan got no letter at all. At a few places it was said that Suranjan wasn't being chosen because he lacked good manners and was not respectful enough to his examiners. This was not true though Suranjan would be the first to admit that he didn't make it a point to say Assalaam Aleikum or Namaskar indiscriminately—to him this was not the only way of showing respect. And it was a fact that those who said Assalaam Aleikum incessantly and made a great show of respect towards their examiners were the first to abuse them the moment they were out of hearing. Yet, it was these boys who were thought to be well-mannered and it was they who passed the interviews. And

Suranjan, who had not feigned reverence, acquired a reputation for impertinence and disrespect. Perhaps it was for these reasons or perhaps it was because he was a Hindu, but there were no jobs forthcoming with the government. He did land a job with a private firm but did not like it and resigned after three months.

Maya, however, knew how to make compromises and survive. She managed quite well with her tuitions and it was likely that she would be able to get a job with a NGO. Suranjan suspected, however, that she was having a relatively easy time of it because of her friendship with Jahangir. Would Maya end up marrying him to show her gratitude? He felt very apprehensive about this. Just then Kironmoyee entered and handed him a cup of tea. Her eyes were swollen and Suranjan realized that she had spent a sleepless night. He did not want to add to her worries by admitting that he had not slept all night, and so he yawned and said, 'I did not realize it was so late already.' Kironmoyee showed no sign that she had heard him; indeed, she didn't seem to be aware of anything around her at all. She simply stood there with the cup of tea in her hand. Suranjan thought she wanted to say something to him, but she did not utter a word. It seemed as though she was waiting for her son to reach out and take the cup of tea from her hands. How wide the gulf between them must have grown for Kironmoyee to stand speechless for so long! Finally, it was Suranjan who spoke. 'Hasn't Maya come back home?'

'No.' It was as though she had been waiting for the question to be asked and it almost seemed as though she would have replied to anything that Suranjan said. She sat down on the bed, near her son. Suranjan guessed that she sat close to him because she felt insecure. He turned away from her sleepless eyes, her unkempt hair and her crushed and creased sari. Raising himself up into a sitting position, he sipped his tea. 'Why isn't she coming home? Are the Muslims saving her? Doesn't she have confidence in us? She does not even enquire about us. Will it be enough to save her own skin alone?'

Kironmoyee did not reply. Suranjan lit a cigarette. He had never smoked in front of his parents before. But today was not a normal day. And when he lit up, inhaled and blew out smoke it did not strike him that he did not normally smoke in front of his mother. Somehow, at this moment, the gap between mother and son had been bridged and the frail wall that separated them had broken down. It had been such a long time since he had reached out to his mother with affection. He suddenly wanted to lie with his head on Kironmoyee's lap like an innocent child and talk to her about the kites that he had flown in his childhood. His uncle Nobin would bring beautiful kites for him from Sylhet. He had the most artful way of making and flying them too. All the kites in the sky would have their strings cut and his kite would reign supreme.

Suranjan gave his mother's lap a yearning look. He blew out a last ring of smoke and asked her, 'Did Kamal or Belal or anyone else come over yesterday?'

'No,' she said cheerlessly.

Kamal had not bothered to enquire after them? That was really strange. Did his friends think that he was dead? Or had they lost interest in saving his life?

Kironmoyee asked, in a choked voice. 'Where were you last night? The two of us were alone at home. Don't you even care about what might happen to us? And what if something had happened to you outside? Goutam had gone out in the afternoon to buy some eggs, and the local Muslim boys beat him up. Two of his front teeth were broken. And I believe they broke one of his legs.'

'Oh.'

'Do you remember, two years back Geeta's mother used to come from Shoni's gym to work for us? She did not have a home to live in because they had burnt down her house. So she worked in other people's houses and made enough money to rebuild her home. She was here this morning with her children to tell me that they've burnt down her new house too. She was asking me where she could buy some poison. I think she's gone mad.'

'Oh.' Suranjan put down his cup of tea.

'If Maya comes back to this house, we'll have more reason to worry about her.'

'That doesn't mean she should stay under a Muslim roof for the rest of her life, does it?'

Suranjan sounded stern. Yes, he too had taken them all to seek refuge in a Muslim home once. But at that time they had no reason to feel so bereft of all hope. They had simply felt that some evil men were up to evil work, the effects of which would surely pass with time. After all every country had its share of such people. But this time everything felt different. It felt as though some deep-rooted conspiracy to victimize them was afoot. Indeed, so suspicious did Suranjan feel that it was difficult to believe that even friends like Kamal, Belal, Kaiser and Lutfor were non-communal. In 1978, hadn't the people of Bangladesh carried out a movement to institute the word 'Bismillah' in the constitution during the Zia-ur Rahman's government? Again, in 1988, didn't the public cry out for the declaration of Islam as the State religion? Otherwise would he make such a declaration?

Secularism was supposed to be one of the strong beliefs of the Bengali Muslim, especially during the war for independence, when everyone had to co-operate with one another to win victory. What had happened to all these people after independence was won? Did they not notice the seeds of communalism being sown in the national framework? Were they not agitated? Agitation it was that had brought about the glorious war that had resulted in their country's independence. But why were all those warm blooded people as cold as reptiles today? Why did they not sense how urgent it was to uproot the sapling of communalism immediately? How could they nurse the impossible notion that democracy could come to stay in a country in the absence of secularism? It was truly ironic that those who had joined hands to strengthen the fight for independence were now the same people who were allowing the perpetuation of communalism.

'Yesterday they destroyed the Shoarighat temple, have you heard about it? Shyampur temple as well?'

Suranjan stretched as Kironmoyee continued to speak in a voice empty of all hope. He said, 'Did you ever go to pray in a temple that you feel sorry when one is destroyed? Let them damage as many temples as they want to. So what? Let all these religious structures be razed to the ground.'

'They are angry when a mosque is destroyed, don't they realize that Hindus will be just as angry when temples are destroyed? Just because one mosque has been demolished must they destroy hundreds and hundreds of temples? Doesn't Islam profess peace?'

'The Muslims know very well that the Hindus of this country will achieve nothing by showing their anger. That is why they go about their plundering without giving it a second thought. Has any

Hindu been able to touch a single mosque? The temple at Naya Bazaar has been lying in ruins for the last two years. Children jump and play on top of it. They piss on it. Does one Hindu have the courage to fist a couple of blows on the shining walls of a mosque?'

Kironmoyee got up silently and left the room. Suranjan realized that she had been building walls around herself that now threatened to shut her in totally. At one time she had not differentiated between Parveen and Archana but now her thoughts and feelings teetered in a precarious balance. And disturbingly a new question had arisen in her mind: Were Muslims alone entitled to the right of being angry and offended?

*

It was no secret that the victimization of the Hindus had begun long before the riots in 1990 and the destruction of the Babri Masjid in 1992. Suranjan remembered that in 1979, on the morning of 21 April, the idol of the Goddess Kali in the historic temple at Saheb Bazaar in Rajshahi district was smashed to pieces by a person called Ayub Ali. After breaking down the temple, the shops of Hindu owners were also destroyed. There were other instances of mayhem visited on the Hindus:

- On 16 April 1979, in the Ramgopal area of Shailakupa subdistrict (of the Jhinaidaha district) the famous statue of Ramgopal in the Ramgopal temple was stolen. The mutilated idol was later found beside the Shailakupa graveyard; its gold and silver ornaments were missing.
- The Jaigopalhaat Kali temple of Purna Lalangar village in Sitakunda was razed to the ground.
- In Uttar Chandgaon, the image in the Kuraisha Chandgaon Durgabari was destroyed.
- Two months after the National Religion Bill was passed, an image made of touchstone and the ornaments that adorned it were stolen from Dakshindihi village of Phultala in Khulna district. When the temple committee's secretary went to the Phultala police station to make a statement on the losses, the police detained and tortured him. A warrant for the arrest of all the committee members was issued. When the district Assistant Superintendent of Police went to further investigate the case, he accused the Hindu residents of the area of stealing the idol.

- On the night of 8 December, in the Dwimukha village of Kalihati subdistrict in Tangail, a raid was made on an ancient temple. A marble Shiv lingam, the images of Annapurna and Radha-gobinda and a Shaligram (ammonite stone worshipped as Narayan) were all stolen. When the police arrived, they were told that Noor Muhammad Talukdar was responsible for the thefts, but the police made no efforts to recover the stolen goods.

- The Hindus of the Burichong subdistrict, Moinamoti Union in Comilla, were sent an open letter by an organization called the Vishwa Islam which told them to leave the country immediately. They were also threatened with dire consequences if they continued to perform their pujas. On 14 April, the local hooligans poured petrol on a banyan tree outside the Kali mandir and set fire to it. Also, a man called Ali Ahmed went around telling the crowds in the market at Moinamoti, that the Hindus of the area must be eliminated by means of riots.

- On 11 March, in the Lalmohon subdistrict of Bhola, at the Sri Sri Madan Mohon gymnasium, devotional songs were being sung in praise of God, when hundreds of people attacked the place. They stormed into the temple, smashed the image of the goddess, and beat up the devotees who were present. After this all the temples in Duttapara were raided; the images of the goddesses were destroyed and the by now familiar pattern of looting and arson followed.

- In Bortia village of Ghior in Manikgunj, it was decided that the grave of Advocate Jillur Ahmed as well as a mosque, would be constructed next to the Sri Sri Kali temple which was more than a hundred years old, a plan that, if implemented, was bound to disturb the prayers of the Hindus.

- Also, in the Muhammadpur union of the Chotkhali subdistrict of Noakhali, the Muslims were planning to convert an ancient Kali temple into a commercial complex.

- In the Ghazipur Municipal Corporation's Phaukal village, on the night of 26 May, the Lakshmi temple was raided and the image of the goddess destroyed.

- In the Kashtasagara village in the main subdistrict of Jhinaidaha district, a mob laid siege to a monastery where religious functions and celebrations commemorating the ending of the Hindu year were taking place. They manhandled the pujari, dispersed the offerings made to the gods, and wrenched the drums from the *dhakis*. The police were informed immediately but no one was arrested.

- In Gopalgunj's main subdistrict, Nijara, Muslims raided Hindu temples and damaged them considerably on 14 March 1979 at 9 p.m. At the Ulupur Shiv mandir, the lock was broken open, and many valuables, including the Shiv lingam, were stolen.

- At Kushtia district, on 17 October 1988, in the area where the police station was located, the image of the goddess Durga was broken.
- In Khulna district, in the main marketplace, before prayers could commence, a group of people smashed the idols.
- At Gobra, in Jessore district, the Durga idol was destroyed.
- Again in Khulna, in the famous Pranabanandaji monastery, idols of Durga were broken on 1 October 1988.
- On 30 September, at the Satkhira Kaligunj bus-stand temple, Durga icons were shattered.
- In the Khulna subdistrict of Dumuria, the Imam of the Jama Masjid in Madhugraam sent a circular to the organizers of the Annual Durga Puja which stated that no ceremonies would be allowed as the azaan and namaaz would have to be carried out daily. This circular reached the organizers on 17 October.
- In the first week of October, a procession was taken out in Khulna district and slogans against idol worship were raised: 'No idol worship will be allowed, break them, smash them,' some of these slogans said.
- In the Mohishkhola village of the Kumarkhali subdistrict of Kushtia, the idol of Kali inside the temple was destroyed on 23 October.
- At the Kaligunj subdistrict of Ghazipur, in the Kaligunj market, the icon of Kali which was being moulded for the puja was destroyed.
- On 30 September in Nakipur district of Shyamnagar, Satkhira, a Kali idol was broken just before the commencement of the puja in the Haritala temple.
- In Pirozepur district's Bhandaria subdistrict, the wall of a Kali temple was broken down to construct a drain.
- In Borguna district's Phuljhuri market, an idol of goddess Durga was damaged by Muslim fundamentalists on the last day (Bijoya Dashami) of Durga Puja.
- In the Bukabunia union of the Bamana subdistrict, a Durga idol was shattered days before the Puja festival started.

And they said Bangladesh was a country that believed in communal harmony! Suranjan laughed out aloud. He was alone in the room. There was only a cat sitting by the door, and it jumped up in alarm at the sound of Suranjan's laughter. Suranjan's attention was drawn to the animal. Hadn't the cat been to the Dhakeshwari temple today? Which community did the cat belong to? Was it Hindu? Presumably it was Hindu, since it lived in a Hindu home. It was a black and white cat, and there was a softness about its eyes. It seemed to pity him. If it had the ability to pity, the cat must be Muslim! Must be a liberal Muslim! They normally looked at Hindus with a touch of pity. The cat got up and left. Perhaps it was going to the Muslim kitchen next door, since there wasn't much food being cooked in this house. In that case the cat had no communal identity. In fact only human beings had racial and communal differences and only they had temples and mosques. Sunlight flooded the room and Suranjan realized that the day was well advanced. It was the 9th of December, and he longed to become a cat.

He could not remember having ever prayed in his life. Nor had he ever visited a temple. Indeed, he had vowed to bring socialism to his country and in pursuit of his dream had gone out into the streets and given speeches, attended meetings. He had espoused the cause of farmers and labourers, lobbied for the socio-economic uplift of the country. In fact, he had spent so much time looking after the interests of others that he had hardly had the time to worry about his family's and his own interests. And yet, it was the same Suranjan at whom they were pointing a collective finger and labelling a Hindu! It was the same Suranjan that the local boys were chasing with cries of 'Catch him, catch him . . .' They hadn't beaten him up today, but maybe they would tomorrow. Just as they had thrashed Goutam when he had gone out to buy eggs, so also when he went to buy cigarettes from Moti's shop round the corner, he might suddenly find himself receiving a hard blow on his back. His cigarette would fall from his lips and when he turned around to see who his attacker was, he would find Kuddus, Rehman, Vilayat, and Sobhan menacing him with sticks and knives. Suranjan shut his eyes and shuddered at the thought. Did this mean that Suranjan was afraid? Perhaps, even though he was no coward!

Getting out of bed, Suranjan went in search of the cat. The stillness of the house shocked him. It seemed as though no one had lived in it for a very long time. In 1971, when they had left the village to come and live in the house in Brahmapalli, the quiet and emptiness of the place had bothered Suranjan. He had missed his kite, his carom board, his marbles and his books and the lack of any activity and people had depressed him and filled him with unease. A similar unease gripped him today. Would his father continue to stay in bed? If his blood pressure had in fact increased, who would call the doctor?

Going to the market, buying medicines, calling mechanics, arranging the newspapers—Suranjan had never done these chores. He did not have much to do with the house. Thrice a day, sometimes twice, he would eat at home and that was the extent of his involvement in the household. He usually returned only late in the evening; if it was too late, and the front door was locked, he would let himself in through a door that opened into his own room. He would ask either Sudhamoy or Kironmoyee for money if he needed it, though he felt ashamed every time he did so. He was thirty-three years of age and still did not have a job. Sudhamoy would say to him, every now and again, 'I will be retiring soon, Suranjan, I think you should do something.' It was true that he did not have it in him any longer to shoulder the family's responsibilities. He continued to support the family by seeing a few patients in the outer room, but it was obvious it was a strain. And all this while Suranjan would wander in and out of the party office, Madhu's canteen, the Ghatak Dalal Nirmul Committee office and the Press Club and other regular haunts, and return home completely exhausted where he would find food waiting for him on the table. He would eat if he was interested, or ignore it otherwise. Gradually the orbits of Suranjan and his family separated and the gap widened with each passing year. But this morning when his mother had come to him with a cup of tea and sat beside him on the bed, he had realized how much his parents still depended on their wasteful, indifferent and totally irresponsible son. He felt remorseful. After all, what had he contributed to his family?

And how far they had come down in life! It wasn't that the once wealthy Sudhamoy was complaining. He was quite content with a simple meal of dal and rice. This was true of Suranjan as well. He could remember being forced to drink milk and eat butter by his mother when he was a child and being scolded when he refused to obey her orders. But today, even if he wanted milk and butter, fish, meat and paranthas, would Sudhamoy be able to provide him with these? However, he had never cared for wealth and luxury; his father had been responsible for inculcating this attitude in him. At a time, when all Suranjan's friends were interested in were clothes of the latest cut, Sudhamoy bought for his son books on the lives of Einstein, Newton and Galileo or books on the French Revolution, the Second World War or the novels of Gorky and Tolstoy.

Sudhamoy had wanted his son to grow up with distinction. But this morning, as he searched for the cat, Suranjan wasn't sure whether he had distinguished himself in any manner, whether he had achieved anything at all! He was not greedy, and did not long for material things. He was also quite selfless and was always concerned about the well-being of others. Was this an achievement? Confused and pre-occupied, Suranjan crossed the veranda. Sudhamoy, who had been reading the newspaper, caught sight of his son and called out to him: 'Suranjan.'

'What is it?' he asked.

'Have you heard that Joshi, Advani and eight others have been arrested? They say more than four hundred people have died. UP's Kalyan Singh will be tried. America, in fact the whole world, has condemned the demolition of the Babri Masjid. Curfew has been declared in Bhola, and the Bangladesh National Party, Awami League and many other parties have stepped out to try and restore communal harmony. There are vivid descriptions here of the turn of events.'

Sudhamoy's eyes were soft and full of wonder, very much like the eyes of the cat.

'Actually, do you know what the truth is? Those who are causing these riots are not doing so for the love of any particular religion. Their main aim is to loot and plunder. Do you know why they loot the sweetmeat shops? Simply in order to satisfy their greed for sweets. Likewise, jewellery shops have been broken into because of a love of gold. The riots are quite clearly the result of hooliganism. In fact, there is no real difference between the members of the two different communities. And the rate at which peace marches are being conducted, something or the other will soon be done to normalize the situation. In 1990, you will recall, Ershad's downfall was brought about by this very issue. By the way, Suro, did Ershad compensate the losses of the Hindus, as he promised he would?'

'Have you gone mad, Baba?'

'Actually, my memory fails me nowadays. Those accused in the Nidarabad murder case have been sentenced to death by hanging . . .did you know?'

Suranjan could see that Sudhamoy was trying to convince himself that in this country justice was done to the Hindus. The incident he was referring to had occurred at Brahmanbaria in Niradabad village: Birajabala Debnath and her five children, Niyatibala, Subhash Debnath, Minatibala, Suman Debnath and Sujan Debnath were taken to the Dhopajuri lake, murdered and chopped into pieces with an axe. Later these pieces were stuffed into a drum, which was then sealed and thrown into a lake. On the following day the drum floated to the surface and the dismembered bodies were discovered. It turned out that they had been killed because their murderers were trying to ensure that they would not be suspected of the earlier murder of Birajabala's husband, Sasanka, who had been killed by people who had wanted to acquire his land. Those accused of the murder—Tajul Islam and Chora Badshah—were sentenced to death by the Supreme Court, about four months after the multiple murders. It was sadly apparent that Sudhamoy was referring to the incident only to convince himself that Hindus and Muslims were treated the same and that Hindus were not second class citizens in this country.

'Did you go on the peace march yesterday? How many people were there, Suranjan?'

'I don't know.'

'Barring the Jamaatis, all the other parties were out yesterday, weren't they?'

'I don't know.'

'The government must be providing police protection?'

'I don't know.'

'In the Shankhari Bazaar area, the roads are said to be lined, from one end to the other, with trucks filled with police.'

'I don't know.'

'The Hindus are opening up their shops, aren't they?'

'I don't know.'

'They say the situation is very bad at Bhola. Is it true, Suranjan? Or are they exaggerating?'

'I don't know.'

'They must have beaten up Goutam for personal reasons. Is it true that he is a ganja addict?'

'I don't know.'

Suranjan's dispiritedness and stonewalling gradually dampened Sudhamoy's enthusiasm and desire for information. He held his newspaper up in front of his son's eyes and said, 'You don't read the newspapers, do you?'

'How will it benefit me?'

Sudhamoy ignored the question and said: 'Just about everywhere they are protesting against the riots. Everyone is trying to prevent the situation from getting any worse. So, will the Jamaatis have enough strength to break the police barricades and force their way into the temples?'

'What have you got to do with temples? Have you suddenly become religious in the last stage of your life? How will it affect you even if all the temples are smashed to pieces? Let them destroy all the temples that come their way. I will be very happy.'

Sudhamoy was embarrassed. Suranjan was aware that he was hurting his simple, good-natured father but he was impatient with his view of the situation. As members of the second class Hindu minority, it was foolish, he thought, to try and see themselves as equal to the Muslims who were the first class citizens of this country. They had never been conventional Hindus. They had accepted the Muslims as their brothers and their friends . . . but to what end? What good had it done Sudhamoy and Suranjan? Despite everything, the only identity that they had was their Hindu one. They had always been non-believers, and they had spent their lives professing humanity and humanitarianism . . . but what good had that achieved? They still had to live with the fear of being insulted and of course physically wounded. They still had to cringe with fear at the prospect of being charred by the flames of communalism.

Suranjan remembered the day when as a student in the seventh standard, a friend called Faroukh had taken him aside during the lunch break and said, 'I have brought something delicious to eat. I won't tell anyone about it; you and I will eat it quietly up on the roof, okay?' It was not as though Suranjan was famished, but he had approved of Faroukh's proposal. They had climbed up to the roof where Faroukh had opened his tiffin box, taken out a kebab and given it to Suranjan. The two of them had chatted happily as they ate the kebabs. In return for the treat, Suranjan thought that he could ask his mother to make some delicious coconut sweets for his friend. He had asked Faroukh, 'Did your mother make this? I must treat you to my mother's cooking one of these days.' To his surprise, once they had finished eating, Faroukh had cheered aloud. Before Suranjan could react, he was bounding down the stairs, and before long he and the rest of the class were yelling with joy over the fact that Faroukh had made Suranjan eat beef. Everyone had gathered around Suranjan, laughing at him and teasing him. Some of them had pinched him, others had slapped his head, some pulled at his shirt, and a few had even tried to take off his shorts. He had seen a few poking their tongues out at him, and others, exhilarated beyond measure, had filled his pockets with dead cockroaches. Suranjan had been shattered. His eyes had brimmed over with tears. These hadn't been prompted by any shame he felt from eating beef but from the sadistic pleasure his classmates were having at his expense. He had felt a deep sense of isolation. The idea that he was one kind of human being and that all of them were of another kind, had crossed his mind for the first time. He had gone home that day and broken into uncontrollable tears. 'They plotted to feed me beef . . .' he had said to his father when he was asked why he was crying.

Sudhamoy had laughed at this, and said, 'Is this any reason for you to cry? Beef is a delicacy. I'll go to the market tomorrow and buy some beef, and all of us will eat it together.'

The next day Sudhamoy had made good on his promise. Kironmoyee had cooked the beef after a good deal of cajoling on Sudhamoy's part who had explained to his wife, at great length, the futility and illogicality of observing such customs. Even saints and sages did not have these prejudices, Sudhamoy had argued. Besides, he pointed out, they were only depriving themselves for spicy fried beef really did taste good. By and by, Suranjan's childhood sense of shame, fear, regret and prejudice had ceased to bother him.

Sudhamoy's family looked up to him in every way, and on his part, Sudhamoy had brought up his children well. Indeed, Suranjan regarded his father as an extraordinary human being. With reason, for in these difficult times it was rare to find someone with so much honesty, simplicity, purity of thought and deed, love, and above all so strong a sense of secularism and dislike for communalism.

Now, Suranjan left his father's room quietly. He was not interested in reading the newspaper—he wasn't interested at all in the views of various intellectuals against communalism nor did he want to look at pictures of peace marches. He did not need the sense of reassurance his father seemed to get from things like this. He would much rather look for the cat. The cat that had no identity. After all, cats did not belong to any specific community and Suranjan wished all over again that he was a cat.

*

Sudhamoy had returned from the internment camp after a few days. Was it seven days? Six? He hadn't been able to tell for sure. All he knew was that he had always been extremely thirsty during his imprisonment. So thirsty, in fact, that even with his hands and feet bound and his eyes blindfolded, he had tried to roll himself forward, in the hope that he might bump into a pot of water. But where was water to be found in the camp? The Brahmaputra was brimming with water, but all the pots in the camp were empty. When he begged for water, the sadistic guards would laugh at him. One day, however, they did give him water. They took off his blindfold and forced him to watch them urinate into a jug. When the jug was put to Sudhamoy's lips, he had turned his head away in disgust, but one of them had forced his mouth open while the other poured the contents of the jug in. Those who were watching the spectacle had broken into harsh laughter as the warm, salty liquid had trickled down his throat. Sudhamoy had felt at the time that he would rather have drunk poison!

They had then suspended him from a wooden beam and thrashed him. With each blow they had told him to become a Muslim; to read the kalma and announce he had converted to Islam. But Sudhamoy had held firm. Just like Kunta Kinte, the black boy in Alex Haley's *Roots*, who was mercilessly whipped for refusing to accept he was Toby, so too did Sudhamoy refuse to call himself a Muslim. His enraged tormentors finally said that whether he accepted or not, they'd make a Muslim out of him. One day, after Sudhamoy had again thwarted their efforts, they jerked up his lungi, and mutilated his penis. Sudhamoy had seen the blood and the severed foreskin and heard the harsh laughter before he had lost consciousness. After this incident, he had entertained no hope of returning to his family alive. The other Hindus in the camp had all agreed to read the kalma and convert to Islam in the hope that they'd be spared, but they were murdered regardless. Surprisingly enough, Sudhamoy's life was spared, perhaps because he had been 'converted' so radically. The torture did not stop, however, and it was a crushed and broken human being who was finally thrown out of the camp.

Even today, it amazed Sudhamoy that he had managed to reach his home with his ribs and legs broken and bleeding from his severe wounds. Where had he found the strength and will to keep going? Perhaps it was the same inner strength that still kept him alive. When he had reached Brahmapalli he had fallen at the feet of Kironmoyee. She had shuddered at the sight of the bleeding, broken body that lay in front of her but finding unexpected strength within her had gathered up her husband and two children and taken them to safety. She had not broken down, had not allowed the pent-up tears to flow.

All through the months that followed she had not allowed herself the luxury of breaking down. When Muslim friends had said to her, 'Let me call the maulvi—read the kalma and become Muslims . . . it will be the safest thing for you to do. Explain to Maya's father,' she had displayed the same strength of will her husband had shown in the camp. Late into the night, after everyone had gone to sleep, she would continue to watch over Sudhamoy, tending to his wounds, bandaging them with pieces of cloth she had torn from her saris. In all this time, despite the tremendous burden she bore, Kironmoyee did not weep once. It was only when the village they were in celebrated the sweet victory of independence, that she had ignored everyone around her and throwing herself into Sudhamoy's arms, cried bitterly. She had cried like a child—lustily, and with no inhibitions whatsoever.

As he looked at Kironmoyee now, Sudhamoy sensed that she was storing her tears just as she had done for nine long months during 1971. Suddenly one day she will burst, he thought, and her unnatural calm will dissolve. He had no doubt that dark clouds of grief had gathered in her heart but he knew she would wait for a moment like the declaration of Joi Bangla to let herself express her emotions freely. She would have to wait for the freedom to smear her forehead with sindur, to wear a pair of sankhas, for him to wear a dhuti and for them all to be unconditionally free, to be her true self again. When would these despairing nights, so like the ones in 1971, pass?

To make matters worse, Sudhamoy's patients had deserted him as well. In the past, there had always been at least six to seven of them even when it rained but now no one came. He found it tedious to sit indoors all the time starting every time a procession passed screaming, 'Naraye takbir, Allahu Akbar . . . . Hindus leave the country if you want to live.' Despite his optimism, and faith in his countrymen, he was aware that the fanatics could at any time bomb their house or set it on fire. It was quite possible that their belongings would be plundered and it was even possible that they would be murdered. He wondered if there was really an exodus of Hindus from the country. He knew that a number of Hindus had left the country in 1990, but as the new census had not made separate estimations of the number of Hindus and Muslims, there was no way of knowing how many Hindus were left. Dust had collected on the books in the shelf. Sudhamoy tried to blow it off without much success. He picked up the corner of his kurta and used it to dust off the grime. Just then he noticed a copy of the 1986 yearly census which also had records of the years 1974 and 1981. This was the story it told:

In 1974, the total population in the hill areas of Chittagong was five lakhs and eight thousand. The Muslims living there amounted to 96,000 in that year. In 1981, the number of Muslims went up to 1,88,000, and the overall population of Chittagong went up by five lakh eighty thousand. In 1974, the Hindus had numbered 53,000 and this figure had increased to 66,000 in 1981. The rate of increase among Muslims was around 87.05 per cent, while the Hindus had increased at the rate of approximately 18.87 per cent. In 1974, in Comilla, the estimated number of Muslims was 5,250,000 and in 1981, the number had increased to 6,300,000. The number of Hindus in 1974 was 5,64,000 and in 1981 this had increased to 5,65,000. The rate of increase in the number of Muslims was roughly twenty per cent, while Hindus had increased at the rate of around 0.18 per cent. In Faridpur, the population had increased by 17.34 per cent. The Muslims numbered 3,100,000 in 1974, and in 1981 there were 3,852,000. The rate of increase was around 24.26 per cent. In 1974, the number of Hindus was 9,44,000 and in 1981 this had decreased to 8,94,000. The rate of increase was -5.30 per cent. In Pabna, the population had increased by 21.63 per cent between 1974 and 1981. There were 2,546,000 Muslims in 1974, and in 1981 the figure had gone up to 3,167,000. The rate of increase was 24.39 per cent. On the other hand, there were 2,60,000 Hindus in 1974 and in 1981 their numbers had decreased to 2,51,000. The rate of increase was -3.46 per cent. In Rajshahi, the population had increased by 23.78 per cent. The Muslims had increased by 27.20 per cent. In 1974 Hindus numbered 5,58,000, and in 1981 they numbered 5,03,000. The rate of increase among Hindus was -9.68 per cent.

Sudhamoy noticed an interesting fact on page 120: In 1974, the Hindu population was 13.5 per cent of the total population. In 1981, the Hindus constituted only 12.1 per cent of the population. Where had the rest gone? Was leaving the country the only solution? Shouldn't they have stayed back and fought for their rights in their own country? Sudhamoy cursed the migrating Hindus for being cowards.

He was not feeling too well. When he had taken the census book down from the shelf his right hand had felt weak. Now when he tried to return the book to the shelf, he found he hadn't the strength to do so. He called out to Kironmoyee, but even as he did, he felt a peculiar heaviness in his tongue. Terror enveloped him, hard and unyielding. He tried to take a step forward and realized that his foot wasn't responding. Weakly he called out, 'Kiron . . . Kiron . . .'

His wife had just begun to cook some dal. When she heard Sudhamoy call out, she went to him. Sudhamoy tried to reach out to her but his hand dropped slackly down. He whispered: 'Kiron, please lay me down on the bed.'

Kironmoyee was surprised by the change that had come over her husband. Why was he trembling so much? And why was his speech so slurred? She helped him on to their bed. 'What is the matter with you?' she asked.

'Where is Suranjan?'

'He's just left. I tried to ask him to stay, but he wouldn't listen to me.'

'I don't feel well at all, Kiron. Please do something.'

'Why is your speech slurred? What is happening?'

'I have no feeling in my right hand, and my right leg isn't responding either. Am I getting paralyzed, Kiron?'

Beginning to be afraid now, Kironmoyee took hold of Sudhamoy's arms and said, 'God forbid! No, no, you must be feeling this way because you're weak. You haven't been sleeping properly and you haven't been eating well either.'

Sudhamoy tossed restlessly on the bed. He said, 'Kiron, tell me, am I dying? Do I look as though I am going to die?'

'Whom will I call? Shall I call Haripada-babu?'

Sudhamoy clutched Kironmoyee with all the strength that he had in his left hand and cried out in despair, 'No . . Kiron . . .don't even move . . you must stay beside me. Where is Maya?'

'You know, she has gone to Parul's house. She hasn't returned yet.'

'Where is my son, Kiron? My son?'

'Stop raving in this manner.'

'Kiron, open all the doors and windows.'

'Why should I open the doors and windows?'

'I need some light. Some fresh air.'

'Let me go and call Haripada-babu. You lie down quietly.'

'All those Hindus have left their homes and gone. You won't get them. Call Maya.'

'How will I send word to her . . . tell me? There isn't anyone here.'

'No . . . no . . . Don't even move one step, Kiron. Call Suranjan.'

After that it began to be difficult to make out Sudhamoy's slurred and inaudible muttering. Kironmoyee was now truly alarmed. There was obviously something badly wrong with her husband. But what could she do? Should she scream to attract the attention of the people from the neighbourhood? They would help her, after all she had known them for many years now. But even as she thought this, she realized it would not work. Which neighbour would help her? Haider, Goutam or someone from Shafiq Sahib's house? Kironmoyee felt completely helpless. The stench of burnt dal floated into the room.

*

As with his previous journey across town, Suranjan was unsure about his destination today as well. He thought he might go to Belal's house. But just as he crossed Kakrail, he was horrified to see the burnt-out shell of a familiar shop called Jalkhabar. Charred tables and chairs from the place were strewn all over the pavement. Suranjan looked at the scene with foreboding and abruptly changed his mind as to his destination. He would go to Pulok's house in Chamelibagh. He hailed a rickshaw and asked to go to Pulok's apartment. Pulok worked for a NGO and it had been a long time since Suranjan had met him. Right next door was Belal's home, where they had spent many evenings laughing and talking with one another. And yet he had not found the time to meet his college friend!

No one answered the door bell. But Suranjan refused to be put off and continued to ring the bell. Finally, someone inside the house asked in a barely audible voice, 'Who is it?'

'It's me—Suranjan.'

'Which Suranjan?'

'Suranjan Dutta.'

The sound of a padlock being opened could be heard. Pulok himself opened the door and said in a low voice, 'Get inside.'

'What's the big idea? Why do you have to have so much security? Couldn't you simply invest in a spy-hole?' Pulok did not reply. He shut the door and double-checked the padlock to see that it was properly locked. Suranjan was amazed. Pulok spoke now, still keeping his voice low. 'How come you are out of your house?'

'I felt like it.'

'What do you mean? Aren't you afraid at all? What if this foolhardiness costs you your life? Or are you just feeling adventurous?'

Suranjan flopped on to a sofa and said, 'Whatever you say.'

He could see that Pulok was truly afraid. He sat down on another sofa, breathing heavily, and asked, 'Are you keeping track of everything?'

'No.'

'Things are very bad at Bhola. Tajmuddin,Golokpur in the Borhanuddin police station, Chhoto Dauri, Shambhupur, Daasherhaat, Khaasherhaat, Darirampur, Padmamon and Moniram villages have all suffered heavy losses. Almost 50,000

Hindus in no less than 10,000 families have been finished off completely. Mobs set fire to their homes, after looting and plundering everything they could find of any value. At least 500 million takas worth of property has been lost, two people have died and two hundred have been hurt. People don't have clothes to wear and food to eat. Not a single home remains standing and many hundreds of shops have been looted. At the Daasherhaat market, not a single Hindu shop has been spared. And the streets are full of homeless people who have to somehow cope with the cold and hunger . . .

'Also, the Madanmohon Thakurbari and its adjoining mandir, Lakshmigobindo Thakurbari and its mandir, and the Mahaprabhu gymnasium have been burnt to cinders. In fact, in the Borhanuddin Daulatkhan, Charfashion, Tajmuddin, and Lalmohon police station areas, not a single temple or gymnasium has been spared. All the houses have been systematically looted and torched. In an area called Ghuinaarhaat, Hindu homes over a two mile area have been burnt down. On the 7th night, the gymnasium at the Daulatkhan police station was set on fire. The gymnasium at Bohranuddin Market was destroyed. Fifty homes in the Qutuba village were reduced to ashes. At the Charfashion police station, Hindu homes were looted. It seems a man called Aurobindo Dey was knifed as well.'

'Where is Neela?'

'She is very very scared. How about you?'

Suranjan shut his eyes and relaxed. He wondered why he had not gone to Belal's house, instead of coming here? Was he actually becoming communal, or was the situation making him so?

'I can only say that I am alive.'

He opened his eyes when Pulok's six-year-old son, who was lying on the floor, began crying. Pulok said, 'Do you know why he is crying? The children next door, who used to play with Alok every day, have refused to play with him today. It seems the Hujur asked them not to mix with Hindu children.'

'Who is this Hujur?'

'Hujur is the maulvi who comes to their house to teach the children Arabic.'

'But the man next door is Anis Ahmed, isn't he? He is with the Communist Party if I remember right. Are you saying that he's teaching his children Arabic?'

'Yes,' said Pulok.

Once again Suranjan shut his eyes. He tried to put himself in Alok's place. He could imagine the little boy shivering and weeping over things he could barely comprehend. At a stroke he had been deprived of the friends he had played with every day. Suranjan remembered how Maya had come from school one day, crying. She had said, 'Teacher has turned me out of the class.' All the schools were required to hold compulsory classes in religion. And Maya had been asked to leave the Islamiat class. She was the only Hindu girl, and she did not even have books on that particular subject. Nor was there a Hindu teacher in school to teach her separately and so she had had to stand outside the classroom, feeling forlorn and very isolated.

Sudhamoy had asked her, 'Why did they turn you out of the class?'

His daughter had replied: 'Because I am a Hindu you see.'

Sudhamoy had held his daughter close. He was so shocked, hurt and insulted that he had been unable to talk for a while. He had gone to the religious instructor's house the same day and said, 'In future, please don't send my daughter out of the class. You must not let her think that she is different.' After that Maya had been allowed to take the class and she had been much happier. Indeed, she was so taken with religious instruction that even when she played alone, she could be heard chanting '*Alhamdo Lillahe Rabbil Aalemin. Ar Rahmanir Rahim. Malike Yaumiddin.*' When she had heard her daughter say this, Kironmoyee had panicked and asked her husband, 'What is she doing? Is it compulsory to give up one's race and religion just to get a fair share of education?' Sudhamoy was anxious too about this new development. It had been all right to secure mental peace for his daughter by allowing her to be taught the tenets of Islam, but this was a new problem: What if Maya had genuinely become interested in Islam. So he had sent a written complaint to the school headmaster, stating that religion was something very personal and that it must not be a compulsory part of the school curriculum. Besides, if as a parent, he was not willing to allow his children to acquire knowledge about any religion at all, how then could the school authorities compel them to follow the dictates of any one religion? He had suggested that instead of having religion as a subject of study, it would be far more profitable to create an entirely new subject, which would include the teachings of great men as well as a study of their lives. This would benefit the students of all communities alike and not give the minorities an inferiority complex. The school authorities, however, had ignored Sudhamoy's proposal and the system remained unchanged.

Neela entered the room. She was a slim, beautiful girl. Normally she was exquisitely turned out, but today she was grossly unkempt. There were dark circles under her eyes, which were full of fear and anxiety. Nervously she began, 'Suranjan-da, why haven't you been to our house for such a long time? Don't you want to know how we are, whether we are alive at all? We always get to know when you come to visit them next door . . . ' At this point she suddenly broke down and sobbed.

Why should she cry just because Suranjan had not been coming to their house? Was it a sense of helplessness born from communal discrimination that made her cry? And did she feel that Suranjan, Pulok and Alok also felt as insecure and unhappy as she did?

Suddenly, Suranjan felt very close to this family. Five days ago he had spent hours at Belal's house, chatting with his friend and generally having a good time. But he had not felt the need to visit Pulok and his family; now he felt differently.

'Why are you so nervous? They won't be able to do much in Dhaka. The police are on guard in Shankhari Bazaar, Islampur and Tantibazaar.'

'But the police were there the last time too. They plundered the Dhakeshwari temple and set it on fire in their very presence. The police did nothing about it, did they?'

'Hmm . . .'

'What made you come out on the streets today? It's just not possible to trust Muslims. You may think someone is your friend, but it wouldn't be surprising if he suddenly came and chopped off your head.'

Suranjan allowed himself the comfort of shutting his eyes again. Did it help to reduce the sufferings of his heart and soul when he shut both his eyes? Outside there was a good deal of screaming and shouting. Perhaps they were destroying some Hindu's shop. With his eyes shut he could sense something burning, just as he could see in his mind's eye a host of fanatics dancing about crazily with axes and crowbars in their hands. The previous evening he had visited Goutam. His friend had been lying down and there were bruises under his eyes, on his chest and on his back. He had put a hand on Goutam's heart and had sat quietly beside his bed. He had not felt the need to speak. Goutam had said to him. 'Dada, I did not do anything. They were returning from the masjid following their afternoon prayers. I had gone to buy some eggs because there were no provisions at home. I did not think there was anything to be afraid of, since it was just a local shop that I'd gone to. There I was paying for the eggs, when I was suddenly stunned by a kick on my back. There were at least six or seven of them. What could I do all by myself!? The shopkeeper and all those who were passing by just stood and laughed while they beat me up. Even when they threw me on the ground and thrashed me, I did not say anything at all. They kept abusing me all the while: "Bloody low caste Hindu . . . . " they called me. "We'll kill you, you bastard. You think you'll get away with breaking our masjid? We'll see to it that the whole lot of you are chucked out of this country."' Suranjan had listened quietly. He had wanted to say something reassuring but words had failed him. He had felt the thumping of Goutam's heart. Had his heart been behaving the same way too? Perhaps it had, at least once or twice.

Neela brought tea. While they were drinking the tea they talked about Maya.

'I am really worried about Maya. What if she suddenly decides to marry Jahangir?'

'Good God, Suranjan-da! Is that right? Please stop her before it is too late. You know how it is . . . we often make hasty decisions when we're pressured by circumstances.'

'Let's see. Maybe on my way back home I'll pick her up from Parul's house. You know, I see a definite change in Maya. Perhaps the desire to survive will compel her to change her name to something like Farida Begum . . . . It is very selfish.'

Neela's eyes seemed to reflect the stark reality of their collective situation. Alok had fallen asleep. His cheeks bore signs of his tears. Pulok had got up and was pacing the floor nervously. Some of his restlessness communicated itself to Suranjan. They had by now forgotten their tea, and it grew cold. Suranjan had, in fact, been waiting for the tea but it is strange how these thirsts gradually evaporate into nothingness. He wanted to shut his eyes and think. This country, all said and done, was his and his father's as much as it was his grandfather's, and great-grandfather's! Why, in spite of that, did he feel so isolated? Why did he have the feeling that he could not exercise his rights in this, his own country?

He did not have the right to speak freely, nor could he move about as he pleased or wear the clothes that he desired. He could not, in short, do anything of his own free will. It seemed as though he had been strangled by someone. Involuntarily, his hands reached up to his throat, and he pressed it hard with both his hands. Even as he felt his breath escaping him, Suranjan loosened his grip and shouted aloud in despair, 'Pulok, I just don't feel right . . . .'

Beads of sweat had collected on Pulok's forehead. Why sweat on such a cold wintry day? Suranjan's hands reached up to his own forehead. He was shocked to find it sweating too. Was it out of fear? Nobody was beating them up, nor were they actually being strangled. Then why were they so scared? Why did their hearts beat so fast?

Suranjan went to the telephone and dialled the number of Dilip De; his friend had once been a famous student leader. Fortunately, he was at home.

'How are you, Dada? Is there any problem? Has anything major happened?'

'No, there isn't any problem as such, but somehow I don't feel reassured. Anyway, why should I be the only one to face problems? The whole country is on edge.'

'Yes, of course.'

'How are you? I am sure you've heard about the situation in Chittagong!'

'What's happening there?'

'Three temples at the Sandip police station, at Bauria, two at Kalapania, three at Magdhrai, two at Dheuria, one at Harishpur, one at Rahmatpur, one at Paschim Sharikaith and one at Maitbhanga have been demolished. In Paschim Sharikaith a man named Sucharu Das was beaten up mercilessly and robbed of fifteen thousand takas. Two men were knifed and two houses were looted in Tokatoli. One house in Kochua in the Potia police station area, one mandir in Bhatikaine . . . .'

'How did you manage to get such a detailed report?'

'You forget that I am from Chittagong. Whether I look for information or not, it comes to me. Three houses in Boilchhari in the Banshkhali police station area and three houses in Purva Chambal have been destroyed. Five homes in Sarafbhata union of Rangunia police station, seven homes in Paira union, a temple in Shilok union, a temple in Badamtoli at the Chandanaish police station have been destroyed. Another temple at Joara was looted and plundered and at Boalgaon in the Anwara police station area, four temples and a house were destroyed. At Tegota, sixteen homes were razed to the ground and the Medhoshmuni's Ashram at Boalkhali was set ablaze.'

'I have heard that Kaibolyadhaam, Tulsidhaam, Abhaya Mitra Samshan, Samshan Kalibari, Panchanandhaam, altogether ten Kali mandirs were torched,' said Suranjan.

'They have also raided the Sadarghat Kalibari and Golpahar Samshan mandir. All the shops on Jamal Khan Road and Sirajjudaula Road were damaged. In Enaiyat Bazaar, Hindu shops and homes on K.C. Dey Road and Brickfield Road were looted and burnt. Thirty-eight houses in the Malipara area of Kaibolyadhaam and more than a hundred homes in the Sadarghat Jelepara were demolished. At Idgaon, Agrabad, Jelepara and Bahaddarhaat Manager's colony, many homes were looted and destroyed. The worst cases of loot and plunder occurred at Meerersarai and Sitakunda. Seventy-five families were devastated in the Satbari village of Meerersarai, ten families of the Masdia union, four families in Hadinagar, sixteen families lost their homes and three temples were demolished at Besarat, twenty homes at Wadepur, twelve homes in Khajuria and twenty-seven homes in Jafrabad were attacked and destroyed. One family at the Muradpur union in Sitakunda, twenty-three families of the Mahalanka village of Baraia Dhala union, eighty families in Baharpur, three hundred and forty families of Baroipara, Narayan mandir, twelve families of Banshbaria, seventeen families in Barabkund are homeless; fourteen homes in Fahradpur and two mandirs in Barabkund have been looted and put to the flames . . . .'

'How much longer do you want me to hear you out, Dilip-da? I don't feel like it anymore.'

'Are you unwell, Suranjan? Somehow your voice sounds different.'

'I don't really know.'

Just as he was putting down the receiver, Pulok asked him to phone to see if Debabrata was all right. After Debabrata, Suranjan called Mahadeb Bhattacharya, Asit Pal, Sajal Dhar, Madhabi Ghosh, Kuntala Chowdhury, Saral Dey, Rabindra Gupta, Nikhil Sanyal and Nirmal Sengupta to find out how they were. He was speaking to all these people after a very long time, even though he knew them well; now he felt a strange kinship with them all.

The phone rang. Suranjan picked it up irritably. It was for Pulok, from Cox's Bazaar. After Pulok had finished with the phone call, he said, 'At the Jamaati Shibeer in Cox's Bazaar, they've burnt the national flag.'

Suranjan was surprised at his own indifference to the information. He should have been full of sorrow and regret, but strangely enough was totally uninterested in the besmirching of the national flag. After all, it wasn't his flag, was it? It was odd he felt that way about the matter, and he tried to pull himself together and reproach himself. How could he be so petty and selfish? But the feeling of indifference would not go away, and where he should have been beside himself with anger, he felt nothing.

Pulok came and sat beside Suranjan. He said, 'Don't go home today. Stay with us. You can't tell what might happen when you are out on the streets. None of us should go out at this time.'

Lutfor had given him similar advice the previous evening. But Suranjan fancied he could see that Pulok's advice was sincere and felt whereas Lutfor's had been a manifestation of his arrogance and power.

Neela sighed in despair. 'I don't think we can continue to stay in our own country. Today we are safe, tomorrow we may be victims. What terrible uncertainty we all have to live with! I really feel it would be preferable to live a life of poverty than one which is so uncertain.'

Suranjan was about to accept Pulok's offer to stay, when he suddenly remembered that Sudhamoy and Kironmoyee were alone at home, and decided to leave. He said, 'I'll take a chance anyway. At the most I will become a martyr at the hands of the Muslims. An unclaimed body will be found lying under the flowers and the leaves of the nation. People will turn round and say, ... it's just an accident ... What do you say?' Suranjan laughed out aloud, but Pulok and Neela did not even smile.

Out on the streets Suranjan found a rickshaw. But it was only eight in the evening and he did not feel like going home. He thought with some bitterness about Pulok's good fortune in finding a nice girl and settling down well. Only Suranjan had been unable to achieve anything. Once in a while he had the urge to marry and lead a settled family life. After Parveen's marriage, he had thought of renouncing this option altogether. But, two months ago, he had met a girl called Ratna and the old urge had flared up again. He had not of course found the time and the opportunity to tell Ratna how much he liked her, but there was no question that he would have liked to have expressed his fondness for her.

Soon after they had met for the first time, Ratna had asked, 'What do you do with your time?'

'Nothing,' Suranjan had said in an offhand manner.

'You are not in service, nor business, nor trade . . .?'

'No.'

'Weren't you involved in politics?'

'I've quit.'

'I was told you were a member of the Youth Union?'

'I don't like all that anymore.'

'What do you like?'

'To move around. To meet people.'

'You don't like trees, rivers . . .?'

'Yes, I do. But most of all I like people. There is a romance or a mystery within every man . . . And I love to explore those unknown recesses of the human mind.'

'Do you write poetry?'

'No, not at all. But I do have quite a few poet friends.'

'Do you drink?'

'Sometimes.'

'You smoke a lot, anyway.'

'Yes, I do. But I don't have enough money.'

'I hope you know that cigarette smoking is bad for you.'

'Of course I know. But there is nothing I can do about it.'

'Why haven't you married?'

'No one has chosen me.'

'No one?'

'Someone did . . . but ultimately she didn't take the risk.'

'Why?'

'Because she was Muslim, and as you know, I am called a Hindu. To marry a Hindu, she would not have had to convert to Hinduism, but I would have had to call myself something like Abdus Sabber.'

Ratna had laughed when she heard this. She had said, 'It is best not to marry. After all life is short, and it is best to live it without any ties and commitments.'

'Is that why you have not married either?'

'Precisely.'

'I suppose it is good in a sense.'

'If both of us have the same outlook, our friendship will be very strong.'

'To me friendship means something pretty vast. Just because a few interests match it is not possible to become friends.'

'Does one have to pray to earn your friendship?'

Suranjan had laughed and said, 'Since when have I become so fortunate?'

'You seem to have very little confidence in yourself.'

'It is not that. I have enough faith in myself, not in others.'

'Why don't you try trusting me?'

That day Suranjan had been very happy. He wanted to recapture it in his mind, and remember Ratna, for he needed to cheer himself up. In recent times, whenever he had been down in the dumps, he'd think of Ratna. He wondered how she was. Should he go to Azimpur just once? He would simply go and ask after her health. Would she be a bit embarrassed to see him? Suranjan wasn't sure about what he should do. It was a fact that in these troubled times, Hindus were trying to get together for reassurance and safety. Wouldn't Ratna think that that was the reason he had come to see her, to enquire about her safety? And so perhaps she wouldn't find it strange to find him on her doorstep.

He asked the rickshaw puller to turn towards Azimpur. As he moved off, Suranjan thought again about Ratna. She was not very tall and did not quite reach up to his shoulder. She was fair and had a round face. There was a sadness in her eyes, which Suranjan found surprising. He often wondered what had caused it. He took out his pocket diary to confirm her address.

Ratna was not at home. An old man opened the front door a crack and asked, 'What is your name?'

'Suranjan.'

'She has gone out of Dhaka.'

'When? Where?' Suranjan was a little ashamed of his eagerness for news about her.

'Sylhet.'

'Any idea when she'll be back?'

'No.'

Had she gone to Sylhet on official work? Or was she on holiday? Or had she run away from Dhaka? Or . . . had she not gone at all? Were they saying Sylhet to put him off? But he had given his name and Suranjan was clearly a Hindu name . . . they should not have been afraid. These thoughts filled his mind as he walked the streets of Azimpur. Nobody recognized him as a Hindu. Most of the people who walked by had caps on their heads; agitated young men stood around conferring, others just loafed about but nobody recognized him. Suranjan was amused. If any of these people so much as guessed that he was a Hindu, they would pick him up and deposit his corpse in the graveyard for sure. He had no illusions about that, for there was no way he could defend himself on his own. Once again, he thought he could hear his heart thumping out aloud, as it had by Goutam's bed. He could feel the sweat break out on his forehead. It was a strange feeling for even as his body felt cold from the icy wind that pierced his thin shirt, beads of sweat collected on his forehead.

Suranjan walked on until he reached Palashi. Here he thought he would call on Nirmalendu Goon to find out how he was doing. His friend rented a room in a housing colony for fourth class employees of the Engineering University. Suranjan had great respect for Goon who was honest and cultured and did not hesitate to speak his mind. When he knocked, the door was flung open by a twelve-year-old girl. Nirmalendu Goon was sitting on his bed, intently watching television. The moment he saw Suranjan he sang a line from one of Tagore's songs, that went, 'Please do come into my humble room . . . '

'Is there anything worth watching on TV?'

'I am watching commercials. Sunlight battery, Zia silk sari and Peps Gel toothpaste. I also watch Hamad Nath, and Koran'er Bani.'

Suranjan could not help laughing. 'Is this how you spend your day? I don't suppose you've been going out, have you?'

'A four-year-old Muslim boy lives in my house. We virtually depend on him for our survival. Yesterday I went to Ashim's house. He walked ahead of me and I followed him.'

Suranjan laughed once again and said, 'But the door was opened without anyone enquiring who it was. Suppose it was someone else?'

It was Goon's turn to laugh. He said, 'Last night, at about two, some young men were standing in the middle of the road, making preparations for a procession. In fact they were discussing which slogans to use to abuse Hindus effectively. All of a sudden, I yelled out, "Who is there?" and they moved away quietly. You know, a lot of people mistake me for a maulvi, because of my hair and my beard.'

'Have you been writing poetry?'

'No. What's the point? I've stopped all that.'

'Is it true that you gamble in the Azimpur market at night?'

'Yes. I spend some time there. But I have not been going there recently.'

'Why?'

'I don't even get off my bed. I am too scared that they'll catch me the moment I do!'

'Are they showing anything on TV? I mean, have they said anything at all about the temples that are being destroyed?'

'No, not at all. If you watch TV, you'll get the impression that this is a country where communal harmony prevails. No riots have broken out here, and it's only in India that such things happen.'

'The other day someone was saying there have been no less than four thousand riots in India. Even then the Muslims in India have not left their country. But the Hindus here have one foot in Bangladesh and the other in India. To put it differently, the Muslims in India are fighting for their cause, while the Hindus in Bangladesh are running away.'

Goon spoke gravely. 'The Muslims in India are in a position to fight, because India is a secular State. Here, power is in the hands of the fundamentalists. There is no scope to fight in this country. The Hindus here are second class citizens. Since when do second class citizens have the power to fight?'

'Why don't you write about these things?'

'I have often felt like writing on these matters, but the moment I do, they'll abuse me for being an apologist for India. Actually I feel like writing on a whole lot of topics, but I deliberately do not do anything. What's the point anyway!'

Goon went back to the TV. Geeta came in with some tea. Suranjan did not feel like having any, because Goon's views had had a considerable effect on him.

Suddenly Goon laughed and said, 'You are going around enquiring after everyone, what about yourself? Are you perfectly safe?'

'Dada, do you ever win anything at gambling?'

'No.'

'Then why do you play?'

'If I don't, they start abusing me in the name of my parents. So I have to play.'

Suranjan burst out laughing, as did Goon. He had a good sense of humour and the ability to be at home anywhere. He would be equally comfortable gambling in a casino in Las Vegas as he would be in the slums of Palashi getting bitten by mosquitoes. He never seemed to mind anything, never showed his irritation. He was quite happy in his tiny room, spending his days enjoying small insignificant pleasures. Suranjan wondered how he could live so happily? Was his happiness in fact a facade for all the sorrows that he was hiding in his heart? Was he compelling himself to be happy because there was no getting away from the grim realities of life?

Suranjan got up. The sense of pain and suffering which had already found root in his heart was now growing. Was suffering infectious?

He left Palashi behind and headed in the direction of Tikatuli. He decided against taking a rickshaw, because he had only five takas with him. He bought a cigarette at Palashi crossing. When he asked for a Bangla Five, the shopkeeper gave him a strange look. Suranjan's heart sank. Did the shopkeeper guess he was a Hindu? And did he know that ever since the breaking of the Babri Masjid, every Hindu could be beaten up with impunity? He quickly paid for the cigarette and moved on. He was surprised by the way he felt, especially as he had never really felt this way before. To think he had left the shop without lighting his cigarette, just because he thought they would make out that he was a Hindu!

One's identity as a Hindu or a Muslim was not of course written on one's body . . . but Suranjan was apprehensive of being recognized as a Hindu by the manner in which he looked, spoke and walked. As he moved into Tikatuli, a pariah dog howled loudly and without warning. Suranjan nearly jumped out of his skin in fright. At the same time, he heard a group of boys say, 'Catch . . . Catch . . . .' Without looking back he ran as fast as his legs could carry him. His body broke into a sweat, and his shirt buttons came undone, but he kept running. After he had run quite a distance, he stopped at a corner and looked back furtively. There was no one in sight. Had he fled for no reason at all? Were those words not meant for him after all? Was he beginning to hear things? Or were these auditory hallucinations?

Since it was quite late in the night, Suranjan did not knock on the front door. Instead he unlocked his own door and walked into his room. As he did so, he heard cries of 'Bhagavan . . . Bhagavan . . .' interposed with wails. For a moment he wondered if some relative or Hindu friend was visiting. Possibly. Still turning this possibility over his mind, he walked into his parents' room and found Kironmoyee bowed before a clay idol in one corner. She was saying fervent prayers and every now and again would bend low and wail mournfully, 'Bhagavan . . . O Bhagavan . . .' Suranjan was so surprised by this unexpected tableau that for a moment, he did not know what to do. Should he pick up the clay idol and throw it out? Or should he, with his own hands, pull up Kironmoyee's stooping head? It made him sick to see a head bent in such humility.

He went over to Kironmoyee, helped her up and said harshly, 'What is the matter with you? Why are you sitting with an idol? Will this idol redeem you?'

Kironmoyee sobbed uncontrollably. 'Your father's hands and feet are paralyzed. His speech is getting slurred.'

Suranjan turned to look at his father. He was lying down and muttering indistinctly. Suranjan sat beside his father and took his right hand. There was no sensation in it whatsoever, and it lay limply in his own. The gravity of the situation dawned on Suranjan. Something like this had happened to his grandfather as well. The doctors had said it was a stroke. His grandfather was prescribed a lot of pills and the physiotherapist used to come and exercise his hands and feet. Sudhamoy stared blankly at Suranjan and Kironmoyee.

None of their relatives were close by. Who could he go to? In fact, they didn't have any close relative left in the country. Suranjan felt very lost, helpless and desperate. As the son, he was expected to shoulder the family's responsibilities. But he was the useless, prodigal son. To this day, he had continued to loaf about, looking for something constructive to do. He had not been able to stick to any job, nor was he able to establish a business of his own. If Sudhamoy remained sick in bed, there would be nothing for them to eat. They would end up in the streets, should this happen.

'Did Kamal or the others come over?'

'No,' said Kironmoyee shaking her head.

It was incredible. Nobody had come to find out how he was! And to think he was all over town, enquiring after everyone's well being. Everyone was in good shape, except his family and himself. Come to think of it, it was quite possible that no other family he knew had faced so much poverty and loss and uncertainty as his own! Suranjan gripped his father's useless hand and felt very sorry for him. With all the odds stacked against him, had he paralyzed himself on purpose?

'Hasn't Maya returned?' Suranjan asked suddenly.

'No.'

'Why hasn't she returned?' Suranjan shouted. His unexpected vehemence startled Kironmoyee. She stared at him. Whatever his faults, she had never really heard him raise his voice. What had come over him? There was nothing wrong with Maya's going to Parul's house. On the contrary it was reassuring for she would be safe there.

Suranjan walked about the room restlessly and said, 'Why does she have so much faith in Muslims? How long will they let her live?'

Kironmoyee was completely baffled. Here was Sudhamoy, fighting for his life, and all Suranjan could think about was Maya seeking shelter in a Muslim household.

Suranjan muttered under his breath. 'A doctor has to be called. Who will pay for his treatment? When two unimpressive young boys threatened him, he had sold property worth one million for a mere 200,000. Doesn't he feel ashamed to live like this now, a helpless pauper?'

'Do you think he did what he did only because of those boys?

He sold because he had to face litigation as well,' Kironmoyee said sharply.

Suranjan kicked a chair in disgust.

'And your daughter goes off to marry a Muslim. She thinks those Muslims will put her on a pedestal and give her all the sustenance she needs. She wants to be rich.'

Suranjan walked out of the house. There were two doctors in the neighbourhood. Haripada Bhattacharya lived at the Tikatuli crossing, and there was Amjad Hussain two houses from where he stayed. Whom should he call? Suranjan walked about distractedly. And why had he abused Maya? Was it because she had not returned? Or was it because she was so dependent on Muslims? Suranjan wondered whether he was beginning to show traces of communalism. He began to have doubts about himself as he walked up to the Tikatuli crossing.

Day Four

Haider came to Suranjan's house not so much to find out how he was, but to gossip. Haider was with the Awami League. At one time, Suranjan had joined him to start up a small business but he had abandoned the project when he realized that it was going nowhere. Haider's favourite subject was politics. Suranjan, too, was very fond of politics, but lately he had lost interest in it. What Ershad had done, what Khaleda was doing, what Hasina might do, all this was of far less importance than a long and undisturbed rest. Haider was expatiating on the subject of Islam as the national religion.

'By the way, Haider,' Suranjan said, propping himself up on the bed, 'what right does your country or your parliament have to discriminate between people belonging to different religions?'

Haider was sitting on the chair with his legs up on the table, flipping through the pages of a book. When he heard Suranjan's question, he burst out laughing. 'What do you mean "your" country? Isn't this your country too?'

Suranjan smirked. He had used the word 'your' on purpose. Now he laughed and said, 'I am going to ask you a few questions, and I expect you to give me straight answers.'

Haider took his legs off the table and said: 'The answer to your question is "no". That is, this country does not discriminate between people following different religions.'

Suranjan took a long drag at his cigarette and asked, 'Does the country or parliament have the right to favour or patronize any one religion over other religions?'

Haider answered 'No' without any hesitation.

Suranjan asked his third question. 'Does the country or parliament have the right to be partial?'

Haider shook his head.

'Does parliament have the right to alter the most important clause, that of secularism, in the Constitution of the Peoples Democratic Republic of Bangladesh?'

Haider heard him out carefully, and said, 'Certainly not.'

Then Suranjan said, 'The sovereignty of the country is based on the equality of the people in terms of rights. In the name of constitutional amendments, are we not damaging that very base?'

Haider looked at Suranjan suspiciously. Was he joking ? Why did he have to ask questions which had already been answered?

Suranjan asked his sixth question. 'By declaring Islam as the national religion, aren't the citizens of this country who are not Muslim deprived of the nation's support?'

Haider frowned and said, 'Yes.'

As they talked it was obvious that both Suranjan and Haider knew the answers to the questions. Moreover, Suranjan was fully aware that Haider and he had always had similar views on these matters. The reason why Suranjan was putting Haider on the spot, with these questions related to the 8th constitutional Amendment, was to find out whether or not Haider's communal instincts were surfacing.

Stubbing out his cigarette in an ashtray, Suranjan said,'My final question is: During the last phase of the British regime, India was divided into two separate nations. That was complicated enough.Today, why has Bangladesh again been drawn into the whirlpool of the two-nation controversy? Who will derive any benefit from the situation?'

Haider did not answer this time. Instead, he lit a cigarette, blew out some smoke, and said, 'Actually, even Jinnah ignored the question of two nations or two races as part of the national framework. He declared, "From this day onwards, Hindus, Muslims, Christians and Buddhists will not be identified by their respective religions, but by their identity as Pakistanis."'

Suranjan sat up straight and said, 'We were better off as Pakistanis, don't you think?'

Somewhat excited by this, Haider suddenly got up and said, 'No . . . . Pakistan was not good at all. As long as it was Pakistan, none of you had anything to look forward to. After Bangladesh was born, you allowed yourselves to believe that you would be honoured with the rights and facilities that are due to first class citizens, because this is after all a secular State. But when you discovered that your dreams and hopes were far from satisfied, even in the newly-created Bangladesh, then you were really hurt.'

Suranjan burst out laughing. Still chuckling, he said, 'Even you had to say, "your hopes, your dreams"! Who is this "you"? Hindus, isn't that so? After all these years of non-believing, you bracket me with Hindus?'

Suranjan swung himself off the bed and began to pace the floor restlessly. In India more than 650 people had died. The police had apparently arrested eight fundamentalist leaders. Among them were the President of the BJP, Murli Manohar Joshi, and L.K. Advani. As a mark of protest against the demolition of the Babri Masjid, a Bharat Bandh had been declared in India. In Bombay, Ranchi, and some other cities of Karnataka and Maharashtra riots were widespread. Suranjan clenched his fists in disgust at the Hindu fanatics. If he had the strength, he would line up all the fanatics from every corner of the world and shoot them. The communalists of Bangladesh had announced that, 'The Indian Government is responsible for the demolition of the Babri Masjid . . . and for this fault of the Indian Government, the Hindus in Bangladesh should not be held responsible. We have no ill-feelings towards the Hindus in this country, nor towards their temples. Let us all rise up in the true spirit of Islam and maintain communal harmony.' Their message was publicized through television and radio broadcasts. Ironically, however, these broadcasts proved to be only a facade. On the day of the hartal, as a measure of protest against the demolition of the mosque, all hell broke loose. The trail of disaster the marauding hooligans left behind was unprecedented. In the name of protest, the killers of 1971 had ransacked and set fire to the Ghatak Dalal Nirmul Committee as well as the office of the Communist Party. Why? A delegation from the Jamaat-i-Islami party had met the BJP leaders. What had they discussed? What conspiracy had they planned? Suranjan tried to guess the answers to these questions. All over the subcontinent, in the name of religion, riots were rampant. The minorities were brutalized, and Suranjan being a minority himself, understood their plight full well. No Christian in Bangladesh could be held responsible for the atrocities that were being perpetrated in Bosnia, Herzeigovina. Similarly, no Hindu in Bangladesh could be blamed for the troubles visited on Muslims by their Hindu countrymen. How could Suranjan drive in this simple logic ? Who would listen to him?

Haider said, 'Come, come, get ready. We'll go and join the human Chain that is being organized in support of communal harmony.' Human Chain! The winning of independence and all the dreams that were associated with it, was clearly the result of national unity and a vision everyone shared. The effort to preserve independence, and the sovereignty of their State, also called for a fraternal spirit. Therefore, a movement had been started in 1971 to fight all communal and fascist influences and strengthen the spirit of friendship and amity all over the country. An effort had been also made to establish world peace by calling for an International Brotherhood through the efforts of a National Integration Committee. It was this committee that had organized the meeting for the Human Chain all over the country.

'What has that got to do with me?' Suranjan asked.

'What do you mean? Hasn't it got anything to do with you at all?' Haider asked in surprise.

Suranjan's reply was cool and calculated. 'No,' he replied.

Haider, who had been standing up, was so shocked that he flopped down on a chair. He lit another cigarette, and asked, 'Can you get me a cup of tea?'

Suranjan lay down on his bed and said, 'There is no sugar in the house.'

The march to form the Human Chain was to start at Bahadur Shah park and end at National Parliament House. From eleven in the morning to one in the afternoon all traffic was diverted away from that route. Haider was about to say something more about the Human Chain when Suranjan stopped him and asked, 'What did Hasina say at yesterday's Awami League meeting?'

'You mean the peace meeting?'

'Yes.'

'In order to maintain communal harmony a peace brigade was proposed in each locality.'

'Will this save the Hindus, meaning us? Will our lives be spared?'

Haider looked appraisingly at Suranjan without saying anything. Suranjan had not shaved that morning nor had he brushed his hair. Abruptly, Haider changed the subject.

'Where is Maya?' he asked.

'She has gone to hell.'

Haider was shocked. Recovering, he attempted to make a joke of it. He smiled and said, 'Can you tell me what this hell is like?'

'Snakes bite, scorpions sting, the body is enveloped in flames and is gradually burnt to cinders, but you do not die.'

'Great! You seem to know much more about hell than I do.'

'I am bound to. After all, it is we who are engulfed by the flames.'

'Why is the house so quiet? Where are your parents? Have you sent them away somewhere?'

'No.'

'Have you noticed something, Suranjan? The Jamaatis are projecting Gholam Azam's[*] plea for justice in a different light, by using the Babri Masjid as a pretext.'

'Perhaps. But I can tell you one thing. I don't feel for Gholam Azam the way you do. It wouldn't affect me in the least whether or not he were sentenced to death.'

'You have changed.'

'Haider, even Khaleda Zia has demanded that the Babri Masjid be rebuilt. Can you tell me why she does not talk about temples being rebuilt?'

'Do you really want temples to be built?'

'You know that I am not in the least interested in temples or mosques. But when the question of building afresh arises, why should it only be mosques?'

Haider lit another cigarette. He couldn't understand why Suranjan would want to stay home on the day of the Human Chain. Earlier this year, on 26 March, when the People's Court had come into being, it had been Suranjan who had come and woken up Haider. On that day, it had been pouring with rain. Haider hadn't wanted to leave the house and had said to Suranjan, 'Why don't we just stay at home today and eat some muri?' But Suranjan had not agreed. 'You have to participate,' he had said, standing up. 'Get

---

[*] Gholam Azam, a Pakistani politician, had sought political asylum in Bangladesh. However, it was alleged in some quarters that he was engaging in anti-national activities. The various political parties in Bangladesh were divided in their response to the issue—some believed the charges levelled against Azam and demanded that he be severely punished, while others dismissed the charges altogether.

ready immediately. If we back out, everything will be lost.' So they had braved the wind and the rain, and had gone out that day. And today it was the same Suranjan who was expressing his dislike for meetings and assemblies. The Human Chain was just a farce, he said.

Haider tried from nine to eleven that morning to convince Suranjan to join the Human Chain. He did not succeed in his mission.

*

Kironmoyee fetched Maya from Parul's home. No sooner had they arrived in the house, than she started crying, with her face on her father's chest. Sudhamoy could not console her but in the next room Suranjan seethed with anger. He hated pointless tears. Had tears ever achieved anything in this world? What was needed was urgent medical attention. Suranjan had bought medicines for three days as prescribed by Dr Haripada and perhaps there were more medicines in Kironmoyee's cupboard that she didn't know about.

Suranjan's anger was mixed with self-pity. He felt no one in his family cared for him and all because he was jobless at the moment. He had never managed to hold down a regular job it was true but that was because he hated working for someone else. Now, as he pondered over whether or not he should revive his old business links with Haider, he felt very hungry. Again, he felt sorry for himself. Whom could he ask for food at this unearthly hour? Neither Maya nor his mother had bothered to come to his room to find out if he was hungry. It was a fact that he, on his part, found it a chore to enquire about dinner, but did they have to ignore him just because he was unemployed and lazy?

He had not visited his father today. This was also symptomatic of the relationship he had with the rest of the family. He made hardly any contribution to the family and yet he expected a lot from them. His usual routine was aimless and irresolute and consisted mainly of hours of loafing about with friends and assorted companions. On the home front it was one of confrontation or total indifference. Politically he had abided by the party directives, often blindly committing to memory the tenets of Marx and Lenin. How did that benefit him or the family?

Haider had left. That was fine by him. He had decided he

would not entirely quit the political scene but he did not see why he should ally himself with the Human Chain? He did not believe that such an action would release him from his recent deep-rooted sense of a separate existence. Of course, it wouldn't. What was plain to see was that much of Suranjan's indecisiveness and anger sprang from a pervasive lack of faith.

Haider and he had been friends for many decades. And through much of their association they had debated the benefits and advantages of logic, the rational mind, and the human conscience. They had jointly appealed to their fellow citizens to protect the cultural heritage of their nation, and had agitated for human rights. Today, Suranjan suddenly realized that all their efforts had been unnecessary. Instead he could have either engaged in a life filled with drinking binges and other hedonistic pursuits or he could have been a completely responsible member of the family. It was idealism that was useless and which gave rise to all these uncalled for worries and needless anxiety! Ruminating in this fashion, he lit a cigarette. His attention was drawn to a thin book lying on top of the table. He had never seen the book before. It was about the communal conflict of 1990 and he opened it and was soon engrossed in it.

- On 30 October 1990, at 1 a.m., the residents of Panchanandhaam Ashram woke up to the sound of a slogan-shouting procession. The processionists broke open the front gate and breached the boundary wall, abused the ashramites, poured kerosene on a temporary shed and started a fire. One by one, all the idols were broken, including the top of the shrine over the sadhubaba's grave, and all the religious books were burnt. The Sanskrit Language Institute was housed on the same plot as the Ashram. The crowd ransacked the book shelves, burnt the valuable books and looted whatever money they could find. On the same day, around midnight, approximately 2,500 armed people attacked the Sadarghat Kalibari with bricks, entered the main temple and broke and destroyed the idols. All the shops and hamlets alongside the Chatteswari Mayer mandir were looted and destroyed. The cremation area of Golpahar was consigned to the flames and the Kali idol (Swasan Kali) was destroyed. A news broadcast by the Voice of America on 30 October night resulted in an assault on Kaibolya Ashram. Every idol and every room in the ashram was torched; the inmates of the ashram fled to the hills. Those who failed to leave were beaten with iron rods or brutalized in other ways. The temple was damaged badly.

Something similar occurred at the Haragouri temple; the idols were smashed, all the valuables looted and the religious scriptures burnt to ashes. The area around the temple was left in a shambles and the entire population of the place was rendered homeless. An armed gang attacked the Krishnagopalji temple on Chatteswari Road in the evening. Their total booty was two kilos of silver, 250 grams of gold and other precious items including the idol. The precious sculpture of the cow at the gate and the surrounding pine trees were not spared either. Ilias colony of Bahaddarhaat was turned into a ghost town—all Hindu houses were looted, the people of the area irrespective of sex and age were brutalized.

- Large-scale looting and arson took place in many areas of Chittagong, including the Dasbhuja Durgabari at College Road, the Baradeshwari Kali mandir of Korbanigunj, the Paramahangsa Mahatma Narsingha mandir at Chakbazaar, the Barsa Kalibari and Durga Kalibari at Uttar Chandgai, the Sidheshwari Kali mandir at Sadarghat, the Dewaneshwari Kali mandir of Dewanhaat, the Uttar Patenga Samshan Kalibari of Katghar, the Magadeshwari idol was broken and Rakhsha Kali mandir of Purva Motherbari, the Milan Parishad mandir of Mogultuli, the Durga mandir, the Shivbari and Hari mandir of Tigerpass, the Sadarghat's Raj Rajeshwari Thakurbari, the Kali mandir and Durgabari of Jalalabad, the Napitpara Swasan mandir of Kul Gaon, the Karunamoyee Kali mandir of Katalgunj, the Jaikali mandir of Chandgaon's Nathpara, the Dayamoyee Kalibari and Magadeshwari Kali mandir of Nazirpara, the Kalibari of Paschim Baklia, the Brahmamoyee Kalibari of Katalgunj, the Bara Bazaar Shreekrishna mandir of Paschim Baklia, the Shiv mandirs of Himangshu Das, Satindra Das, Rammohan Das and Chandicharan Das, the Krishna mandir of Monomohan Das, the Tulsidhaam mandir of Nandankanan, the Dakshin Halishahar mandir of Port Area, the Golpahar Mahasamshan and Kalibari of Panchlaish, the Jelepara Kali mandir at Aman Ali Road and the Anandamoyee Kali mandir at Medical College Road.
- Other areas that were destroyed and plundered included the Bura Kalibari of Nalua of Satkania, the community Kalibari and Durga mandir of Jagoria, the Chandimandap Magadeshwari temple of Dakshin Kanchara, the Madhyabari Kalibari of Dakshin Charti, the community Kalibari of Madhyanalua, the temple at Charti, the Rup Kalibari and Dhara mandir of Barnakpara of Dakshin Charti, the Jalakumari temple of Paschim Matiadanga, the Krishnahari temple of Badona Deputyhaat, the Durnigar Mahabodi Bihar of Bajalia, the

famous Milan mandir and Krishnamandir of Boalkhali of Kodurkhil, the Jagadananda Mission of Aburdandi, the community Magadeshwari mandir of Paschim Shakhpura, the Mohinibabur Ashram of central Shakhpura, the Kali mandir of Dhorla Kalaiahaat, the community Jagadhatri mandir of Kodurkhil, the Rishigraam Adhipati of Kok Dandiya, the Bigraha mandir, the Magadeshwari Dhanpota and Sebakhola of Kodurkhil's Saswat Choudhury, the community Kalibari of Potiya, the Hari mandir and Jagannathbari of Dwijendra Das of Nolua in Satkania, the community Kalibari in Satkania's Dakshin Charti Dakhshinpara and the Dakshin Brahmandanga's community Kalibari.

- A hundred-strong communal crowd attacked the Mirzapur Jagannath Ashram (a place for meditation and study) in Hathazari subdistrict of Mirzapur at about 11 in the night. All the idols were destroyed and all the ornaments of Lord Jagannath were looted. The next morning the crowd set fire to the corrugated tin roof. The police who had been alerted to a second attack retreated in the face of the violent crowd. When a fresh complaint was lodged with the police they drew attention to their limitations and took no further action. That evening about forty to forty-five armed people attacked the unarmed villagers. They fled. The gang forcibly entered homes and temples in the area, destroyed idols and decamped with valuables.

- Armed gangs destroyed the idols at Dhairahaat Hari mandir at Chandnaish subdivision. They did the same with Jagannath's chariot. The Matri mandir and the Radhagobinda mandir at Pathandandi village of Borokal union were destroyed. At 12 midnight, 400 men from Boalkhali destroyed all the family temples at Kodurkhil union, and demolished the homes of Himangshu Choudhury, Paresh Biswas, Bhupal Choudhury, Phanindra Choudhury and Anukul Choudhury. The ancient Rishidhaam Ashram of Banskholi subdistrict was destroyed. All the rooms were burnt down and the books were reduced to ashes.

- Fundamentalists attacked the Jagannath Ashram of Sitakunda on 31 October. Shri Shri Kali mandir of Battala, built around 200 years ago, turned into a prize target. The head of the idol was broken and its silver crown and gold ornaments were stolen. Hindus were in the majority at the Charsarat village. On 1 November, around two to three hundred people arrived and literally looted the entire village. Whatever they could not carry away, they consigned to the flames leaving behind ashes and mute, half-burnt trees. Finally, before the marauders left they warned the villagers to leave by the 10th, failing which they would face even more calamitous attacks. Goats and cattle were killed and the granary was completely burnt. About 4,000 Hindus suffered enormous losses. More than seventy-five per cent of the houses were burnt to the ground, numerous goats and cattle killed and many women raped. The estimated loss was over twenty-five million takas. Approximately 200 people armed with lathis and iron rods attacked the Satbaria village temple and destroyed all the idols inside. The people in the adjacent villages came to know of the destruction and fled. Many of them took shelter in the neighbouring jungles. The invaders looted every house. The community Durgabari of Satbaria was razed to the ground. The temple and the residences of Khajuria village met with identical fate. The peasants lost everything. The raiders set Sailen Kumar's wife afire and the poor woman was critically injured. A few devotees were at prayer in the Shiva temple. When they were discovered by the hooligans they were taunted and abused; the idols in the temple were destroyed and as the mobs left they urinated on them for good measure.

Suranjan's eyes misted over. He could feel the urine of the thugs on his body. He flung the book away in disgust.

*

Dr Haripada had trained both Maya and Kironmoyee to exercise Sudhamoy's limbs and help him regain his strength. Sudhamoy's condition began to improve because of physiotherapy and the medicines. But he would never be his old self again and the person who was most affected by this was his daughter, Maya. She lost much of her ebullience at seeing her strong, zestful father lying in bed like a log of wood. She would wince with anguish every time Sudhamoy called out in his choked voice, 'Maya . . . Maya . . . ' Yet even as he lay there, a mere shadow of his former self, his expressionless eyes always seemed to communicate something to his daughter.

Her father had always advised her to be a straight arrow, and true to herself. He had himself always been honest to a fault and vehemently opposed to any of society's strictures that he found limiting. Kironmoyee often reminded him that their daughter had come of age, and that they should think of marrying her off, but

Sudhamoy always opposed the idea. 'She will have to study further . . .' he would say, ' . . . then take up a job, and if after all that she still wishes to get married, she may.' Kironmoyee would accept her husband's argument with a resigned sigh and then bring up her other favourite topic—despatching Maya to her maternal uncle in Calcutta. After all, Anjali, Abha, Neelima and Shibani were all Maya's contemporaries, and they had all gone to Calcutta for further studies, she would argue, to which Sudhamoy would retort angrily, 'Why should she go? Is there any regulation in this country forbidding education? Have schools and colleges been abolished?'

'Our daughter has grown up. I am unable to sleep at night. Didn't those boys obstruct Bijoya on her way to college?'

'Such things are happening to Muslim girls as well. Are you telling me that Muslim girls are not raped or kidnapped?'

'Yes, what you're saying is true. But still . . . .'

Eventually, Kironmoyee realized that Sudhamoy would never agree with her plans for Maya. Even if they had lost their ancestral home, they still had the soil of the country to plant their feet squarely on. This in itself was enough for her husband. And to be fair, Maya had never shown any eagerness to go to Calcutta. She had been to her aunt's house only once, and she had not enjoyed herself at all. She had found her cousins vain and egoistical and she was looked down upon by them. They would never invite her to join in their activities and she would spend much of the day alone, thinking of her home in Bangladesh. According to the original plan she was to spend her Puja holidays in Calcutta, but long before her holidays were over she had pleaded with her uncle to be sent back.

Her aunt had said, 'But Didi has sent you for ten days.'

'I miss my home . . . .' Maya had said, her eyes brimming with tears. Calcutta during the Pujas was always full of lights, gaiety and entertainment, but it held no charm for Maya. She had returned within seven days even though Kironmoyee had hoped she would begin to like the place and stay on.

Maya sat at Sudhamoy's head and thought of Jahangir. She had spoken to him twice on the telephone from Parul's house. Somehow, it had seemed his old enthusiasm for her company was missing. Apparently, he had an uncle in America and he had been asked to stay with him and study further. Jahangir told her that he was already making arrangements to leave. Maya was so shocked she had almost screamed. Collecting herself nervously, she had asked, 'Are you really going away?'

'Come on, it's America after all. Of course I'll go!'

'What will you do there?'

'For the time being, I'll keep myself busy with this and that, until I get my citizenship.'

'Won't you come back?'

'What will I do when I get back? Can any sane person stay in this godforsaken country?'

'When are you going?'

'Next month. Chacha's pushing me. He's afraid I might get involved in local politics.'

'Oh.'

Not once during the conversation did Jahangir ask what Maya would do in his absence. Was he expecting Maya to join him, or at least wait for him? Their four-year-long love affair, their leisurely meetings at restaurants, their frequent discussions on marriage on the banks of the Crescent Lake . . . how could his dreams of America make him forget all this? How could Jahangir's visions of grandeur make him forsake his living prize, Maya? Sitting beside Sudhamoy, Maya couldn't help but think of Jahangir. Try as she might, she could not forget him. And so to her own troubles, Maya added the pain of her near-paralytic father.

Kironmoyee's agony was even more deep-seated, and impossible to alleviate. Suddenly, in the middle of the night, she would wake up crying. Why she cried, or for whom she cried, were secrets she would not divulge. The tears would eventually dry up and she would silently carry on with the household chores—cooking, cleaning, seeing to her husband's ablutions.

Kironmoyee had stopped using sindur in the parting in her hair and loha and sankha on her wrists as was expected of every married Hindu woman. Sudhamoy had asked her to stop in 1971 and Kironmoyee had finally ceased using them altogether in 1975. Sudhamoy, too, had given up his beloved dhuti. He had gone to the tailor Taru Khalifa to have a set of pajamas stitched. When he had come home that day, he had complained of a headache and fever as well. Kironmoyee knew that Sudhamoy always felt feverish whenever he was upset.

What confused and surprised Maya was the manner in which Suranjan stayed aloof from the family even at this time of crisis. He would stay in his room all day long. He was not particular about his meals, nor did he ask for food when he was hungry. Strangely he was not even concerned about his sick, dying father. His friends would visit him in his room, where they would sit and make loud conversation. He would leave the house whenever he pleased, without telling anyone where he was going, or when he would return. Didn't he have any responsibility at all? his sister thought bitterly. No one was asking him for money, but as a son wasn't it his duty to at least help take care of his father? He could fetch medicines, call the doctor, or at the very least, sit beside Sudhamoy to keep him company and give him support. For all they knew Sudhamoy probably wanted his son to come and be with him every now and again just to show he cared.

Sudhamoy had improved considerably under Dr Haripada's medication and therapy. His speech was less slurred, but he had still not recovered the use of his paralyzed limbs. The doctor assured them that with regular exercise, his condition was sure to improve further. Maya was constantly with her father, attending to his every need. She was able to spare so much time, because she had stopped giving her tuitions. The mother of her last student, a girl called Minati, had announced one day that her daughter would not be taking any more tuitions from her, because she was going off to India.

'Why India?' Maya had asked.

Minati's mother had smiled joylessly and said nothing in reply.

Maya remembered something else about her erstwhile student. Minati had studied at the Bhikarunessa School. One day, as she was teaching her maths, Maya had heard her muttering under breath, *'Alhamdo Lillahe Rabbil Aalemin . . . Ar Rahmanir Rahim . . .'*

Maya had asked her in surprise, 'What's all this you're saying?'

Minati had replied unhesitatingly, 'Why, we recite passages from the *Sura* during assembly . . . .'

'Is that right? So they have *Sura* recitations for assembly in your school?'

'Yes, two *Suras*. After that we sing the National Anthem.'

'What do you do when the *Sura* is being read?'

'I read as well. I also cover my head.'

'Isn't there a prayer for Hindus, Buddhists and Christians?'
'No.'

Maya had found this very perturbing. It seemed immoral that one of the capital's most famous schools should make no provision to have the prayers of all faiths read out in the morning assembly.

She recalled the other girl she had taught. She was called Sumaiya and was a relative of Parul's. One day she had suddenly said to Maya, 'Didi, I won't be tutored by you anymore . . . '

'Why not?'

'Abba says he will find me a Muslim tutor.'

'Oh, I see.'

This was how Maya had lost both her students. She hadn't mentioned this to anyone at home for they would worry needlessly. As it was, Suranjan took money from the family funds, and if Maya began to do the same how would Kironmoyee manage?

Kironmoyee was in the kitchen cooking rice and dal. She would also have to make some soup and fruit juice for Sudhamoy but who was to fetch the fruit? She wondered resentfully how her son could lie in bed all day when it was evident that he was required to help. Maya was upset with her brother for another reason as well. She had begged and pleaded with him on the 7th to find them all a refuge, but Suranjan had not lifted a finger to help. They were still in great danger but all her useless brother did was laze about. Frustrated and depressed by her brother's indifference, indeed the general apathy that seemed to have gripped her family, Maya too had begun to stop planning ways in which they could tide over this crisis. She had gradually become passive and had learnt to accept things, for if Suranjan did not so much as bother about their safety and well-being, what could she do? After all she did not know anyone to whose house they could move to be safe and secure. Even at Parul's house she had not really been comfortable. Parul was definitely a very good friend and no one ever questioned her presence in their house. But this time around, the look in the eyes of Parul's people was not the same. Even though they knew her so well, for the first time they seemed to look at her as a stranger. Their look seemed to ask the question, 'Why are you here?' Parul too would say that her house wasn't secure enough for Maya to spend too long there.

How unfair, thought Maya, that the question of safety arose only with her, and not with someone like Parul? Would Parul ever have to come and seek shelter in Maya's house? Maya was doubtful that this would ever happen.

On one occasion, some relatives who had been visiting Parul's family house interrogated her, 'What is your name?'

'Maya.'

'What is your full name?'

At this time Parul had intervened and hastily said that her friend's name was Zakia Sultan. Later she had explained why she had had to disguise Maya's name. 'They are different from us . . . sort of like high priests. I wouldn't be surprised if they went around saying, "They are giving shelter to Hindus."'

'Oh.'

Maya had tried to understand the episode from her friend's point of view but she had still felt very hurt. Was it a crime to give shelter to Hindus? The whole business also threw into sharp relief a question that had been bothering her for some time now. Why did Hindus have to take shelter anyway? Maya had passed her exams with distinction, and had earned a star in her Intermediate exams, whereas Parul had merely obtained a second division. And yet, on many occasions, it seemed as though Parul was the one who held all the cards.

'Baba, fist your fingers. Try and lift your hands.'

Sudhamoy obliged like an obedient little boy and Maya was encouraged to see that some strength had returned to his fingers. She took hold of her father's hands.

'Isn't Dada going to eat?'

'Who knows? I just saw him sleeping.' Kironmoyee seemed totally indifferent to Suranjan's welfare.

Kironmoyee did not eat herself, but kept Maya's share of food for her. Maya was exhausted and was nodding off when all of a sudden, she snapped alert. Slogans filtered into the room which was dark and gloomy as all the doors and windows were closed. 'Hindus, if you want to live, leave this country and go away.' Sudhamoy also heard the chants and his fingers in Maya's grip tightened, another indication of his returning strength.

*

Suranjan's stomach cramped with hunger pangs. Earlier, whether he ate or not, a bowl of rice would be kept waiting for him on the dining table. It was obvious that his family's concern for him had dwindled but he decided that he would not tell anyone he was hungry. He walked out into the courtyard, washed his face in the bathroom and wiped his face with a towel that hung on a wire rack. Coming back to his room he changed his shirt, and walked out of the house. Out on the street, he could not decide where he wanted to go. Should he go to Haider's? But Haider would not be home at this hour. In that case should he go to Belal's or Kamal's? Perhaps, but what if they thought he had come in search of refuge? Or sympathy? No, he decided, he would wander around the city by himself. After all, the city was his own. At one time he had not been able to bring himself to leave Mymensingh. And then, one night, Sudhamoy had sold the house to Raisuddin, without informing his son. When he had woken up the next morning, he hadn't the faintest idea, that this, the place of his birth, fragrant with the smell of kamini flowers and endowed with a crystal clear pond in which he swam so often, this "Dutta Bari" (or Home of the Duttas), was no longer his. When Suranjan had learnt that they would have to leave the house within the next seven days, he was so incensed that he had stormed out and hadn't returned home for the next two days.

Suranjan had never really understood why he was often so touchy and what it was that injured his pride. Sometimes, he felt his entire family, and he did not exclude himself, was to blame. At other times, he felt that Parveen was at fault. It galled him to think that at one time she had been in love with him. Often she would come running to his room to say, 'Come, let's run away . . . '

'Where to?'

'Far away, to the hills.'

'Where are the hills? You have to go to Sylhet or Chittagong to get hills.'

'We'll do that. We'll make our own house.'

'What will we eat? Grass?'

At this Parveen would laugh and throw herself down on Suranjan and say, 'I won't be able to live without you.'

'These are the kind of frivolous things that girls usually say. Actually they don't die.'

And Suranjan had been right. Parveen had not died. On the contrary, like an obedient child, she had taken the marriage vows her parents had asked her to. Two days before she was to be married, she had come to tell him that her family wanted him to convert to Islam. Suranjan had laughed and said, 'You know very well I don't believe in religion.'

'No, you must become a Muslim.'

'I don't want to be a Muslim.'

'Which means, you don't want me either!'

'Of course, I want you. But why must I become a Muslim just for that?'

Parveen's fair face had instantly reddened with anger. Suranjan was aware that pressure was being brought to bear on Parveen by her family to leave him once and for all. He wondered whose side her brother was on. Haider, her brother, was a friend of his, but had never commented on their relationship. Suranjan was very uneasy about Haider's noncommittal attitude, but there was no way in which he could force the issue.

Suranjan made no move to convert to Islam, and consequently Parveen also extinguished her dreams of living in the hills with him. Could dreams be so easily drowned—just as clay images, built for the pujas, were submerged in water? Were dreams only meant to give people a temporary feeling of happiness?

Parveen was married to a Muslim businessman but the marriage soon ran into trouble. Haider said to him one day, 'Parveen might divorce her husband.'

Divorce, within two years? Suranjan had wanted to say, but didn't. He had elided Parveen from his mind, but the news of her possible divorce had gladdened him and revived memories of her. Had he kept the name Parveen gently, ever so carefully, wrapped in the safety of moth balls in the vault of his heart? Perhaps. How long had it been since he had last seen her? Nostalgia drenched him, and with an effort he turned his thoughts now to Ratna. Ratna Mitra. She was a beautiful girl, and she would suit Suranjan well. So Parveen was going to become a divorceé . . . . How was that supposed to affect him? She had married a Muslim, someone her family approved of. And everyone had expected everything to take off smoothly from there, almost as if it was guaranteed that if marriages were matched in terms of religion and caste they would last. So why was it necessary to come back? Didn't her husband take her to the hills? Hadn't her dreams been fulfilled? And where did he fit into all this? He was an unemployed Hindu youth, who did nothing but roam the streets. So how could he be an eligible boy? Suranjan caught a rickshaw at the Tikatuli crossing. Parveen would not leave his mind. From the vault in his heart, her face kept leaping out and engaging his attention. Often when they were together, she would kiss him and he would hold her tight and say to her, 'You are a little sparrow.'

Parveen would double up with laughter, and say, 'You are an ape.'

Was he really an ape? But of course he was, why else would he be stagnating? Five years had drifted by, like the irregular clusters of water hyacinths that grew in slimy ponds, but had he profited from the passing of time and life? Not in any way! No one had said to him as Parveen had, 'I like you very much.' The day Parveen had said this to him, he had asked her, 'Have you laid a bet with someone?'

'What do you mean?'

'You know . . . whether you can say these words to me?'

'No, not at all.'

'Do you really mean what you say?'

'I always mean what I say.'

And to think that same girl, who had spoken with so much confidence, had begun to crumble, the moment her family broached the topic of marriage. All her fantastic dreams had evaporated, her individuality and the things she had wanted to achieve—everything had gone. He found it very depressing to think that not once on the day of her wedding had Parveen protested, 'I want to marry the ape who lives in that house!' His home was only two buildings away from hers. Kironmoyee and Maya had gone for the wedding, Suranjan had not.

He told the rickshaw puller to go to Chamelibagh. Dusk had fallen over the city. He was very hungry now. He had suffered from indigestion in the past but now he felt bilious as well. His father had prescribed antacids, but he hated medicines that whitened his lips. Besides, he invariably forgot to take the tablets with him when he went out. He decided he would go to Pulok's house and eat something. Pulok would certainly be home considering he hadn't ventured out for the last five days.

The first thing Suranjan said when the door was opened to him was, 'Please give me something to eat. I don't think any food has been cooked in our house.'

'Why?'

'Dr Sudhamoy Dutta has suffered a stroke. His wife and daughter are busy nursing him. Sudhamoy Dutta, son of the affluent and wealthy Sukumar Dutta, is today unable to pay for his own treatment.'

'Actually, you should be doing something constructive. You know, like getting yourself a job.'

'Oh I've tried! But you can't get jobs in a Muslim country. Besides, who wants to work under these illiterates?'

Pulok was shocked. He said, 'Are you abusing Muslims, Suranjan?'

'You have no reason to panic. I am abusing them all right, but only to you. Do you think it will be at all possible to abuse them to their face? Won't they wrench this head of mine from my body?'

In a short while, Neela served some rice and vegetable curry and asked in a concerned voice, 'Suranjan-da, haven't you eaten anything at all today?'

Suranjan smiled weakly and said, 'Who cares about what I eat?'

'I think you should get married.'

'Marriage?' Suranjan choked on his food. 'Who will marry me?'

'It's not fair that you should stop thinking about marriage just because of that girl, Parveen.'

'No, no . . . it's not that. Actually I was oblivious of the fact that I might have to marry one day.'

Pulok and Neela smiled ruefully.

Suranjan was not enjoying the food, it seemed as if his tastebuds had given up on him. But he ate anyway to allay his hunger.

'Can you loan me some money, Pulok?' he asked as he ate.

'How much?'

'As much as you can afford. At home no one tells me anything about the financial situation. But I think my mother's purse is empty.'

'Well, okay, I'll give you what you need. Meanwhile, have you been keeping track of the latest situation all over the country? Bhola, Chittagong, Sylhet, Cox's Bazaar and Pirozepur?'

'I know what you're going to tell me . . . they've demolished so many temples, looted and burnt down Hindu homes, killed or beaten up Hindu men, raped their women . . . . If there is something new, please tell me.'

'Does all this seem normal to you?'

'But, of course, it's normal. What else do you expect from this country? You sit with your back exposed, but you react when they clobber you! That's hardly fair.'

Pulok who was sitting opposite Suranjan at the dining table lapsed into silence. After a while, he said, 'They've burnt the home of Chaitanyadeb in Sylhet. They haven't even spared the old library. My brother has come from Sylhet with the latest information. Kalighat Kalibari, Shivbari, Jagannath gymnasium, Chali Bondor Bhairavbari, Chali Bondor Samshan, the gymnasium of Jatarpur Mahaprabhu, Meera Bazaar Ramakrishna Mission, the Balaram gymnasium at Meera Bazaar, Nirmalabala Students' Home, Bondor Bazaar Brahmo mandir, Jinda Bazaar Jagannath gymnasium, Gobindoji gym, the Narasingha gym of Lama Bazaar, Naya Sadak gym, Debpur gym, Tilagarh gym, Biyani Bazaar Kalibari, Dhaka Dakshin Mahaprabhubari, Gotatikor Shivbari, Mahalaxmibari Mahapeeth, Fenchugunj, Sharkarkhana Durgabari, the Shahjibari at Bishwanath, Bairagi Bazaar gym, Chandograam Shiv mandir, Akilpur gymnasium, Companygunj Jeevanpur Kalibari, Balagunj Jogipur Kalibari, Jakigunj Aamloshi Kali mandir, Barohata gym, Gazipur gym and the Birsri gym have all been demolished. Benubhushon Das, Sunil Kumar Das and Kanubhusan Das were burnt alive.'

'Is that right?'

'All kinds of things are happening, Suranjan. I really don't know how we are going to survive in this country. In Chittagong, the Jamaatis and the BNP have joined hands to destroy houses and temples. They have taken away utensils and clothes from as many Hindu homes as possible, and they've also drawn out all the fish from their ponds. For days, the Hindus have not had anything to eat. In the Khajuria village of Sitakunda, the Jamaati Camp people told Kanubihari Nath and his son, Arjunbihari at gun point, that if they failed to hand over at least twenty thousand takas, they would be evicted from their own home. They fled their homes. The daughter of a teacher in Meerersarai College, Utpala Rani Bhowmick, was abducted in the middle of the night and was returned almost at dawn. Aren't we going to protest about any of this?'

'Do you know what will happen if we do protest? Remember that song by D. L. Roy . . . "So I have kicked you, but how can you be so audacious as to feel any pain because of that?"'

Suranjan leaned back on his chair and shut his eyes.

'They've ruined many thousands of homes at Bhola. This morning, curfew was lifted for about twelve hours, and in that short space of time, men armed with shovels, rods and crowbars raided the Lakshminarayan gym for the third time. Policemen just stood by and watched the whole thing happen, more amused than alarmed. At Borhanuddin more than one and a half thousand people have been attacked and least two thousand homes have been damaged. At Tajmuddin, a total of two thousand two hundred houses have been completely destroyed and two thousand partially. Two hundred and sixty temples were destroyed at Bhola.'

Suranjan laughed and said, 'You just gave us an itemized report like a journalist. Are you sorry these things happened?'

Pulok stared at Suranjan, flabbergasted. He said, 'Don't you feel sorry?'

Suranjan laughed uproariously. 'No,' he said, 'I don't feel sorry at all.'

Pulok looked bemused by this. He said, 'Actually, I have a number of relatives staying there. I can't help but worry about them.'

'The Muslims have done their bit; but it does not become Hindus to seek retribution! I am afraid I cannot sympathize with you, Pulok. I am really sorry.'

Pulok looked at Suranjan strangely. Then he left the room. He returned with two thousand takas which he gave Suranjan. Stuffing the money into his pockets Suranjan asked, 'How is Alok? Have his friends included him in the team?'

'No. He is by himself all day long. He doesn't have anything to do but watch all his friends playing in the field, while he suffers alone in his room.'

'You know something, Pulok? Those whom we think of as non-communal, or as our own people, and as our friends, are highly communal deep down. We have mixed and mingled so much with the Muslims of this country, that we never hesitate to say Assalaam Aleikum, Khuda Hafiz, *paani* instead of *jal*, and *gosol* instead of *snan*. We respect their religious practices, and avoid drinking tea or smoking in public during the month of Ramzan. In fact, we do not even go to their restaurants on those days. But how close are they to us actually? For whom do we make these sacrifices? How many holidays do we get for the pujas? Yet, Hindus are pushed, are expected to work long hours in the hospitals, while they enjoy the two Id holidays. The 8th Amendment has been passed and the Awami Leaguers have raised a hue and cry, but that's about all. Hasina herself has covered her head, just as they do after returning from Haj. They are all the same, Pulok . . . . all the same. The only options left to us now are either suicide or migration.'

Suranjan moved to the door. His mother had recently asked him to go and meet Raisuddin in Mymensingh. He had bought their house for such a paltry sum of money that perhaps he would help them out of their financial difficulty. But Suranjan hadn't wanted to ask Raisuddin for help. In any case, he had always hated borrowing but times were bleak and they had the grocer's and other bills to pay. Instead of going to Raisuddin he had decided he would ask Pulok for a loan, possibly because Suranjan had helped him out earlier. Or again, it was possible that being a fellow Hindu, Pulok would understand better than anyone else the trials and hardships of the minorities. Indeed, over the past few days, Suranjan had resolved not to ask any Muslim for help.

Saying his goodbyes to Pulok and his family he wandered off in the direction of home. As he walked, he thought of the way he was treated at home. No one seemed to want to give him much responsibility. Perhaps, they thought him a patriot who was concerned only about the country's good, and who had no time for anything else. Perhaps, they thought there was no point in disturbing him. Today he would give the money to Kironmoyee. He was amazed at the way his mother held the family together. She never complained about anyone, not even her useless son. They had passed through so many bad patches, but Kironmoyee had never ever complained.

Suranjan suddenly felt that this life was really not worth living. There was Sudhamoy suspended between life and death, having to be waited upon constantly. What was the point in living such a life? Why should Suranjan himself be living? For a fleeting moment, he thought of buying a few ampoules of Pethydryn and giving himself a fatal shot. For a moment he could clearly visualize his death. He would be lying dead in bed, but his family wouldn't know that. They would think he was tired and resting, and therefore not to be disturbed. Eventually, Maya would come to him and say 'Dada, wake up. We must do something for Baba . . . .,' and then her Dada would not answer her.

As he walked along, thinking these thoughts, he noticed a procession passing through the Bijoy Nagar crossing. It was a march for communal harmony. They chanted slogans that emphasized the fraternity between Hindus and Muslims. Suranjan could not help a cynical smile.

Before going home, he went to Goutam's house. He was feeling better, but he still looked scared and started at the slightest noise. It was indeed ironical that someone like him who kept himself busy with his medical course, and had no interest in politics, and what is more had no enemies in the locality, should have been beaten up so ruthlessly because the Babri Masjid had been demolished in India!

Goutam's mother, who was sitting nearby, whispered into Suranjan's ears, careful not to be overheard, 'We are going away.'

'Going away? . . . ' Suranjan was taken aback.

'Yes, we are making arrangements to sell the house.'

Suranjan did not want to know where they were going. If he sat there any longer, he might even have to hear the horrible truth that they were about to leave the country. So he pushed back his chair, and quickly got up to leave. But Goutam's mother stopped him and said, 'No, son, don't go yet. God knows if we will get to meet before we leave. Sit down, let us talk for a while . . . ' Her voice was choked with tears.

'I am sorry, Mashima, I have some work at home. I'll come and see you another time.'

Suranjan did not turn to look at Goutam, nor did he look at his mother. With eyes downcast, he walked out, failing, as he did, to conceal a sigh of despair.

Day Five

Birupaksha was a studious young man who belonged to Suranjan's political party. That morning Suranjan had not yet got out of bed, when Birupaksha walked into his room.

'It's ten already, and you're still in bed?'

'I am not sleeping, just lying down. When there is nothing to do, it's best to lie down. We don't have the guts to demolish mosques, so the only option we have is to lie down.'

'You're quite right. They are destroying hundreds of temples, but if we even threw a stone at a mosque can you imagine the consequences! The Pakistanis just reduced the four-hundred-year-old Romona Kalibari to dust, but there was no assurance from any government that it would be rebuilt!'

'Hasina is always talking about the reconstruction of the Babri Masjid, but in Bangladesh even if there is some hope of compensation for the Hindus, nothing is ever mentioned about the rebuilding of temples. They do not seem to realize that Hindus have not drifted into Bangladesh with the flood waters. We are as much citizens of this country as anyone else. We have the right to live, as also the right to protect our own lives, property and places of worship.'

'It is not as though all the looting and plundering is because of the Babri Masjid issue. On the morning of 21st March 1992, in the village of Bagerhata, the daughter of Kalindra Haldar, Putul Rani, was kidnapped by Mokhlesur Rahman and Chand Mia Talukdar, who lived in the same area.

'The Upazila Parishad Chairman of the Potuakhali Boga union, Yonus Mia, and UP member, Nabi Ali Mridha tortured the Moni Kanailal families so much that they were forced to flee the country . . .

'In Rajnagar village, a person named Biren was kept confined and forced to part with his property. To date, there is no sign of Biren. Similarly, they tortured Sudhir in order to take away his plot of land. Sudhir left the country. Chandan Seal of Sabupura village was personally abducted by the chairman. No news of him till this day. And at Boga village, the paddy crop of Chittaranjan Chakravarty was stolen. When Chitta-babu filed a case, he was told to withdraw the complaint, else he would be killed.'

Suranjan lit a cigarette. He found that, despite himself, he was being drawn into the conversation. He drew at his cigarette and said, 'On the 1st of April, some people tried to force Swapan Chandra Ghosh of Jalkhabar, at gun point, to hand over a cash subscription. When he refused, they beat up his staff, broke open the cash box and made off with twenty thousand takas. But then such incidents are taking place in Muslim shops as well. This business of asking for subscriptions is really becoming a menace. Take, for instance, the case of Maniklal Dhupi of Siddiq Bazaar. People like Shahabuddin, Siraj Parvez, Salahuddin who are all from the same area have forcibly taken possession of his property. They are now trying their best to get hold of the rest.'

Suranjan was quiet for a while, then said, 'Stealing crops, abducting women, raping them, confiscating property, threatening to kill, beating up people and throwing them out of their own houses, out of the country as well. . . all these things are not just happening in and around us, but all over the country. How much do we really know about the tortures that have taken place. Do we know the exact number of people who have been forced to leave their homeland?'

'In Senbagh, Noakhali, Krishnalal Das' wife, Swarnabala, was kidnapped by Abul Kalam Munshi, Abul Kasem and some others. They assaulted her and left her lying unconscious in the neighbouring paddy fields,' Birupaksha said.

Suranjan got up from bed and went to have a wash. On the way to the bathroom he stopped to ask Kironmoyee for two cups of tea. He had given his mother the two thousand takas the previous night. Surely she would not think her son was completely irresponsible now. She looked somewhat relaxed today, perhaps because her financial situation was temporarily better. When he got back to his room, Birupaksha was sitting on the chair looking worried. Suranjan told him to cheer up. He himself was feeling much better now. He considered going into Sudhamoy's room to see how he was doing. Meanwhile, Maya came in with two cups of tea.

'Hey, you seem to have grown thinner in the last few days. Didn't they give you enough to eat at Parul's home?' Maya ignored the question and walked out. She was very annoyed with her brother. Sudhamoy was sick and it was certainly not appropriate to be laughing and joking at this hour. Maya's coldness sobered him up immediately and he went quiet.

Birupaksha brought him out of his thoughts. He said, 'Suranjan-da, you don't believe in religion, right? I know that you don't pray, and that you eat beef as well. Why don't you tell them you are not a pure Hindu, that you are half Muslim?'

'The fact is that I am a real human being. That is what they object to most of all. Strangely enough, there is no dispute between Hindu fanatics and Muslim fanatics. You must have noticed the similarities between the Jamaatis in this country and the BJP in India. Both parties are trying to establish their strength in their respective countries. "In India, it is not the BJP but the Congress that is responsible for the riots. . ." Do you know who made this statement? The Nizami himself at the Baitul Mokarram congregation . . .

'One thousand people have died in the riots in India. The Vishwa Hindu Parishad, the RSS, the Bajrang Dal, the Jamaat-i-Islami groups have all been banned. Meanwhile, they have called a strike in Sylhet, Section 144 has been promulgated in Pirozepur, curfew has been imposed in Bhola, and there is a fair scattering of marches for communal harmony all over the country. In these processions, curiously enough, the slogans include lines like, "Nizami, Advani, bhai, bhai . . . ." followed by other chants which point to the similarities between the two. Today all the parties have come together on a peace mission to protest communalism. Apparently, in England too, there have been raids on temples. Tofael Ahmed has just returned after a survey of Bhola, and he feels that the Bangladesh Rifles [BDR] should be sent to that place. The whole area is in very bad shape.

'And, finally, what is the point of all this? After everything has been burnt to cinders, what can the BDR do? Collect the ashes? Where was Tofael on the 6th? Why didn't he arrange for protection on that very night?'

Suranjan was visibly excited now. He said, 'And don't think the Awami League consists of saints either.'

'Is it possible that the Awami League has not tried to stop the riots because they wanted this government to take the blame for the breakdown in law and order?'

'I don't know. It's possible though. Everyone needs votes. In this country, it is only vote-based politics that survives. No one bothers about ideals. By hook or by crook, votes must be acquired. The Awami League thinks that it will surely get the Hindu votes. What do they call it? Vote bank, I think . . . . Do you know, in some places they have themselves instigated destruction.'

'I've also heard it said that the places from which the Awami League normally wins were terrorized by the BNP, who destroyed temples and at the same time asked the locals—where are those people you voted for? In like fashion, the Awami League destroyed BNP strongholds and asked the people a similar question. The BNP have done this in Bhola, while at Maheshkhali Ghior and Manikgunj, the Awami League have been responsible.'

'Yes, politics is a factor, but nothing has ever been achieved by leaving out the fundamentalists. By the way, is it true that there have been identical editorials in all the newspapers? Apparently they have all appealed for communal harmony?'

'Don't you read the papers?'

'I don't feel like reading them.'

At this point, Maya came into the room. She put an envelope down on the table and said, 'Ma asked me to give you this. She said she won't need it.'

Before he could ask what she had returned, Maya had left the room. Suranjan opened the envelope and found the two thousand takas that he had given his mother last night. Suranjan was very insulted. What did Kironmoyee think she was doing? Was it her pride that made her refuse his contribution? Or did she think her unemployed son had robbed someone of the money? Suranjan was so disturbed that he didn't feel like talking to anyone, not even to Birupaksha. He wanted to be left alone.

*

Kironmoyee's father, Akhil Chandra Basu, was a well-known

lawyer. He had married off his sixteen-year-old daughter to a young doctor, and had left with his entire family for Calcutta. He had hoped that his daughter and son-in-law would join them sooner or later. Kironmoyee, too, was herself quite hopeful about this possibility, especially because she thought that with most of their family in Calcutta, Sudhamoy too would choose to migrate. But it was a strange family she had married into. She had stayed with her parents-in-law for six years. In that time, a slew of friends and relatives had packed up and left, but her husband had not once suggested leaving the country. Kironmoyee would secretly shed tears. And from Calcutta, her father would write:

> My dear Kiron,
> Have you finally decided not to come after all? Ask Sudhamoy to think it over once again. We were not happy to leave our country either, but we were compelled to do so. It is not that we are very happy here. We yearn for our motherland too, but we have to be practical and realistic. I am rather worried for you.
>
> > Your father

Kironmoyee would read these letters all by herself, and cry. Sometimes at night, she would try and convince Sudhamoy to leave. 'Most of your relatives have left, so have mine. If we continue to stay here in the middle of all this trouble, no one will help us even if we ask for a glass of water.' At this Sudhamoy would laugh and ridicule Kironmoyee. 'You have to beg for water! I'll give you the whole of the Brahmaputra. Let's see how much you can drink. Surely relatives do not hold more water than the Brahmaputra?'

No one in her husband's family beginning with Sudhamoy's father, Sudhamoy himself and even Suranjan, would even think of leaving Bangladesh, and so Kironmoyee had no alternative but to abide by their decision. After all that the responsibility of keeping the family afloat through all the crises that visited it had devolved upon her. She did not make a fuss. Her latest sacrifice had involved selling a pair of her gold bangles to Dr Haripada's wife. She had not of course discussed the matter with anyone in the family. After all, gold was not so precious that it could not be sold if the need arose. At the moment, Sudhamoy's treatment and speedy recovery was the prime concern.

When she had the time to think about it, Kironmoyee could

not think from which bottomless spring inside her so much love flowed for her husband. It wasn't a physical bond, for they had not made love to each other since 1971. He would often say to her, 'Kironmoyee, I think I have cheated you, isn't that right?'

And though Kironmoyee understood what he was trying to say, she would say nothing in reply, although what she really wanted to say was, 'No . . .I have not been cheated. Who said so?' But she could not find the right words to express herself and so would say nothing. And Sudhamoy would say with a despairing sigh, 'Are you going to leave me and go away, Kiron? You know, I feel very scared sometimes.'

There was no question of that. She would never leave him, ever. After all, was sex the only significant aspect of a relationship between a man and a woman? Was everything else insignificant? Were the thirty-five years of wedlock of no value at all? Was it so easy to ignore the sorrows and joys that together went towards completing the circle of a family's achievements. No, Kironmoyee would say to herself. This life of ours does not come back to us, so we must make the best of the good things and the bad. Unfortunately for them, a part of their lives had become sterile but she was able to accept it. And whenever Sudhamoy woke her up in the middle of the night to apologize for his inability to make love to her or to ask whether she suffered because of his inadequacy, she would always say: 'No, why should I be suffering?'

But she knew Sudhamoy was filled with pain and frustration at his inadequacy, especially when he buried his face in his pillow. Kironmoyee, on her part, would turn her face to the wall and spend a sleepless night. Sometimes Sudhamoy would say to her, 'If you wish to begin a new life, I wouldn't mind.'

It would be incorrect to say that Kironmoyee had never felt desire. When Sudhamoy's friends came to visit, and they sat around talking, their shadows would sometimes fall on Kironmoyee's lap, and almost involuntarily she would wish that those shadows were real. And how wonderful it would be, she would think, if a shadow made of flesh and blood could rest its head on her lap.

However, Kironmoyee's physical cravings did not last very long. Her body soon became used to the deprivation. And in any case, life did not stop at any point but moved on, and as it passed and age caught up with her, her past longings faded to a distant shadow. Since that time, twenty-one years had passed and she no longer felt deprived in that regard. Sometimes she would think: What if I had gone away to another man and he too had proved incapable? Or, even if he was a good lover, would he have been as large-hearted and good as Sudhamoy?

Kironmoyee knew that Sudhamoy loved her very much. She felt it in many ways and it filled her with a sense of well-being. He never ate without her, and he always put the larger portion of fish on her plate. And, if it should happen that the maid was on leave (this was before they were reduced to their present state) he would offer to help with the washing up and general house-cleaning. In the evenings, if Kironmoyee sat by herself looking lonely, he would offer to comb the knots out of her hair. Or he would ask her to go to Romona Bhavan and buy herself a couple of saris. 'You don't seem to have enough saris to wear at home . . . .' he'd say. Or he'd say 'If I had enough money, Kiron, I would build a huge house for you. You could have walked barefoot in the courtyard. There would have been all kinds of fruit trees in the garden, seasonal vegetables and flowers as well. The bean plants and the gourds would have entwined themselves on their supports and the scent of the hasnuhenna would have drifted into your room. Actually, the Brahmapalli house would have suited you best, but you know my problem. Money was just not important for me, it was not my goal. It's not as though I could not have made money. Your father was reassured of my financial standing, judging from my house. Now, I don't have the house, nor do I have wealth. I know it is almost a hand to mouth situation at the moment. I can manage, but I am sure you suffer, Kiron.'

Kironmoyee understood from all this and more that this straightforward, simple soul really and truly loved her. If one was to lose some small pleasures in life, perhaps even major pleasures, and in exchange be given the opportunity to love such a person there would be no question about which was the better deal. Certainly, ever since the age of twenty-eight some of her desires had not been fulfilled but deep in her heart and soul a whole sea of love tossed and turned, washing away the physical wounds every time they showed up.

Her thoughts turned to her son. Suranjan had given her some

money. In all probability, he had taken a loan. She knew he probably felt unworthy because he did not have a job but she did not yet have her back to the wall, she could manage. She still had some money left because Sudhamoy had never kept any money for himself but had promptly handed over what little he earned to his wife. Moreover, she still had some of her gold ornaments to fall back on. It was because of this that she had returned Suranjan's money to him, little 'realizing how much this would offend Suranjan. And so she had stared at him in surprise, when he had barged into her room and said, 'Did you think I've robbed somebody of that money? Or are you ashamed to take money from someone so useless and unemployed? Yes, I know I can't do anything for you all . . . but I wish I could. Couldn't you have understood that much?'

His words had pierced her heart and she had gone very still.

*

Suranjan knocked on Ratna's door. She opened the door herself, and did not seem surprised to see him. Almost as though she had been expecting him, she took him straight through into her room. She was wearing a simple cotton sari. He thought a red bindi on her forehead would have suited her . . . and maybe a thin line of red sindur in the parting of her hair. Suranjan did not believe in the precepts or badges of religion, but he had always liked sankha, sindur and the sound of conch-shells. His family did not practise the traditional forms of their faith, but there were no restrictions on joining in the festivities during the pujas.

Ratna left him to go and get some tea. All she had said to him this far was 'How are you?' Suranjan had been less than talkative as well. Words failed him for he realized he had come to love someone after Parveen. For the first time in days, he had shaved, put on an ironed shirt, and even used some cologne.

Ratna's parents were quite old. She had a brother who was married with two children. Ratna lived with all these people. The children, to whom he had not been introduced, were naturally very curious about him. They hung around near the door, peeping in occasionally. Suranjan called a seven-year-old girl to him and asked what her name was.

'Mrittika,' she said brightly.

'What a lovely name. How are you related to Ratna?'

'She is my aunt.'

'Oh.'

'Do you work in my aunt's office?'

'I don't work. I just roam around.'

Somehow, Mrittika seemed to like the expression, roam around. She was preparing to make further conversation, when Ratna entered the room with a tray on which there was tea, biscuits, hot gram and two varieties of sweets.

'Just look at that!' Suranjan said. 'They say it's hard to get food in Hindu homes these days because they are unable to go out. But that seems to be far from true in this house. With such a spread you can open a shop! So? When did you return from Sylhet?'

'Not Sylhet. I'd gone to Habigunj, Sunamgunj, Maulvi Bazaar. Right in front of my eyes at Habigunj, they burnt three mandirs.'

'Who has been doing the damage?'

'Who else? Muslims wearing caps and sporting beards. After that they destroyed the Kali temple in the shopping centre. A relative of mine, Tapan Dasgupta, happens to be a doctor. His consulting room was looted and destroyed. On the 8th, they destroyed two temples at Sunamgunj. On the 9th, four temples, and fifty shops were looted then burnt to the ground. At Maulvi Bazaar, in Rajnagar and Kulaura, six temples and a gym were completely destroyed. At Brahman Bazaar, seven shops were looted.'

'Must have been Hindu shops.'

Ratna could not help laughing. 'But of course.'

She pushed the tea and hot gram towards Suranjan and said, 'Do you think it is possible to stay in this country?'

'Why not? Is this country the property of the Muslims?'

Ratna smiled. A touch of sadness brushed her smile. 'It seems they are selling off properties at a paltry price, if at all, in Bhola.'

'Who is leaving Bhola? Hindus?'

'Without a doubt.'

'Then why don't you say so?' Suranjan asked as he dug into the hot gram.

He knew there was no need for her to spell out the fact that those who were being victimized were Hindus. Despite this, he had insisted so that she would say it was 'Hindus' who were being driven away, not simply people who lived in those areas.

Whatever she may have understood, Ratna said nothing but stared unflinchingly at him as he ate. Suranjan's mind was focused on only one thing. Today he had come mentally prepared to tell her without any inhibitions, 'I like you very much. If you are interested, I'd be happy to marry you.'

Just then Ratna got up to fetch a glass of water. The hem of her sari touched his hand as she walked past. He thrilled to that touch. He thought: Ratna could so easily become my wife! He did not want to marry her in order to stabilize his wasteful, squandering life but because he knew he would really enjoy the experience. They would lie next to each other all day along and he would play with her fingers and they would talk about the times when they were naked babies, and before long, all the walls that were between them would be broken down. He did not really want Ratna as a wife, but more as a friend.

But what of her? What was hidden in the depths of her eyes? Suranjan felt a little frustrated that he didn't know. He said, 'I came to find out if you were all unhurt.'

'Unhurt? The word has one meaning for men and quite another for women. What did you really come to see?'

'Both.'

Ratna laughed and lowered her head. She did not have a pearly glamour about her when she smiled, but it was a treat to watch her all the same. Suranjan could not take his eyes off her face. He wondered if he was too old beside her. Did men begin to look a little worn at his age? Was he totally unsuited for marriage? As these thoughts ran through his head he noticed that Ratna was again staring at him. There seemed to be a distinct look of infatuation in her eyes.

'Are you still firm on your decision not to marry?' Ratna asked with a smile.

Suranjan took some time before he answered. 'Life is like a river, did you know that? Does the river stop flowing at any point? Decisions also change once in a while. They do not stay unchanged all the time.'

Ratna heard him out, and as Suranjan rose to go, she laughed prettily and said, 'Thank God!' Considering the plight of the Hindus, and with the situation in general being what it was, it seemed a little inappropriate to hear the words, 'Thank God.'

But Suranjan wasn't grumbling. He had no need to ask her what she meant because he knew exactly why she had made the remark. Ratna had begun to give him a sort of clean, pure happiness and he wanted to hold her slim little fingers in his own and say, 'Come, let's go to the saal forests, where you and I can lie down together, and the moon will protect us. We'll ask the moon not to hide her glow . . .' And he wanted to say 'Let us change those fixed ideas and decisions we have made and do something together.'

But he was unable to say any of these things and the moment passed. Ratna saw him off down the stairs and said, 'Please come again. Because you came, we now have the reassurance that there is someone to stand by us. At least we are not alone . . . .'

Suranjan could feel clearly the stirring of the spring that the joyful little sparrow Parveen had once awoken in his heart. He could see that he was beginning to float away into that heaven of happiness that Parveen had once opened up for him.

Day Six

Suranjan picked up the newspapers with his morning cup of tea. He was very relaxed today. He had also had a good night's sleep. He called out to Maya after he had glanced at the newspapers.

'What's the matter with you, Maya? Why do you look so glum all the time?'

'Nothing's the matter with me . . . . You're the one who has been behaving strangely. You haven't sat beside Baba even once.'

'I can't handle such things. I find it very depressing to see a man who used to be so hale and hearty just lying there like a log! And what makes it even worse is seeing the two of you sitting there crying. By the way, why did Ma return the money I gave her? Has she got a lot of money?'

'Ma has sold her jewellery.'

'Well, that's good. I don't like ornaments at all.'

'You don't like them? Then why did you give Parveen Apa a pearl-studded ring?'

'Oh, I was raw and immature at that time. Didn't have much intelligence then, if you ask me . . .'

'Well, have you matured now?' Maya asked and smiled.

Suranjan was delighted to see the smile, for it had been a long time since he had seen his sister happy. To prolong the smile he showed her the front page of the newspaper, he was reading. 'Look . . .' he said, 'we live in a country where people of every religion and caste live in harmony. Stop communalism, and punish those who have set about on mass rampage of killing, looting and plunder . . . This is the urgent message of the All Party Peace Mission. In India, the spread of hatred is now limited. The forced occupation of the land in and around the Babri Masjid has been declared unlawful by the High Court. Narasimha Rao has declared that the demolition of the Babri Masjid is entirely the doing of the

UP Government and the Centre is in no way responsible. The states of West Bengal, Gujarat, Maharashtra are still under the supervision of the army. The leftist forces have declared total war against communalism. Today, there is a meeting at the Paltan junction, called by the CPB. The Awami League has declared the formation of a Peace Brigade to maintain communal harmony. The City Coordination Committee has demanded that those who were responsible for instigating riots, be arrested. The Committee for Total Eradication of Communalism has also called a meeting. The All Party Peace Procession is due at Tongi. The Cultural Conglomerates have raised the slogan, "Bangladesh will surely put an end to communal forces." Fifteen eminent citizens have declared that it is the responsibility of all citizens to maintain communal peace and harmony. Colonel Akbar has declared that the strength of the fascist Jamaatis has to be curbed. In Barisal, a committee for Combined Communal Amity has been formed. The Dhaka University Teacher's Union has declared that if communal harmony is disrupted, the sanctity of the forthcoming Victory Month will be destroyed. Twenty-eight people have been arrested in Dhamrai, for the plundering of temples. Jyoti Basu, CM of West Bengal, has said he feels deep regret that India has lost face in the sight of the world.'

'You've read out the good news only . . . . ' protested Maya sitting cross-legged on the bed. She took the newspaper from him and said, 'What about the rest of the news? 10,000 families in Bhola have been rendered homeless, seven hundred homes in Chittagong have been burnt to ashes. In Kishoregunj, temples have been destroyed. In Pirozepur, Section 144 has been imposed. In Mirsari, Sitakunda, seven hundred homes have been torched.'

'I won't listen to any bad news today, because I'm in a good mood,' Suranjan declared firmly.

'Why? Because Parveen Apa is going to be divorced? She had come over yesterday. She said her husband beats her every night.'

'And now what? They were convinced that she could be happy only with a Muslim. No, no my good mood has nothing to do with Parveen. This time, no more Muslims . . . . So that just before we decide to marry, neither of us will need to ask with choked voices, "Can you change your religion?"'

Maya laughed heartily. It had been such a long time since he had heard that lovely laugh!

Suddenly, Suranjan became serious and asked, 'How is Baba now? Isn't he going to be up and about soon?'

'He's relatively better. He is able to speak quite well now. With support he goes to the bathroom as well. He has even started eating semi-solid food. Oh, incidentally, last evening Belal Bhai came and enquired about you. He met Baba. He said you should not go out these days, it's very risky.'

'Oh.'

Suranjan suddenly jumped up. Maya thought she knew the reason for his urgency and said, 'What is it? Are you going out somewhere?'

'Am I the kind of person to stay home?'

'If you go out Ma will worry a lot. Dada, please don't go. I am just as worried and scared too.'

'I have to return the money to Pulok. Have you got some money? After all you have a job. Come on, give me some money for cigarettes from your funds.'

'No, I will not give you any money for cigarettes. I don't want you to die early.'

Even as she said this, Maya went and got him a hundred taka note. He looked at his sister with affection and remembered something that had happened many years ago. Maya had been quite small then and had broken down when some of the girls in her school had teased her, 'Hindu, Hindu . . . . Hindus eat cow's head . . . .' She had asked Suranjan, 'Am I a Hindu, Dada?' And he had said, 'Yes.'

Maya had then said, 'I don't want to be a Hindu anymore. They tease me for being one.'

Sudhamoy, who had overheard this exchange said, 'Who said you are Hindu? You are a human being. There is nothing superior to that.' At that moment Suranjan's heart bowed in respect to Sudhamoy. He dealt with many men, but there were none as noble, patient, understanding and considerate as his father.

In 1964, Sudhamoy had coined the slogan, 'East Pakistan, stop them . . . oppose them . . . .' to stop a riot. Fortunately, it had not spread further because of the intervention of Sheikh Mujib. In fact, the riot had actually been clandestinely instigated by supporters of the Ayub Khan government in order to give it a lever to pre-empt the blossoming of anti-government movements. Pleading that the riots were against it, the government had moved the courts, and had sued the students and political leaders heading the agitation. Sudhamoy was one of the accused. It was not like Sudhamoy to be lost in nostalgia, but almost involuntarily the past came back to him in snatches. And usually these forays into the past plunged him into melancholy. His involvement with the country, its welfare, its future . . . where had it all led to? The management of the country's affairs since 1975 had been gradually taken over by fundamentalist elements. The people were aware of this, but nobody seemed to want to react. Did this generation have no sense of values? Where had the spirit of the past gone? That spirit which had propelled the youth in 1952 to stage mass protests to make Bengali the language of the nation? The young men of that time had invited mass slaughter in the name of their cause. Where were the counterparts of those who had sacrificed their lives in the 1969 mass uprising? Where were the three million patriots of 1971? Who had inherited their courage, their sense of mission? Where was that feeling of enthusiasm, of excitement that had propelled Sudhamoy into the movement? Where was that dynamism today? Why did the skin of these youngsters feel as cold as a serpent's, and why was communalism being so cordially ushered into a secular country? How was it that no one seemed to realize what a dangerous period was in the offing? Beset by these thoughts, Sudhamoy tried to get up from his bed but failed. The pain, and the failure that he was experiencing was etched into his worn face.

The Law Ministry of the Awami League, moved in the parliament, the much hated 'Enemy Property Act' of Ayub Khan under a different name, 'The Acquired Property Act'. Under the previous regime, the property of Hindus who had left the country was declared 'Enemy Property'. In other words, were Sudhamoy's uncles enemies of the country? His uncles had land as well as huge mansions in Dhaka as well as in the neighbouring suburbs, Sonargaon, Narshindi, Kishoregunj and Faridpur. On some of these, educational institutions, veterinary hospitals, family planning offices, income tax offices and the like were set up. When Sudhamoy was a child, he regularly visited one uncle called Anil, who lived at Ramakrishna Mission Road in a huge mansion. There were ten horses in his stables, and he remembered Uncle Anil making him ride one of them.

Today, Sudhamoy Dutta lived in a dark damp house in Tikatuli, even though in the neighbourhood there was a huge house, that had once belonged to one of his uncles but which had been requisitioned by the government. Had the renamed law, that is, the Acquired Property Act, been designed to favour the closest living inheritors of those who had fled, much of the sufferings of the Hindus who had stayed would have been alleviated. Sudhamoy had suggested this to many important and high ranking officers without any success. It was yet another of the many failures he had experienced and now he was exhausted. All this, and now he was doomed to lead a partly paralyzed existence. He found no reason to live anymore and was sure that if he were to die silently in bed, no one would be affected. On the contrary, Kironmoyee would be spared sleepless nights and continuous suffering. As he lay abed, he couldn't help thinking again about the failure of the government to protect its Hindu citizens.

Two considerations after the 1965 war between India and Pakistan—the attitude of the fascist Pakistani government towards East Pakistan as a dominion and its intensely communal character—had led to the 'Enemy Property Act.' After independence, the same act had been cleverly perpetuated, to Sudhamoy's chagrin, by another name. Sudhamoy could not help feeling that this was a shameful act by the newly independent Bengali nation. The act had quite clearly stifled the fundamental, human and democratic rights of its citizens. The failure to award equal rights, under the cover of a cleverly planned and renamed act, devastated almost twenty million Hindus. They were practically uprooted from their homes and pushed out into the cold. If under such provocation the Hindus felt unsafe, could anyone blame them? The seed of communalism was rooted deep in their soil; once again, was it their fault?

The constitution of the country provided the same protection and guaranteed the same rights to all its citizens. Yet the Enemy Property Act was clearly a violation of the constitution, and was also a sign of disrespect to the independent character of the country as also its sovereignty. The constitution was clear enough about the provisions made with regard to fundamental rights. These provisions read as follows:

26.(1) All existing law inconsistent with any provisions of this Part, and any law so made shall, to the extent of such inconsistency, be void.

26.(2) The state shall not make any law inconsistent with any provisions of this Part, and any law so made shall, to the extent of such inconsistency, be void.

27. All citizens are equal before law and are entitled to equal protection of law.

28. (1) The state shall not discriminate against any citizens on grounds of religion, race, caste, sex or place of birth.

31. To enjoy the protection of the law, and to be treated in accordance with the law, and only in accordance with the law, is the inalienable right of every citizen, wherever he may be, and of every other person for the time being within Bangladesh, and in particular, no action detrimental to the life, liberty, body, reputation or property of any person shall be taken except in accordance with law.

Clause 112 clearly stated: 'All authorities, executive and judicial, in the Republic shall act in aid of the Supreme Court.'

The relevant clauses of the Pakistani Defence Law, 1965, which defined enemies of the state ran as follows:

a. any state, or sovereign of a state, at war with, or engaged in military operation against Pakistan, or

b. any individual resident in enemy territory, or

c. any body of persons constituted or (incorporated) in enemy territory, or in or under the laws of a state at war with, or engaged in military operations, against Pakistan, or

d. any other persons or body of persons declared by the Central Government to be an enemy, or

e. any body of persons (whether incorporated or not) carrying on business in any place, if and so long as the body is controlled by a person who under this rule *is an enemy,* or

f. as respect any business carried on in enemy territory and individual or body of persons (whether incorporate or not) carrying on that business.

This was further classified in Clause 169.1 which stated enemy subject as:

a. any individual who possesses the nationality of a state at war with, or engaged in military operation against Pakistan, or having possessed such nationality at any time has lost . . . without acquiring another nationality, or
b. any body of persons constituted or incorporated in or under the laws of such state.
169.4. 'Enemy property means: any property for the time being belonging to or held or managed on behalf of an enemy as defined in rule 161, an enemy subject or any enemy firm, but does not include the property which is 'Evacuee property' under the Pakistan (Administration of Evacuee Property) Act, 1957 (XLL of 1957).'

It went on to say:

Where an individual enemy subject dies in Pakistan any property which individually before his death belonged to or was held by him, or was managed on his behalf, may not-withstanding his death continue to be regarded as enemy property for the purpose of rule 182.

After 1947, when communal riots broke out in East Pakistan, millions of Hindus left for India. The then Pakistani government enforced the East Bengal Evacuees (Administration of Property) Act VIII of 1949, the East Bengal Evacuees (Restoration of Possession) Act XXIII of 1951, and the East Bengal Evacuees (Administration of Immovable Property) Act XXIV of 1951. The 1951 East Bengal Evacuees (Administration of Immovable Property) Act XXIV stated:

The evacuee property committees constituted under this Act shall not take charge of any evacuated property

1. If the sole owner or all the co-sharer owners of the property, object to the management of such property by the committee on the ground that he or they has or have

made other arrangements for the management and utilisation of the property and if the committee is satisfied that the arrangement so made proper and adequate, or
2. if an objection is filed and allowed under this section.

This law further stated that the property shall be vested only on the applications of the evacuees and it shall be vested with the right to dispose of property as he likes.

In 1957, the Pakistan government made further changes in this law and enforced the Pakistan (Administration of Evacuee Property) Act XII of 1957. According to this law, 'properties of the person who is resident in any place in the territories now comprising India or in any area occupied by India and is unable to occupy, supervise or manage in person his property in then Pakistan or is being occupied, supervised or managed by a person.' This law had not put the Hindus in as much trouble as did the East Pakistan Disturbed Persons and Rehabilitation Ordinance 1964.

As a result of the Indo-Pak war in 1965, the Pakistan government declared a state of Emergency and the Pakistan Constitution of 1962, and the power of the law as stated in chapters 1 and 2 including those pertaining to fundamental rights was reduced. On 6 September 1965, like the Defence of Pakistan Ordinance No. XXIII, the Defence of Pakistan Rules 1965 was enforced.

In the Defence of Pakistan Rules 1965, Clause 182 states, 'With a view to preventing the payment of money to an enemy firm, and to provide for the administration and disposal by way of transfer or otherwise of enemy property and matters connected there with or incidental thereto, the Central Government may appoint a Custodian of enemy property for Pakistan and one or more Deputy Custodian and Asstt. Custodians of enemy property for such local areas as may be prescribed and may, by order—vest or provide for and regulate the vesting in the prescribed custodian such enemy property as may be prescribed.' On the basis of this, under the Pakistan Defence laws and rules all such property came under the jurisdiction of the government. Such enemy property of which the owner was either imprisoned during the war or on whom certain restrictions were placed, was as a consequence considered unprotected. Responsibility for such property was temporarily taken over by the government and a promise was made to the owners that all their property would be returned to them. A new law was passed by the Central Government called the Enemy Property (Custody and Registration) Order 1965. Later another law—the Enemy Property (Land and Building) Administration & Disposal Order—was passed in 1966. According to these laws the entire responsibility of settling compensation, maintenance and management, as well as accounts in regard to the property in question would for the time being be given to a particular government officer.

After the Indo-Pak war the earlier laws on Enemy Property —(Continuance of Emergency Provision) Ordinance No:1 of 1969—were extended. Following the war of independence, despite the fact that India was considered a friendly power, and there was no war between the two countries, the President's Command No:29/1972, or the Bangladesh Vesting of Property and Assets Order was promulgated. As a result, the said enemy property which was entrusted to the Pakistan government, was now transferred to the Bangladesh government. In fact, the promise that had been made by the Pakistan Governing Body of 1969, on the basis of the Enemy Property (Continuance of Emergency Provision) Ordinance to the people who were property owners, that all their property would be returned with due respect, was most callously broken. As in the Pakistani regime, so too in independent Bangladesh, the management of 'Enemy Property' continued unobtrusively and illegally, to be in the hands of the Bangladesh government. When the distressed public appealed for their lawful rights, the Enemy Property (Continuance of Emergency Provision) Ordinance was farcically repealed by Act XLV of 1974 and renamed the Vested and Non-Resident Property(Administration) Act XLVI of 1974. According to this, all the property that was hitherto under the Pakistan government, was declared to be property belonging to those who had ceased to be permanent residents or had acquired foreign citizenship. Simultaneously, a committee was formed for the maintenance and protection of such property by the government. This committee did not only take over the charge of all the 'Enemy Property' that had been listed by the Pakistan government, but over and above this it also took under its jurisdiction such property which had never been considered Enemy Property. However, before the law was put into action the 1976 Ordinance No:XCIII was enforced. According to this law: 'Those properties which were vested under the Act shall be administered, controlled, managed and disposed of, by transfer or otherwise, by the Government on such officer or authority as Government may direct.' After this, within a year, on 23 May 1977, a circular was brought out, which stated: '10 kathas of vacant non-agricultural land shall be given in long term lease to a person deserving to get it, realising full market value as premium and proper rent, that non-agricultural lands situated in business centres shall be settled in open auction with the highest bidder.' In other words, almost fifteen to twenty million people in Bangladesh, who owned non-agricultural land, would have their lands auctioned off, and the government on its part would enjoy the benefits of long term taxes from it. In the 37th paragraph of the instruction, it was stated that if officers from the Revenue Department could locate such property or provide information related to it, they would be given special awards. In the 38th paragraph it was stated that the district officers(revenue), associated with this job, subdivisional officers and circle officers (revenue), land officers and land reform officers would all be given high honours. The greed for awards drove these officers into a frenzied search for such property, and in the process, they succeeded in turning out innumerable Hindus from their ancestral homesteads.

After 1966, the East Pakistan government had carried out an official survey which revealed that the property of those Hindus who had left the country for India during the mass exodus of 1947 and after the riots of 1950 and 1954 was listed as Enemy Property. They had left with the assurance that their homes, orchards, ponds, family crematoriums, temples, agricultural and non-agricultural lands would be duly returned to them. Apart from them, those Hindus who had not left for India, but had gone outside the subcontinent with temporary residence in India, had also had their properties enlisted as Enemy Property. However, the properties of those Muslims who were staying either in India or abroad were not attached. No survey was made of their property. According to the rules of the Hindu joint family system, after the demise of the Karta (or head of the family), the surviving members would enjoy the property. However, the government ignored all these traditions and laws and usurped such properties.

Sudhamoy thought of Niyaz Husain, Fazlul Alam, Anwar

Ahmed and many others who had left for the US or the UK with their families, leaving behind distant relatives or tenants in their houses. Their properties were not considered Enemy Property at all. Thinking of such injustice Sudhamoy struggled to get out of bed. His body broke into a sweat. No one was at home. Where had Maya, Kironmoyee and Suranjan gone.

*

Suranjan walked down the streets of old Dhaka and thought nostalgically of how well he still remembered Mymensingh, despite having lived in Dhaka for so many years now. After all, he was born in that city, that was where he had spent his childhood and his youth. When he dipped his feet into the waters of the Buriganga in Dhaka, his thoughts lingered with the Brahmaputra in Mymensingh. If a person wanted to deny the fact of his birth, only then would he deny his birthplace, or the river that flowed by his birthplace. Goutam's family was leaving the country and going away. They were beginning to feel that this country was no longer a safe place for them to live in. If they truly felt that, why did they weep so much at the prospect of leaving? Five years back, Suranjan's uncle from Calcutta had visited them at their home in Brahmanbaria, and had broken down and wept like a child. Kironmoyee had asked Suranjan whether he had wanted to go to Calcutta with his uncle and he had vehemently rejected the idea.

About four to six years ago, Suranjan had had to go to Mymensingh on party work. Sitting at the window in the train, he had stared hungrily out at the lush green paddy fields, rows and rows of trees, clay huts, stacks of hay, small children who splashed about naked in the ponds trying to catch fish in their improvised fishing nets, and innocent farmers who looked up every time the train whizzed past. Suranjan had been overwhelmed by these sights and had felt he had come to the very heart of his country. The poet Jibanananda Das had been so impressed by this beauty that he had not wanted to go looking for beautiful landscapes anywhere else in the world.

But Suranjan's enthusiasm had waned when he saw that the station called Ramlakshmanpur had been renamed Ahmed Bari. Soon after that he noticed that Kali Bazaar had been renamed

Fatema Nagar, and Krishnanagar was now called Aolianagar. The whole country was being Islamized and now they could not even spare the small railway stations in Mymensingh!

He fancied that the reason Brahmanbaria was now known as B.Baria, Barisal Brojo Mohon College was called B.M. College, and Murari Chand College was referred to as M.C.College was because people did not, under any circumstance, want to say a Hindu name, and, therefore, resorted to abbreviations. Suranjan was worried that in no time these abbreviations themselves would give way to names like Muhammad Ali College, and Sirajuddaula College! He remembered the furore that had erupted when the name of the Jinnah Hall of Dhaka University, had been changed to Surya Sen Hall after twenty-one years of independence. Those who were against the very spirit of independence had declared that Surya Sen was a dacoit and that it was wrong to name a hall after a dacoit! This was just an excuse to change the name, they argued. He would not at all be surprised to find out that the government bowed to the whims of the fundamentalists as it remained in power because of them.

In old Dhaka, Suranjan noticed that the Hindu shops which were still intact were all closed. How could they open their shops? Who would reassure them that they had no reason to be afraid? But they had reopened after the riots of 1990 and perhaps the same thing would happen in 1992 because it seemed that the Hindus were thick skinned. That is why they could rebuild their broken homes, and reorganize their broken shops. At least it was possible to rebuild all this by using sand, brick and mortar, but what could they use to join their broken hearts?

His mind skimmed over various instances of destruction in 1990. The Patuatuli Brahmo Samaj, the Sridhar Bigraha mandir at Shankhari Bazaar, the Prachin Math at Naya Bazaar, the Kaithtuli Shamp mandir, were all set ablaze. Patuatuli's famous M.Bhattacharya and Co., Hotel Raj, Dhakeshwari Jewellers, Evergreen Jewellers, New Ghosh Jewellers, Alpana Jewellers, Kashmiri Biryani House, Rupasree Jewellers, Manashi Jewellers, Mitali Jewellers, Soma Stores at Shankhari Bazaar, Ananya Laundry, Krishna Hair Dresser, Tyre Tube Repairing, Shaha Canteen, Sadarghat's floating restaurant called Hotel Ujala, were all looted. The Naya Bazaar Municipality Sweeper Colony was raided and torched. The Dhaka District Court Sweeper Colony was also set ablaze. The Hari Sabha mandir in Chunkutia Purbapara of Keranigunj, the Kali mandir, the mandir at Mir Bagh, the gymnasium at Ghosum Bazaar, Subhadya Ghoshaibagh Durga mandir, the Chandranikarar mandir, Paschim Para Kali mandir, Samshan Ghat, the Ramkanai mandir of Teghoria Pubnadi, the Durga mandir of Kalindi Borishur Bazaar and the Kali mandir as well as the Manasha mandir were all raided, and their idols destroyed. Fifty homes, including the house of Rabi Misra, son of Parimohon Misra in subdistrict Khejurbagh, district Subhadya, were burnt to the ground. The homes of Bhabatosh Ghosh and Paritosh Ghosh from Teghoria and three hundred odd Hindu homes in Mandail Hindu Para and Bongaon Rishipara were plundered and destroyed. Suranjan had witnessed some of these atrocities personally and had heard of the others.

He had been walking around aimlessly for sometime now but he did not really know where to go. Whom could he call his own in the city of Dhaka? With whom could he talk for a while? Maya had reluctantly given him a hundred takas. Somehow he did not want to spend the money. He had thought a number of times of buying himself a packet of Bangla Fives, but the cigarettes would not last . . .in that case what was the point? He had no weakness for money. Whenever Sudhamoy gave him money to make new shirts and trousers, he would spend the money on friends. If one of them wanted to run away and get married, it was Suranjan who would provide the finances. Once, he had given away the money for his examination fees to a boy called Rahmat. This boy's mother was in hospital and there was no one to pay for her medicines. As soon as he had discovered this, Suranjan did not hesitate to give away his examination fee money . . . . He wondered whether he should visit Ratna. Ratna Mitra. Would it be possible for her to keep her maiden name even after marriage? Why did girls always have to give up their names when they married. Before marriage they had to tag onto their fathers' tails and after marriage their husbands'. Stuff and nonsense. Sometimes Suranjan himself felt like removing his own surname, Dutta. It was the distinctions of name, caste, creed and religion that had spoilt the relationship between man and man. A Bengali, whether Hindu or Muslim, must give himself a Bengali name. He had often thought that Maya's name should have been Nilanjana Maya. And his own name could have been . . . could have been . . . something like Nibir Suranjan or Suranjan Sudha or Nikhil Suranjan. If it were something like this, he would not have to be stained by the name of any religion. He had noticed the tendency among some Bengali Muslims to take on Arabic names. Even those who were steeped in Bengali culture often resorted to names like Faisal Rahman, Touhidul Islam, Faiz Chowdhury. But why? Why should Bengali people have Arabic names? Suranjan would name his daughter, Srotoswini Bhalobasha or Athai Nilima. Actually 'Athai Nilima' matched with Maya Nilanjana, so the name could be saved for her daughter.

Suranjan continued to walk in an aimless way. And yet, when he had left the house, he had had the feeling that there were many things to do. All about him the city bustled, with people walking around in a purposeful fashion. Only he was not busy; only he had nothing to do. In this city of terror and panic, he wanted to sit down somewhere and talk to someone. Should he visit Dulal at Banxshal? Or should he go to Mahadev-da's house in Azimpur? Perhaps he could go to Ispahani Colony and meet Kajal Debnath. Why did he think only of Hindus when he was trying to decide on his destination? Yesterday, Belal had come to visit him, he could return that visit surely? The other day, Haider had come over. It wouldn't be a bad idea to visit his house either. But there was one major deterrent as far as visiting their houses was concerned, and that was the possibility of a discussion on the Babri Masjid. What is happening in India, how many people have died, what are the BJP leaders saying, in which cities has the army taken over? Who has been arrested, which parties have been banned, and topics of a similar nature—Suranjan was quite tired of all this. What the BJP was in India, the Jamaat-i-Islami was in Bangladesh. The purpose of both groups was the same,—the establishment of what might be called fundamentalism. If only religion could be taken off the political agendas of both the countries! Religion had forced itself so strongly on the social firmament, that it would be very difficult for the impoverished, weak and tortured people of the Third World to escape its iron grip. He remembered one of Karl Marx's sayings, one of his favourites—'Problems relating to religion are actually a manifestation of practical shortcomings, as also a protest against them. Religion is the sigh of the tortured and the persecuted, the heart of the heartless world, just as it is the soul of a soulless society. Religion is the opium of the masses.' Suranjan muttered these words to himself as he walked the crowded city roads.

He walked down Wari, Nababpur, Tantibazaar, the Court area, Rajani Basak Lane, Gendaria, and Begum Bazaar till the afternoon was almost gone and finally reached Kajal's house. Like all Hindus these days, he was at home. Either they hide and slink about outside their homes, or they sit tight inside their houses. It benefited Suranjan, though. He had nothing to do and was pleased to be able to see his friends in their homes. There were some others, in Kajal's house—Subhas Singha, Tapas Pal, Dilip De, Nirmal Chatterjee, Anjan Majumdar, Jatin Chakravarti, Syedur Rehman and Kabir Choudhury.

'What's new? Quite a Hindu assembly I must say.'

Nobody laughed at Suranjan's comment. Suranjan alone laughed at his own joke.

'What is the matter? Why is everyone so glum? Is it because the Hindus are being beaten up?' Suranjan asked.

'Is there any reason to be happy?' Subhas countered.

Kajal Debnath was a member of an association for the unity of Hindus, Buddhists and Christians. Suranjan did not support the association, because it seemed to him to have a communal flavour. If he had supported such an association, there would have been no point in insisting that politics should be free of religion. Kajal's view was that, after forty years of hopes and expectations, the association had been formed in a last-ditch effort to preserve their self-respect and independence.

'Has Khaleda ever admitted that this country is being raided by communalism?' When one of the members of the group raised this question, another asked, 'What has the Awami League done in this respect? They have given excuses and attempted to explain the situation but this is what the Jamaatis did as well. In the last elections, after the Awami League gained power, a false promise was circulated that the word Bismillah would be deleted from the constitution. Now that they have lost power, they have decided that by going against the 8th Amendment, they will lose popularity. Does the Awami League only wish to win elections or do they want to be principled? If principles mean so much to them, why did they not say anything against the 8th Amendment?'

'Maybe they think it is practical to get into power first and then institute reforms. Syedur Rahman has come out in favour of the Awami League.'

'You can't trust anyone. Whoever gets into power will praise Islam and at the same time criticize India as much as possible. In this country people are very fond of these two things, criticizing and protesting against India, and eulogizing Islam.' Kajal made these comments with a knowledgeable air.

Suddenly Suranjan went off at a tangent. 'But Kajal-da, don't you think it would be better to form a non-communal group rather than this communal association? And why is Syedur Rahman not a member of this group?'

'Syedur Rahman's absence is not due to our failings . . . . ' said Jatin Chakravarti in a grave voice. 'It is the failing of those who have created the so-called idea of a national religion. All these days we had no reason to form a group like this. So why now? Simply because Bangladesh did not come into being on her own. It was the joint effort of Hindus, Muslims, Buddhists and Christians that made her birth possible. Therefore, to declare only one religion as the national religion is to discriminate against the members of other religious communities. Love for one's country does not vary in degree from person to person nor is it distinguished by caste or religion. Loving one's country is a universal feeling. But when certain groups of people find that because they do not owe religious allegiance to the declared national religion, their religion is regarded as secondary, or is perhaps even third grade in status, and when they are also branded second class citizens, then their egos take a tremendous battering. So can you really blame them if their nationalism is converted to communalism?'

Since the answer had been directed at Suranjan, he perforce had to comment. He did so in a subdued voice, 'But, in a modern State, how can you justify the presence of such a communal association?'

Jatin Chakravarti replied immediately. 'Who is responsible for this feeling of communalism amongst the minorities? Won't you say the promoters of the national religion are responsible? If you pick and choose the religion of one particular community and declare it the religion of the nation, then that State ceases to be nationalistic in nature. A country which proclaims a national religion can any day be declared a theocratic State. This country is gradually becoming communal, and it is just a farce to speak of national integration at this time. The 8th Amendment was actually just an eye-wash, and the minorities who have suffered because of it, have begun to understand this.'

'Are you suggesting that the declaration of Islam as the national religion is going to benefit the Muslims in any way? I don't think so.'

'Certainly not. But they don't understand this now, they will one day.'

'Somehow I think the Awami League has a role to play at this juncture,' said Anjan.

Suranjan said, 'In the Awami League bill too, there is no mention of rejecting the 8th Amendment. Anybody living in a democratic country knows that one basic tenet of democracy is secularism. What I don't understand is why Islam should be declared the national religion in a country which has eighty-six per cent Muslims? In Bangladesh the Muslims are in any case religious. It is not necessary to declare a national religion for them.'

Jatin-babu sat up and said, 'There can be no question of compromising on principles. The Awami League has compromised in some way since it feels that there is some sort of malicious campaign against it.'

Subhas had been listening quietly to the discussion. He spoke up now: 'Actually, instead of discussing the BNP and the Jamaatis, we are unnecessarily bothered about the Awami League. Are they doing any better than the Awami League . . . . .?' Kajal interrupted him to say, 'You must understand that there is really nothing to say about known enemies. But it is when those we rely on stumble that we begin to really feel the pain.'

Kabir Choudhury suddenly said, 'So much has been said about secularism, but what hasn't been pointed out is that secularism means the development of a unanimous or similar outlook towards all religions. There is no scope for partiality and secularism, in effect, means the separation of religion from politics.'

Kajal Debnath said rather agitatedly 'When the country was divided, Muslim fundamentalism gave birth to Pakistan. In India, however, the Hindu fundamentalists lost. As a result, India was able to become a modern, democratic and secular State. Muslims in India were given as much respect as the Hindus, and this naturally meant a moral victory for the Muslims in both countries. Since the Hindus were losers in India, they were regarded as a burden on society in Bangladesh and they ceased to be considered an integral part of the social milieu. Actually all this was an excuse to get rid of the Hindus here and ultimately to occupy all their property. Now, all over again, there is a clamouring for Islamization, just as there was during the Pakistani regime. Naturally the Hindus are apprehensive. Unless and until this State is declared a secular State, it will be difficult for the Hindus to survive here. We must insist on the rejection of the Enemy Property law. And there are other things we should fight for as well. There is no Hindu in the administration. Since Pakistani times no Hindu has been appointed to the post of Secretary. There are only a handful of Hindus in the Army, and they never get promoted beyond a point. I don't suppose there are any Hindus at all in the Air Force and the Navy.'

Nirmal said, 'Kajal-da, it is a fact that there are no Hindus of the rank of Brigadier or Major General. Out of seventy colonels there is only one Hindu, there are eight lieutenant colonels out of 450, forty majors out of 1,000, eight captains out of 1,300, three second lieutenants out of 900, only five hundred sipahis out of 80,000. And there are only 300 Hindus out of 40,000 BDRs. Talking of Secretaries, it is not only the Hindus who have been deprived, there aren't any Buddhists and Christians either. Nor are there any among the Additional Secretaries. There is only one Joint Secretary out of a hundred and thirty-four.'

Kajal spoke up again, 'Are there any candidates from the minorities in the Foreign Services? I don't think so.'

Subhas suddenly got up from his stool and said, 'No, Kajal-da, none.'

There was a carpet laid out on the floor. Suranjan sat on the carpet and leaned on a cushion. He was enjoying himself as he listened to the conversation.

Kabir Choudhury added, 'From Pakistani times until today, only Monoranjan Dhar was sent to Japan for a short while as the Bangladesh Ambassador. When it comes to sending students abroad for higher studies, or for training, Hindus are selectively avoided. Hindus don't have any profitable business in their hands.

In fact, if Hindus wish to go into business, it is a must for them to get hold of a Muslim partner. Only then are they granted a licence. Moreover, they are not given any industrial loans by the various organizations.'

'Yes, you're right,' said Anjan. 'I wanted to start up a garment business, tried my best to the extent that I wore out my shoes going from pillar to post, but I didn't succeed. I got no help at all from the bank. Then I asked Afsar to be my partner and finally managed to get a loan.'

'Have you noticed one thing . . . . ?' asked Subhas, 'All TV and radio programmes start with the Quran, because the Quran is regarded as *the* holy text. Extracts from the Gita and the *Tripitak* are also read out, but they are not regarded as holy.'

Suranjan piped up, 'All this is superfluous. I think all this should be done away with. We should insist on banning religious programmes on TV and radio.'

For a while everyone was quiet. Suranjan felt like a cup of tea, but it was unlikely he would get one in this house. He wanted to do nothing more than lie down on the carpet and mull over the problems and the sorrows that were churning inside the minds of all those present.

Kajal Debnath began talking again. 'At all state functions, societies and associations, extracts from the Quran are religiously read out. Why don't they ever read anything from the Gita? In the whole year, the government has reserved only two days as holidays for the Hindus. Nor can they opt for any special holiday. In every public function, there are proposals to construct new mosques . . . never do they speak of constructing temples, nor do they talk about maintaining the existing temples, churches and pagodas in the city.'

Suranjan raised his head and said, 'Does it make you happy to hear the Gita being chanted on the radio or television? Will the construction of new temples prove propitious for us? The twenty-first century is round the corner, and we are still trying to make our presence felt through religion, both in society as well as in matters of State. Instead, why don't we work to free all State policies, social norms and education policies from the infiltration of religion. If we want the introduction of secularism, it does not necessarily mean that the Gita must be recited as often as the Quran is on radio and TV. What we must insist on is the banning of religion from all State activities. In schools, colleges and universities all religious functions, prayers, the teachings of religious texts and the glorifying of lives of religious personae, should be banned. Similarly where religious functions are concerned, all politics should be disallowed. If any political leader takes part in religious functions or serves as a patron, he should be expelled from the party. The government should not be used as an instrument to propagate religion. Under no circumstance must the religion of an applicant be ascertained when he applies for a job.'

Kajal Debnath laughed when Suranjan finished. 'You've become quite progressive in your thoughts. All these proposals are applicable in a secular State, not in this country.'

Subhas, who was waiting for a chance to say something, chose this moment to put in his bit. 'I have organized a meeting today on behalf of the Bangladesh Students Youth Congress Association. I have sent a memorandum to the Home Minister with a proposal to rebuild the damaged temples, contribute towards the rebuilding of the many homes that have been destroyed, compensate the losses of the homeless and the helpless, and most significantly, punish the guilty and ban communal politics altogether.'

Suranjan had stretched out on the carpet now. He propped himself up and said to Subhas, 'This government will not accept even one proposal of yours.'

Kabir Choudhury said, 'I agree. The Home Minister is an out and out traitor.'

Syedur Rehman said, 'It is terrible that traitors like these are now in power. Sheikh Mujib had forgiven them, and Zia-ur Rahman gave them power. Ershad invested them with further powers, and Khaleda has come to power with their support.'

Tapas Pal, who had been patiently waiting for his turn, now said, 'I have just got news from Cox's Bazaar, that the temple at Sebakhola has been destroyed. There was another at Chitamandir which has suffered the same fate. The Central Kali mandir at the Jalalabad Idgaon Bazaar, the Durga mandir at Hindupara, the Manasha mandir and Hari mandir at Machuapara as well as the Club House at Machuapara have been burnt to cinders by the Jamaatis. The Durga mandir at Islamabad, the Boalkhali Durga mandir, the Adaitya Chintahari math, the chief priest's home at the math, and at least five more temples have been set ablaze. The Hari mandir at Boalkhali has been looted. Eight temples at Choufaldandi as well as six homes and two shops were destroyed. In a Hindu locality hundred and sixty-five homes were completely demolished. In the shopping centre, five Hindu shops were looted and Hindus are being beaten up and tortured at sight. They are setting fire to the granaries in a number of Hindu homes. The Bhairavbari temple at Ukhia has been completely destroyed as well. The Teknaf Kalibari, along with the purohit's home, has been burnt down. The mandir at Sarbang has also been demolished. At Maheshkhali, three temples and eleven Hindu homes were set on fire. Four schools for Gita recitals have been burnt down. At the Kalarama Market, the Kali mandir and Hari mandir have both been set on fire. The Kali mandir at Qutabdia Borghop Bazaar, and five others have also been set on fire. Four craftsmens' shops have been destroyed at the market. At the Ali Akbar Dale, fifty fishermen's homes were looted and burnt to the ground. At Qutabdia, three children sustained burns. At Ramur Idgah, the community Kali mandir and the Jelepara Hari mandir were destroyed and later burnt down. Many homes at Fatehkhanrkhul were set on fire . . . . '

Suranjan cut in abruptly and said, 'Oh for God's sake, stop. Instead, why don't you sing a song?'

'Sing!,' Everyone was taken aback. How could anyone sing in these circumstances? Today was not a normal day. Houses, temples and shops were being burnt in the city, and Suranjan was asking for a song!

Once again Suranjan abruptly changed the topic and said, 'Kajal-da, I am really hungry. Could you give me some rice to eat?'

Rice at this hour! What was the matter with Suranjan?

But all Suranjan wanted was a good helping of rice with some dry fish—which would attract a host of flies—he would fan them away with his left hand while he ate. He remembered how Ramratia used to eat his rice and fish at the Brahmapalli house, sitting outside in the courtyard. Ramratia was the sweeper in the Rajbari school. He had brought Maya home from school one day. She had been a very young girl at that time, and on that particular day was suffering from an upset stomach. She did not have the sense to say that she had to go to the toilet, so the result was a white pajama turned yellow, and Maya standing all by herself in the garden, crying her heart out. The headmistress had spotted her and sent her home with Ramratia. Kironmoyee had given him rice to eat, and the relish with which he had eaten it was something Suranjan would never forget. Had he not seen Ramratia eating that day, he thought, he would never have known that something like rice could give so much pleasure. And now, here he was, asking for a plate of rice in front of so many people. Was he going mad? Perhaps he was not mad. Would he have been moved so much by everything he saw and heard around him if he were mad? Here was a grave discussion in progress and if he happened to break down in the midst of it, it would be truly ridiculous. He had been out in the sun all day long. He was hungry and tired as well.

Almost in a trance, Suranjan heard someone say, 'In the Loharkanda village of Narshindi district, the villagers drove Bashona Rani Choudhury out of her own property. They also forced her son at dagger point to sign on a stamped blank paper. They left with the warning that if anyone got to know about this deal, they would kill Bashona Rani and her two sons.' Suranjan wondered if Bashona was like Kironmoyee: as soft, gentle and peace loving?

'In the Ramzanpur village of Madaripur, Sabita Rani and Pushpa Rani were raped by the henchmen of Yunus Sadaar. In Khulna, Dumuria, Archana Rani Biswas and Bhagabati Biswas were accosted on their way home from the market by thugs who raped them. Who were the ones who did all this? Who? Their names were Madhu, Saokath, Aminur. In Chittagong, at Potia, Uttam Das, the son of Parimal Das, was murdered by Badshah Mia, Nur Hussain and Nur Islam. Uttam's people had filed a case but the only result of that was that the local people were now conspiring to turn them out of their ancestral property. Sabita Rani Dey, a student of Borlekha College in Sylhet, was sitting and studying at night when Nizamuddin, along with his goondas, came into the house, picked her up and made off with her. Nothing has been heard of Sabita Rani since. In Bogura, Nripendra Chandra Dutta's daughter, Shefali Rani Dutta, was not only abducted, but also made to convert to Islam. The administration was of no help when they were requested to look into the matter. In the Suro and Baghdanga villages of Jessore, the attackers surrounded the homes of the Hindus. On whim, they would select victims to beat up. And all through the night they raped eleven Hindu girls.'

'And then?'

Somebody amongst them must have wanted to know. Whoever it was, did his eyes dilate with fear and disgust or with some other feeling? Suranjan's eyes were shut. He was sleepy and not in the least inclined to find out how his companions were reacting to the information that was spewing forth. The gruesome catalogue of destruction resumed.

In Noakhali's Ghosh Bagh area, Sabitribala Roy, her husband Mohonbashi Roy and their young daughter had been turned out into the street. One day, Abdul Halim Noon of Alipur, and Abdur Rub Bachhu Mia had suddenly barged into Sabitribala's house, and demanded 18,000 takas of the money that they had saved up for the marriage of their daughter by selling a fertile plot of land. They had then threatened them with further dire consequences, if they failed to sign their remaining land over to them and leave for India. When they left, they even took the cows in the cowshed with them. What would have happened if Sabitribala and family had not left for India? Their daughter would have been killed . . . . In Shaapmari village of Sherpur, 360 milkmen's families were tortured so much by the fundamentalists, that they left the country. At Kishoregunj, Kotiadi, Charuchandra Dey Sarkar, Sumantomohon Dey Sarkar, Jatindramohon Dey Sarkar and Dineshchandra Dey Sarkar were deprived of vast areas of land by Muslim thugs by means of fake legal documents. Ranjan Rajbhar of Dapuria, Mymensingh, almost lost his ancestral property, once again through fake documents. Ranjan's sisters, Malati and Ramrati, were both married off to Muslims and within months of being wed were both turned out. In the Balighata village of Jaipur, Narayan Chandra Kundu was deprived of twenty bighas of land by shrewd Muslim leaseholders. What is more, they even built homes on that property.'

Suranjan was now very sleepy but he was still registering what the others were saying.

'In Chorgorkul of Narayangunj, Ali Master, Abul Basar and Shahid Morol, surrounded six Hindu homes with sten-guns and ultimately looted and destroyed them. They took away everything from Subhas Mondol, Santosh, Netai and Khetramohon, including their ancestral land.'

Someone called out to Suranjan. 'Wake up, Suranjan, wake up, and eat. The rice has arrived.'

It must be Kajal-da who was calling out to him. Maya would often summon him in this manner, 'Dada, come along, rice has been served, come and eat . . . .'

He would buy a lot of sleeping pills tonight with the money Maya had given him, he thought vaguely. It seemed as though he had not slept for a very long time. As soon as it was dark, the bed bugs would start biting. His bed was full of bed bugs. He remembered how Kironmoyee would clean his bed of bugs when he was a child. He made a mental note to ask Maya to clean out his bed for him that very night. The bugs bit him all through the night; they even bit him in the head. The very thought of it made his head ache. He felt sick. In between someone (it was probably Tapas) said that in his neighbourhood thirty temples were damaged, and all the houses in and around the temple were burnt. Picking up on this note, someone else stated in poetic style: 'Listen to me . . . let me tell you about Noakhali . . . .' He went on to say that in Sundalpur village seven homes and the Adhorchaand Ashram were looted and set on fire. Three houses in Jagonananda village suffered the same fate as did three others in Gangapur. Ragrogaon village, Daulatpur village, Ghoshbagh, Maijadi, the Kali mandir at Sonapur, Binodpur gym, Choumuhini Kali mandir, Durgapur village, Qutabpur, Gopalpur, Sultanpur Akhanda Ashram and some temples in the Choyani Bazaar were demolished. Babupur Tetuia, Mahadipur, Rajgunj Bazaar, Tongirpar, Kazirhaat, Rasulpur, Jameendarhaat, Choumuhini Porabari were destroyed and in Bhabordi village ten temples and eighteen houses were torched. In Rajpur village of Companygunj, nineteen houses were looted and the ladies there were molested. Biplab Bhowmick of Ramdi village was chopped down today.

If only Suranjan could plug his ears with cotton wool! All around him, the only topic was the Babri Masjid and tales of arson and destruction. If only he could have some peace and quiet around him.

It would have been perfect if he could escape to Mymensingh where there had been much less mayhem. If he could have bathed in the waters of the Brahmaputra all afternoon perhaps the burning sensation in his body would have eased somewhat. He got up with a start. Most of the people in the room had already left. Suranjan was also about to leave when Kajal-da said, 'The food is on the table. Aren't you going to eat? How come you are sleeping at this hour? Are you unwell?'

Suranjan stretched and said,'No, Kajal-da, I don't think I'll eat. I don't feel like it. You're right, I'm not feeling too good.'

'Come on. What do you mean?'

'I don't really mean anything. But tell me, what can I do? At times I am ravenously hungry, but before I have eaten my hunger subsides. It must be acidity. I feel sleepy, but I just cannot sleep.'

Jatin Chakravarti put an arm around Suranjan's shoulders and said,'You are breaking down, Suranjan. Pull yourself together. We can't let this happen to any of us. After all we have to survive.'

Suranjan was standing with his head lowered and Jatin-da's words sounded like Sudhamoy's advice. It had been a long time since he had sat by his sick father. He decided to return home immediately. This is what always happened when he visited Kajal-da. There would always be a lot of people around and there would inevitably be a long rambling discussion on politics and other related matters well into the night.

He left without eating. It had been quite a while since he'd eaten at home and he thought he would do so today in the company of Maya, Kironmoyee and Sudhamoy. Barriers had been created between him and the rest of his family, but the reason for this was Suranjan himself. He decided to break down all the barriers today. He would once again laugh and talk with everyone and feel just as happy and content as he had felt in the morning. They would talk about old times, about his childhood days when he had sat in the sun and eaten steamed rice cakes. There would be no rigid differences in identity—father, son, brother, sister—everyone would be friends, very close friends. Today he would not go to anyone else's house. Not to Pulok's house, nor Ratna's. He would go directly to Tikatuli, eat whatever was available, sit up till late and talk to everyone and then sleep peacefully.

Kajal-da saw him off at the gate. He said with concern, 'You should not be moving around in this manner. We are not venturing beyond the neighbourhood, and here you are, moving all over town alone. You can never be sure of what might happen.'

Suranjan had nothing to say to this; he began walking with long strides. He had enough money on him to take a rickshaw, but he did not have the heart to spend Maya's money. He had not smoked the whole day and now, at the end of the day, despite his concern about the money, he longed for a smoke. He stopped at a shop, and bought a Bangla Five and lit it. It made him feel like a king. He walked up to the Kakrail crossing and took a rickshaw from there. These days, he thought, the city seemed to sleep rather early, just like a sick man. What was the city's ailment? As he mulled over this, he remembered a friend who had once had a boil on his back. All through the day he would shriek in pain, but he would never treat it as he was mortally afraid of any type of medication, and especially hated injections. Did the city also have a boil on its back? Suranjan thought it did, as he sat in the rickshaw heading for home.

*

'Maya, what is the matter with Suranjan? Do you know where he could be at this hour?' Sudhamoy asked.

'He said he was going to Pulok-da's house. Must have got held up there.'

'Is that any reason for not returning home before dark?'

'I don't know . . . I don't understand. He should have been back.'

'Doesn't he realize that we could be anxious and that he should return home at a reasonable time . . .'

Maya tried to calm Sudhamoy down. 'Never mind. You should not be talking so much. Talking makes you suffer. Just lie down quietly. It's time for you to eat and after that, if you want me to read to you, I'll be happy to do so. You must sleep at ten after you've taken your sleeping pills. By then Dada will surely be back, so don't worry.'

'You are nursing me back to health too soon, Maya. I could have stayed in bed for a few more days. You know there are drawbacks to being fit too.'

'Like what?' Maya asked as she sat on his bed and mashed the rice that he was supposed to eat.

'You feed me, your mother massages my body, presses my temples . . . . Will I get so much love and care once I am well? Then I'll have to busy myself with my patients, going to the market, perhaps even quarrelling with you . . . . ' Sudhamoy broke into laughter as he said this. His daughter gaped at him; this was the first time since his illness, that he had laughed.

Earlier he had said to Kironmoyee, 'You must open all the windows today. I don't like the room to be so dark and gloomy. Let there be some fresh air too. I haven't felt the winter air at all. Do you think it is only in the spring that we like to breathe in fresh air? When I was young, I used to wander around sticking posters on the walls in the bitter cold of winter with only a thin shirt on my back. I have been all over the hilly regions in Sushong Durgapur with Moni Singh. Do you know anything about the Tonk movement and the Hajong rebellion of those times, Kironmoyee?'

Kironmoyee was mentally much more relaxed. She said to her husband. 'You've told me so much about all this when we were married. If I remember right, you spent a night with Moni Singh in an unfamiliar house in Netrakona.'

'Kironmoyee . . .' Sudhamoy said suddenly, 'has Suranjan worn warm clothes?'

Maya grimaced and said, 'No, of course, not . . . . He's also wearing a thin shirt just like you. He is a modern day revolutionary after all! He is not affected by the winds of nature, he's more busy coping with the winds of time.'

Kironmoyee reacted angrily. 'Heaven knows where he roams around the whole day . . . what he eats . . . whether he eats at all. His indiscipline seems to increase day by day . . . . '

Just then there was a knock on the door. Was it Suranjan? Kironmoyee, who was sitting at Sudhamoy's bedside, got up to open the door. This was exactly how Suranjan knocked, but he normally went straight to his own room using his own entrance, when he returned late. Most of the time the door that led directly to his room was locked from the outside, which facilitated his entry, but he also knew how to open the door if it had been locked from within. Since it wasn't too late, it must be Suranjan.

Maya was mixing dal with rice to feed Sudhamoy. She thought that if she rolled the mixture into soft round balls it would be easier for him to swallow. For days after he had fallen ill, he had survived on a liquid diet. It was only recently that the doctor had allowed him food that was semi-solid. Today they had prepared a thin fish curry to accompany the dal and rice. Maya had been starting to mix the fish with the rice, when the knock sounded on the door.

Kironmoyee went to the door, asked who it was as her husband listened. There was a muttered reply and she opened the door. In a flash, seven young men barged into the house, pushing Kironmoyee aside. Four of them were armed with rods but everything happened so quickly that it was difficult to see what the rest were carrying. They were all about twenty-one years old. Two of them wore caps, pajamas and kurtas and the rest wore shirts and trousers. They wasted no time and, began methodically breaking up everything in the room. Chillingly, not one of them uttered a word and the only sounds were the shattering of tables, chairs, the television set, glass-fronted almirahs, bookshelves, the dressing-table, pedestal fans . . . . Clothes and fabric were torn to shreds. Appalled, Sudhamoy vainly tried to sit upright. His daughter screamed, 'Baba . . . .' A stunned Kironmoyee still held the door open. As they neared the end of their ghastly task, one of the groups pulled out a chopper and menaced them. 'You bastards!' he said, 'Did you think you could get away after destroying the Babri Masjid?'

Frenzied and savage, the young men continued to destroy the earthly possessions of the Duttas. Immobilized and silent the terror-stricken family watched their house being reduced to a shambles . . . . And then the spell was broken for one of the thugs grabbed hold of Maya. Her mother wailed in terror and the invalid Sudhamoy moaned. In a last desperate measure to save herself, Maya caught hold of the bedposts. Her mother came running up and flung herself on her daughter, in a doomed attempt to protect Maya. But their attackers were relentless. They wrenched Kironmoyee off her daughter, broke Maya's grip on the bed and left as swiftly as they had come, carrying their prize with them. Recovering, Kironmoyee ran after them, screaming and begging: 'Please let her go. Please let my daughter go . . .'

Out on the street two autorickshaws waited. Maya's hands

were still soiled with the rice and curry she had been mixing for her father. Her clothes were in disarray as wild-eyed she screamed to her mother for help 'Ma . . . please help me, Ma . . . ' She fought with her captors as she was dragged away, looking back in pain and terror, hoping against hope that her mother would be able to save her. Kironmoyee tried her best. With scant regard for her own safety, she threw herself at the goondas, dodged the shining chopper they aimed at her, and tried to get hold of Maya. But the two men who held her daughter, pushed aside Kironmoyee's attack and bundled Maya into one of the autorickshaws. As the vehicles sped off, Kironmoyee ran after them weeping and screaming, 'They've taken my daughter . . . please save her . . . . '

At the corner of the street, exhausted and at the end of her strength, she stopped. Her hair was wild and dishevelled and her clothes were crushed and creased from her exertions. She noticed Moti Mia whom she knew and pleaded with him: 'Dada, they've abducted Maya. Please help me.' The man looked at her blankly, as did everyone around him. It was as though she were some mad beggar woman spouting rubbish. Gathering up her remaining strength, Kironmoyee ran into the night, in vain and ineffectual pursuit of her vanished daughter . . . .

Suranjan was surprised to find the front door ajar when he returned. As he stepped into the house, he was stunned by the destruction that met his eyes. Tables lay overturned, books were strewn all over the place. The mattresses and sheets had been ripped off the beds, the clothes rack was broken and the clothes lay shredded in heaps all across the room. Suranjan gasped as he moved from room to room. Glass crunched under his feet. He found his father on the floor groaning with pain. Maya and Kironmoyee had vanished. Suranjan was afraid to ask his father what had happened in his absence. Why was he lying on the floor? Why were his mother and sister not at home? As he tried to put his questions, Suranjan noticed that his voice was trembling with shock.

His father said to him in a faint voice, 'They have taken Maya away.'

Shock gave way to anger and fear in Suranjan. 'What do you mean taken her away? Who has taken her away? Where? When?'

His father was unable to reply, his meagre strength rapidly

ebbing away. Suranjan picked him up gently and put him on the bed. He was breathing in short quick gasps, and was wet with perspiration.

'Where is Ma?' Suranjan asked in a whisper.

Sudhamoy's face was the colour and texture of parchment. It was clear that if nothing was done to help him and his blood pressure increased, he would die. Suranjan was in a terrible dilemma: Should he see to his father or should he go looking for his sister? He shuddered in fear and despair. Into his head swam a vision of heaving waters that threatened to swamp him; in moments this was replaced by a vision of a pack of dangerous pariah dogs circling a cuddly, defenceless kitten. He made his decision and headed for the door. Before he left, he gently patted his father's insensate hand and said, 'I will bring back Maya, whatever it takes, Baba.'

Suranjan strode up to Haider's house and knocked loudly on the door. He made such a racket that Haider himself came and opened it. He was amazed to see Suranjan. 'What is it, Suranjan? What is the matter with you?'

At first Suranjan was unable to answer. It was as though the pain and despair that he felt had robbed him of the power of speech.

'They've taken Maya away . . . .' he finally managed to get out, his voice ragged with emotion. He did not have to explain who had taken Maya.

'When did they take her?'

Suranjan did not reply. Why was it important to know when Maya had been abducted? Wasn't it news enough to know that they had taken her. Haider frowned. This was really worrying news. He had been away from home at a party meeting, and had only just returned. In fact, he had been about to change into his night clothes when Suranjan had arrived. He was shocked to see the change in Suranjan. He looked as though everything he lived for had been swept away by flood-waters. He was holding on to the door but his hands began to shake so much that he balled them into fists. Haider, in an attempt to calm his friend, put an arm about his shoulders and said, 'Relax. Let's go inside and decide how we'll tackle this.'

At the touch of Haider's hand, Suranjan broke down. He put

both his arms around Haider and said, 'Bring Maya home, Haider . . . please bring back Maya . . . .'

His agony was plain to see in the great, wrenching sobs that shook his body. Finally, he fell at Haider's feet, making the same pitiful request. Haider looked on aghast. He could never have imagined his tough, hard, cynical friend in this state. He pulled Suranjan to his feet, and though he was famished, decided that food could wait.

'Come on, let's go and see what can be done,' he said. They got onto his Honda motorcycle and sped through the lanes and streets of Tikatuli. Haider went into squalid little houses and well-kept residences, he spoke to suspicious-looking paanwallahs and he conferred with well-fed, well-groomed young men, he went into parts of the neighbourhood Suranjan didn't even know existed but at the end of it he had drawn a blank. Leaving Tikatuli behind they now rode through English Road, Nababpur, Lakshmi Bazaar, Lalmohon Saha Street, Bakshi Bazaar, Lalbagh, Sutrapur, Waiz-ghat, Sadarghat, Parrymohon Das Road, Abhay Das Lane, Narinda, Alu Bazaar, Thathari Bazaar, Parrydas Road, Babu Bazaar, Urdu Road and Chowk Bazaar. They careened through every part of the city that Haider could think of as a potential hide-out but they still found no sign of Maya. They pressed on. Haider knocked on many doors, he talked and he talked to people Suranjan had never seen in his life . . . still nothing. At every stop that Haider made, Suranjan's hopes would rise . . . this time they would surely find Maya! She would be tied up and would probably have been beaten, but she would be found. But what if they weren't just satisfied with beating her and were doing something more? Suranjan kept his ears open, just in case he could hear Maya crying.

As they passed through Lakshmi Bazaar, Suranjan suddenly asked Haider to stop. He thought he could hear Maya crying. They followed the sound to its source and found that it was a baby crying in some house. It was already quite late in the night but Haider and Suranjan continued their search. They didn't spend too long at any one place, for they had a lot of ground to cover. In every alley groups of young men stood watching them with red, blood-shot eyes. Looking at them, Suranjan was sure that these people were responsible for Maya's plight.

'Haider, where is Maya? Why aren't you able to find her?'

'I am trying.'

'We must find her by tonight, we must.'

'I've checked on all the local kingpins. What else can I do?'

Suranjan smoked one cigarette after another. It tore him apart to think that it was with Maya's money that he had bought them.

'Let's go and eat something at Superstar. I am really very hungry.'

Haider ordered paranthas and meat. Two plates. Suranjan made an attempt to eat. He tore the paranthas into pieces, but he could not bear to bring them up to his mouth. As the minutes ticked by, the void in his heart seemed to grow bigger. Haider ate with relish, and after he had finished, lit a cigarette. Suranjan egged him on to continue the search. 'Come on, let's get moving. We still haven't found her.'

'Where else can I look, tell me? You've seen for yourself how carefully we've combed the whole place !'

'Dhaka is such a small place. How can we possibly fail to locate her? Come, let's go to the police station.'

When Suranjan reported the whole incident at the police station, he was heard out by policemen with blank, disinterested looks on their faces. Eventually, he managed to file a written complaint. 'I don't think they'll do anything about it . . .'

'They might,' Haider said.

'Let's go to Wari. Do you know anyone there?'

'I've put the party people on the job. They'll also look around. Now don't worry so much.'

It was obvious Haider had done his very best, but Suranjan wasn't satisfied, and his anxiety drove him on. All through the night, they rode around the old city on Haider's Honda. They went to all the local bootleggers, the gambling joints as well as the smugglers' dens, till it was time for Haider to say his prayers. Suranjan had always liked the sounds of the azaan. But today the sound of it was unbearable. The chanting of the azaan also meant the approach of dawn . . . Maya had still not been found!

Haider brought his bike to a halt at Tikatuli. As gently as he could, he said, 'Suranjan, don't lose heart. Let's see what we can do.'

In their house, Kironmoyee sat amidst the wreckage looking eagerly yet hopelessly at the door. Even Sudhamoy, paralyzed and further weakened by the excitement and a lack of sleep hoped against hope that Suranjan would come back with Maya. But when they saw their tired, grieving son return emptyhanded all hope fled. Did this mean that they would not see Maya anymore? The two of them shook with fear and sorrow. The atmosphere of doom in the house was heightened by the close and smelly atmosphere—a result of the lack of ventilation. All the doors and windows were barred and shuttered. Suranjan did not feel like talking to his parents as they sat there mute, anguished and terrified. Their eyes were full of questions but the only answer was, 'Maya could not be found!'

Suranjan slumped wearily to the floor and stretched out his legs. He felt like vomiting. By now, he thought, they must have gang-raped her. If only Maya would return now just as she had after a two-day-long disappearance as a child of six! The door was open. Everything would still be all right if Maya were to only walk in the door—sorrowful and exhausted, perhaps, but alive and reunited with her devastated family. Let her come back, please, to this small, demoralized and totally ruined household.

Haider had promised to look for Maya the next day. Since he had promised, couldn't Suranjan dream of Maya's return? But why had they abducted Maya? Because she was Hindu? How much more rape, bloodshed and loss of property were the Hindus going to suffer as the price for staying on in this country? Like turtles with their heads drawn in . . . but for how long? If he was looking for answers to these questions, there were none to be had.

Kironmoyee sat with her back against a wall. Not addressing anyone, merely saying the words aloud, she spoke, 'They said, "Mashima, we've come to see how you are. We are from the neighbourhood. Open the door." How old could they have been? Not more than twenty-one or twenty-two. How could I manage against their strength? I went to all the houses in our area, asking for help . . . but they just heard me out, sympathized with me perhaps, but no one helped me. One of them was called Rafiq, I heard one of them who wore a cap, call out the name . . . . She had taken refuge in Parul's house for some time. Perhaps she would have been saved if she had tayed there. Will Maya never come home again? Why couldn't they have burnt down the house instead? I suppose they didn't because the landlord is a Muslim!

Why didn't they kill me instead? At least the innocent girl would have been spared. My life is almost done, her's was just beginning . . . . '

Suranjan's head spun with nausea and a terrible pain. He rushed to the bathroom and vomited uncontrollably.

Day Seven

As the sunlight streamed into the veranda the black and white cat strode across it. Was it looking for food? Or was it looking for Maya? Maya used to walk about with the cat in her arms. It also used to sneak under her quilt and curl up in its warmth. Did it know that Maya was not here anymore?

Maya must be weeping bitterly wherever she was! Did they tie up her hands and legs? And stuff cloth into her mouth? There was a world of difference between a girl of six and one of twenty-one and the reason to kidnap girls at these widely disparate ages would also be different. Suranjan shuddered to think what seven men could do to a twenty-one-year-old girl. Grief-stricken and anxious, he felt stiff and dead. Was Suranjan alive? Yes, of course, he was. Maya was the one who was gone, perhaps forever. It was the way of the world that no one sacrificed his life for another. It was well established that there was no other living creature as selfish as man. And so, why should her relatives die just because Maya had passed on?

It was true that Haider had looked quite hard for Maya. All the same Suranjan felt he had not tried his best! After all Haider was a Muslim, and employing a Muslim to hunt Muslims, was as bad as using a bone to pick up other bones. As he lay in the sun and watched the cat, it suddenly occurred to Suranjan that Haider probably knew who had taken Maya and was only pretending he didn't. When he had wolfed down his food at Superstar there had been no anxiety on his face. On the contrary, he had burped with satisfaction after the meal and had smoked his cigarette with so much ease, that it did not seem as though he was out looking for someone in great danger. And come to think of it, it hadn't seemed as though the search had been of any great importance to him. He remembered that Haider had always wanted to ride around town at night. Had he merely fulfilled his desire that night? Had there been a genuine effort to look for Maya? Or did he merely go through the motions for the sake of friendship. He had hardly been persuasive at the police station. Suranjan doubted that he had left any instructions at all with his party colleagues. Perhaps he thought that Maya was not a number one priority in his scheme of things. Was that because Hindus were second class citizens?

Even now Suranjan found it hard to believe that Maya was gone, and was not in the next room sitting beside Sudhamoy and exercising his arm. He felt that the moment he entered that room he would hear Maya say, 'Dada, aren't you going to do something?' Remorsefully he thought he'd never done anything much for her. Don't all sisters make childish demands of their older brothers—Take me out . . . . buy me this . . buy me that . . . ! Yes, of course, she had asked for all sorts of things, but Suranjan had ignored her. He was too busy, too pre-occupied with himself to care about her. The things he had found important were friends, politics, party meetings . . . . All these years, Sudhamoy, Kironmoyee and Maya had not mattered at all. He was not interested in their joys and sorrows. All that he had been interested in was the future of the country. He had worked hard to remedy the ills he perceived in his country but had he succeeded?

As soon as it was nine, Suranjan ran to Haider's house which was quite close by. Haider was still sleeping, so he waited in the living-room. As he sat waiting, a strange suspicion wormed its way into his mind: he thought that the boy named Rafiq, who had been among the marauders, was someone Haider knew or might even be related to. Suranjan shivered. Two hours passed and Haider finally emerged. 'So, is Maya back?' he asked.

'Would I have come to you if she'd returned?' retorted Suranjan.

'Oh.' Haider sounded indifferent. He was wearing only a lungi. He scratched his bare chest and said, 'It's not all that cold this year, is it?' He scratched himself again. 'There is a meeting at the party president's house today too. They are probably making arrangements for a procession. Just when the Gholam Azam deal was at its peak, all this rioting had to start. Actually the riots were definitely the handiwork of the BNP. They wanted to turn the issue to their advantage.'

'By the way, Haider, do you know a boy called Rafiq? There was someone by that name among the intruders.'

'Where is he from?'

'I don't know. He'll be about twenty-one or twenty-two. He could be from this locality.'

'I don't think I know anyone by that name. Anyway, I'll put my men on the job.'

'Let's go out. I don't think we should waste any more time. I just can't bear to look at my parents' face. As it is, Baba has suffered a stroke. With all this tension, I can only hope nothing worse happens.'

'I don't think it will be right for you to move about with me at this hour.'

'Why? Why won't it be right?'

'Why can't you understand?'

Of course, Suranjan understood why Haider did not wish to be seen with him. Suranjan was a Hindu, and as a Hindu it was not expected of him to try to apprehend Muslims even if they were thieves, thugs or murderers. Also, it may have been asking for too much to expect to be able to effect the release of a Hindu girl from the clutches of Muslims.

Suranjan left Haider's home disappointed. Where could he go now? Home? He did not feel like going into that wilderness. His parents were still nursing the crazy hope that he would come back with Maya. Suranjan did not want to go home without Maya. Haider had said he had told his men to track down Maya . . . . Would they really look for her? After all, they had not lost anything. Who was Maya to them? Why should Muslims have any feelings at all for Hindus? If they did, why was it that only Hindu homes were devastated and burnt? Why was it only Suranjan's home, and Gopal's and Kajalendu's that were targets for plunder?

Suranjan did not go back home. He roamed the streets, in fact the whole city . . . looking for Maya. What was she guilty of, that they should abduct her so ruthlessly? Was it so criminal an offence to be a Hindu? So criminal that one could without a thought ruin and burn their houses, abduct their women and rape them too? Suranjan walked about aimlessly, sometimes he broke into a run. Anyone on the streets who looked about twenty-one years old became a suspect in Suranjan's eyes.

He stopped at a grocer's shop in Islampur to buy some muri. The shopkeeper would not meet his eye and Suranjan was instantly convinced that he was aware of his sister's abduction. He began tramping the city streets again and finally halted at Naya Bazaar to rest by the ruins of the monastery there. He was still very tense and could hardly bear the thought of meeting anyone he knew. And what was the point anyway? They would only continue the discussion on the Babri Masjid. The other day Salim had not hesitated to say, 'If you people can destroy our mosque, why should there be any harm in our burning your temples?' True, Salim had been joking when he said this. But many serious thoughts are expressed through casual jokes.

If only Maya would return home. Perhaps she would. She should come back even if she had been raped. In the hope that he'd find her at home, Suranjan returned. Nothing, however, had changed. Sudhamoy and Kironmoyee still continued to sit and wait for the miracle to happen.

What worse news could there be other than that of Maya's not returning? Suranjan lay down on his bed and hid his face in his pillow. In the other room he could hear Sudhamoy groaning. Later in the middle of the night, the sharp, shrill sound of Kironmoyee crying bore into Suranjan like the droning of crickets and would not permit him to sleep. Why couldn't the three of them take poison and kill themselves? At least their pain and suffering would not continue to pierce and chop them into even finer pieces. It was obvious now that it was pointless for Hindus to try and survive in Bangladesh.

*

Sudhamoy guessed his breakdown was due to cerebral thrombosis or perhaps an embolism. He was certain he would have died if he had begun haemorrhaging, and now he wished it had happened. As it is, he was half dead. Why couldn't his life have been sacrificed and Maya's spared? The girl had so very much wanted to live. She had fled to Parul's house on her own, and it was only his illness that had brought her back to be carried away by those heartless monsters. A deep sense of guilt gnawed at Sudhamoy's heart. Over and over again, his eyes filled with tears. He reached out to hold

Kironmoyee just once, but there was nobody there. Suranjan was not around, and Maya had gone altogether. He was dying of thirst and his tongue and throat were parched and dry.

Kironmoyee, too, had suffered because of him. She had always wanted to perform her prayers in the traditional way but he had warned her that such prayers were not allowed in the house. She had been an excellent singer. But when she began singing in public, people had abused her and called her a shameless Hindu woman. So offended was Kironmoyee by these accusations that she had given up singing completely. When she made this great sacrifice, had Sudhamoy stood by her? How much had he supported her? Maybe he too had felt it would be best to avoid things that were socially unacceptable. For the twenty-one years he had slept beside Kironmoyee . . . . quite literally slept, for there had been nothing else to speak of, he had been guarding her chastity, and helping her be the faithful wife. But why had that been necessary? Wasn't that also a kind of perversion? Kironmoyee had never been all that keen on saris and jewellery. She had never said to him, 'I would like that sari,' or 'Buy me that earring.'

Sudhamoy had often asked her, 'Kironmoyee, are you hiding some sorrow from me?'

And she had always replied, 'No, all I am really interested in is the prosperity and happiness of this family. My own individual happiness is not important.'

Sudhamoy had always been keen on a daughter. Before Suranjan was born, he had put his stethoscope to Kironmoyee's stomach and said, 'I can hear my daughter's heartbeat, Kironmoyee. Do you want to hear it too?' On one occasion he had said, 'It is the daughter who always looks after her parents in their old age. Sons always move out with their wives to live separately, but daughters . . .they even forsake their husbands' homes to look after their parents. I know this for a fact, because I have seen daughters come and attend to their sick, old parents at the hospital. The sons come as well, but only as visitors.'

All through her first pregnancy he would let Kironmoyee listen to her baby's little heart beating through the stethoscope. All over the world, parents yearn for sons, but Sudhamoy only craved a daughter. When Suranjan was a baby, he would dress him up in frocks and take him for walks.

And then Sudhamoy's dreams were fulfilled for Maya was born. He had chosen the name Maya himself saying, 'It is my mother's name. I have lost one mother, but gained another.'

It was Maya who always gave him his medicines at night. Tonight, the hour for his daily dose of medicine was long past. He called out to his beloved daughter: 'Maya . . . . Maya . . . . ' The neighbours were asleep and his anguished wail was only heard by Kironmoyee and Suranjan, who were both awake. It was also heard by the black and white cat.

Day Eight

After the demolition of the Babri Masjid in Ayodhya, Uttar Pradesh, the large scale killing and bloodshed that had spread all over India took a while to subside. The number of people dead had now crossed the 1,800 mark. In Bhopal and Kanpur, there was still violence. To maintain law and order the army was out in the streets of Gujarat, Karnataka, Kerala, Andhra Pradesh, Assam, Rajasthan and West Bengal. The political parties that had been banned, continued to remain inoperative.

In order to maintain peace and harmony, all the parties in Dhaka were spontaneously organizing processions. But all this was a facade. Behind the front, it was a different story.

- In Golokpur, thirty Hindu women were raped. Chanchali, Sandhya, Moni . . . Nikunja Dutta had died. Bhagavati, an old lady, had been so terrified that she had died of a heart attack. In Golokpur incidents of daylight rape were reported. Even women who had taken refuge in Muslim homes were being raped.
- Fourteen hundred *maunds* of betel nuts belonging to Nantu Haldar were burnt to ashes at Das' Haat Bazaar.
- The police, magistrate and DC were mute spectators to the destruction of temples at Bhola city.
- The jewellery of temples was openly looted.
- A Hindu washermens' colony was burnt to cinders.
- At Manikgunj, they destroyed the Lakshmi temple, the community Shiv temple, the goldsmith lanes of Dashara and Kalikhala and the big beverage and cigarette godowns of Gadadhar Pal.
- Three truckloads of people raided the police stations at Twara, Baniajuri, Pukuria, Uthli, Mahadebpur, Joka and Shivalaya.
- Three kilometres from the city, Hindu homes were looted and burnt in the Betila village.
- The century old Naat mandir of Betila was attacked.

- Jeevan Saha's home at Garpara was torched; three cowsheds were burnt to ashes; hundreds of mounds of paddy were lost in the flames.
- Hindu shops at Terosree Bazaar under Ghior police station, and Hindu houses at Gangdubi, Baniajuri and Senpara were burnt down. At Senpara, a Hindu woman was raped as well.
- The Kali temple of Pirozepur, the Debarchana committee Kali mandir, the Manasha mandir, the Sheetala mandir, the Shiv mandir, the Narayan mandir, the Pirozepur Madanmohon Bigraha mandir, the Kali temple of Roykathi, the Krishnanagar Rai Rasaraj Seva Ashram, the Dumurtala Shreeguru Sangha ashram and mandir, the Kali temple at Suresh Saha's home in Dukheri Dumurtala, the Manasha mandir at Naren Saha's house in Dumurtala, the Manasha mandir at the ancestral home of Ramesh Saha, the community Kali mandir at Dumurtala, the temples at the homes of Sucharan Mondal, Gouranga Haldar, Harendra Nath Saha, Narendra Nath Saha, the Kali temple beside the Dumurtala high school, the Ranipur Panch Devi mandir, the community mandir of Hularhaat and Kartick Das' furniture shop, the Kali mandir, the Kalakhali Sanatan Ashram, the Jujkhola Gour Govinda Seva Ashram, the Harisabha Sanatan Dharma mandir, the Kali mandir at the home of Ranjit Seal, the Jujkhola community Puja centre, the community Durga mandir near the Gabtola school, the temple in Bipin Haldar's house at Krishnanagar, the community Kali mandir at Namazpur, the temple and math at Kalikathi Biswas' home, the Lairi Kali mandir, the community temple of Inderhaat under Swarupkathi police station, the Durga mandir at Kanai Biswas' home in Inderhaat, Nakul Saha's cinema hall, the Durga mandir at Amal Guha's home, the temple at Hemanta Seal's house and the Kali mandir at Jadav Das' house at Mathbaria police station were all set ablaze.
- The Shiv mandir at Mistripara in Syedpur was also destroyed.
- The community temple at Rathdanga village of Narail district, the Ghona community mandir, the Kudulia community crematorium, Nikhil Chandra Dey's family mandir, Kalipada Hazra's family temple, Shivprosad Pal's family temple, the family temple at Dulal Chandra Chakraborty's home in Badon village, Krishna Chandra Laskar's family temple, the Taltala village community temple, the family temples of Baidyanath Saha, Sukumar Biswas and Pagla Biswas at Pankabila village, the community temple at Pankabila village, the Narayan Jiu mandir at Purbapara Daulatpur under Lohagara police station were all ransacked and demolished.
- Ten temples at Khulna were razed to the ground.

- Four or five temples along with houses were looted and plundered at Raduli in Paikpara and at Shobonadas and Baka villages.
- Two temples were destroyed in the Talimpur area under Rupsa police station. The Hindu homes adjacent to it were also looted.
- On the night of 8 December, three temples in the Dighlia and Senhati areas were burnt down.
- A group of processionists raided thirteen homes in Sahadevpur village, Feni.
- Twenty people were injured in the Jaipur village of Chagalnaiya.
- At Langalboa village, Gobinda Prosad Roy's home was raided by two hundred people at the instigation of Moazzem Hussain. A person by the name of Kamal Biswas was seriously injured; it was possible he would succumb to his injuries.

These tales of the continuing carnage in Bangladesh were being furnished by Birupaksha, Nayan and Debabrata. They sat in front of Suranjan and chattered on but Suranjan gave no sign that he heard them. He was lying down with his eyes closed. He thought savagely—none of you know that it was not only at Bhola, Chittagong, Pirozepur, Sylhet and Comilla that Hindu homes were looted; there was also a home at Tikatuli which was looted and from where a beautiful girl named Maya was stolen! Women after all were like commodities, and therefore stolen just like gold and silver.

'What is the matter, Suranjan? Why aren't you saying anything?' Debabrata asked.

'I feel like drinking,' Suranjan said, 'can't we fill ourselves to the brim with booze today?'

'Do you mean it?'

'Yes, I do. There is money in my pocket. One of you go and get a bottle of whisky.'

'Do you mean to say you'll sit at home and drink? What about your parents?'

'To hell with my parents! I feel like drinking, so I will. Biru, please go. You'll get it either at Sakura or Piyasi.'

'But, Suranjan-da . . . . '

'For God's sake, go . . . '

The sound of Kironmoyee crying wafted in from the adjacent room.

'Who is crying? Mashima?' asked Birupaksha.

'Being a Hindu, there is no way to avoid tears,' said Suranjan. The three young men present fell silent. They were also Hindus, and they understood why Mashima was crying. Every Hindu's heart was touched by an inexplicable grief these days! Birupaksha quickly went out with the money as though going away would spare him the mental agony the others were experiencing. Suranjan wanted to escape the agony, too—but the route he preferred was alcohol.

Soon after Birupaksha left, Suranjan asked, 'Debabrata, can't we burn a mosque?'

'Mosque? Are you crazy?'

'Come, let's go and set the Tara masjid on fire tonight.'

Debabrata looked from Suranjan to Nayan with dismay.

'There are twenty million Hindus in this country. If we had wanted to, we could even have burnt up Baitul Mokarram.'

'You have never claimed to be a Hindu. Why start today?'

'Yes, I used to call myself a human being, and I believed in humanism. But these Muslims did not let me stay human. They made me a Hindu.'

'You have changed a lot, Suranjan.'

'It's not my fault.'

'What do we gain by pulling down mosques? Will we get back our temples?' Debabrata asked nervously.

'Even if we don't gain anything, we can at least prove that we too can destroy. Shouldn't we make it known that we too are capable of being angry? The Babri Masjid was four hundred and fifty years old, but Chaitanyadeb's house was five hundred years old. Aren't they ruining a five hundred year old monument in this country too? I feel like tearing down the Sobhanbagh mosque. The mosque at Gulshan Part One was constructed by the Saudi Arabians. Why don't we build a temple?'

'What are you saying, Suranjan? Have you gone mad. Don't you remember you used to say that in place of temples and mosques, if there had been ponds you'd have introduced a few ducks into them!'

'I used to say more than that. I used to say, "Let all those brick-built buildings of worship be smashed to smithereens. Let there be no mandirs, masjids, girjas and gurudwaras, and after they are all destroyed, we will build on their ruins beautiful flower gardens and schools for children. For the good of man, the places of worship should be hospitals, orphanages, schools and universities. From now onwards let the prayer homes be Art and Handicrafts Academies, Schools for Fine Arts, Halls for Scientific Discussions. Let our places of worship be converted into rich, green, sun-bathed paddy fields, vast rolling fields, gurgling blue rivers and wild unquiet oceans. Let the other name for Religion be Humanity.'''

'The other day I was reading an article by Debesh Roy on Bade Ghulam Ali,' said Debabrata. 'Apparently, the man had risen up in the midst of his performance and danced to the tune of *Hari Om Tatsat, Hari Om Tatsat*. Even today, Bade Ghulam sings the same song. But those Hindus who have demolished the Babri Masjid and placed the idol of Rama in its place never get to hear this song. The Advanis and the Ashok Singhals do not hear these songs. It never reaches the ears of the Rashtriya Swayamsevak Sangh, or the Bajrang Dal. In spite of being a Muslim, Bade Ghulam Ali's songs are pervaded by the spirit of *Hari Om Tatsat*. Those Muslims who are hell bent on destroying mandirs to avenge the demolition of the Babri Masjid also turn a deaf ear to these songs. All that they understand is that a mosque destroyed will automatically result in the destruction of a mandir.'

'So you mean to say that breaking down a mosque is no real retaliation against the breaking of mandirs? You are being idealistic, like my father. I hate him. I hate the old wretch,' said Suranjan.

He had been lying down all this while, but now jumped up excitedly.

'Calm down, Suranjan, calm down. What you are suggesting is not really a solution.'

'No! Well, for your information, this is the only solution that I am looking for. I too want choppers, daggers and pistols in my hands. I want thick rods. Didn't they go and piss on the ruins of a mandir in old Dhaka? I also want to piss on their mosques!'

'God, Suranjan, you are becoming communal.'

'Yes, I am becoming communal, I am becoming communal . . . So what?'

Debabrata and Suranjan had worked together in the same political party but Debabrata could no longer recognize his old colleague. He was shocked beyond measure by Suranjan's behaviour—he wanted to get drunk, he declared himself to be communal and he even abused his own father. Debabrata was horrified.

*

'Riots are not like floods that you can simply be rescued and given some muri to survive on temporarily. Nor are they like fires that can be quenched to bring about relief. When a riot is in progress, human beings keep their humanity in check. The worst and the most poisonous aspect of man surfaces during a riot. Riots are not natural calamities, nor disasters, so to speak. They are simply a perversion of humanity . . . . ' Sudhamoy took a deep breath after this peroration. His wife sat mute in a corner and clasped her god. The clay image was no longer there, as it had been broken on that fateful day, but she had found a picture of Radha-Krishna somewhere, which she held fiercely, and touched to her forehead occasionally. She wept silently. As he lay immobile, Sudhamoy wondered if Radha or Krishna had the power to bring back Maya. What strength did a picture have, he thought, to rescue Maya from the clutches of the fundamentalists. He was a citizen of this country. He had participated in the language rebellion, fought to drive away the Pakistanis and bring about independence, and this country still could not guarantee him protection. How, then, could Radha or Krishna protect him? Right from his childhood, he thought, it had been his neighbours who had terrorized him: first, they had taken his property, and now they had abducted his daughter. When those whom you have known so well, those whom you have come to rely upon, become a threat to you, how can some God called Krishna save you? If there is anyone who has the power to save you, it is your people who have decided to submerge their differences of caste and creed and be as one.

Sudhamoy called out to his wife in a weak voice. She rose from her corner and stood before him like a zombie.

'Hasn't Suranjan gone to look for Maya today?' Sudhamoy asked.

'I don't know.'

'I believe Haider has put some men on to the job? Did he come today?'

'No.'

'Then, are we meant to give up hope? Will Maya never be found?'

'I don't know.'

'Will you sit beside me for a while, Kiron?'

Kironmoyee flopped down beside him mechanically. She did not reach out to him to comfort him, nor did she look at him. There was the sound of raised voices in the next room.

Sudhamoy asked, 'Why is Suranjan shouting so much? Hasn't he gone to Haider? I could have gone myself. Why did I have to fall sick! Could anyone have touched Maya if I were fit? I would have killed them! If my body had allowed it, I would have found Maya by hook or by crook . . . . ' Sudhamoy struggled to get up but fell back defeated. Kironmoyee made no move to help him. She stared fixedly at the locked front door. When would someone knock? When would Maya return?

'Why don't you go and call your dear son? He's a scoundrel of the first order! His sister is missing, and he has the audacity to drink in the house? Merrymaking? He should be ashamed,' Sudhamoy said in disgust.

Kironmoyee did not go to speak to Suranjan, nor did she attempt to quieten down Sudhamoy. She continued to stare at the door. Occasionally she would glance at the picture of Radha and Krishna in the corner of the room. At this moment no human being could console her. If only God would look towards her!

Sudhamoy wanted to be able to stand up just once. He wanted to tell the world, like Jonathan Swift, that all of us believe in hating each other, but few of us know how to love each other. The history of man has been stained by religious wars and crusades. In 1946, Sudhamoy had chanted a slogan proclaiming Hindu-Muslim brotherhood. Even today the same slogan was heard. Why was it necessary to chant such a slogan for such a long time? For how many more centuries would this slogan resound in the subcontinent? Did we still need to enlighten our people? Would the stupid bigots who were responsible for strengthening communalism ever respond to this slogan? If men did not learn to eradicate communalism from their hearts, no slogan would help, that was inalienable.

*

Suranjan had been to Haider's house. He was not in and Suranjan was told he had gone to Bhola to survey the damage suffered by Hindus there. Suranjan could see it in his mind's eye: Haider being compassionate towards the victims, Haider making speeches at various places and people complimenting him. They would praise him for his compassion and non-communal attitude and the Awami League would be assured of Hindu votes! But, Suranjan thought in a fury, he was not in the least concerned about Maya next door, even though he had gone all the way to Bhola to express his sympathies for others like Maya!

Suranjan uncorked the bottle he held, filled his glass and tilted it to his lips. His companions were not too keen on drinking but they had agreed to keep Suranjan company. On an empty stomach the liquor was having a devastating effect.

Suranjan said: 'I used to love going for walks in the evenings. Maya wanted to go with me too. One of these days I must take her to Shaalbon Vihar.'

'From 2 January, the Ulema Mashaekhs will be going on a long march,' said Birupaksha.

'What long march?'

'They intend to walk upto India and rebuild the Babri Masjid.'

'Will they include Hindus in the long march? If they do, I am willing to go. Will any of you go too?' Suranjan asked.

The others did not respond, though they exchanged meaningful looks.

Somewhat irritably, Debabrata said, 'Why do you keep harping on Hindus and Muslims so much? You are really obsessed with Hinduism nowadays.'

Suranjan ignored the question and said instead: 'Tell me, Debu. We all know that in the case of men it is possible to detect whether a person is a Muslim or not, by finding out if he has been circumcised. But what about women? Take Maya, for instance. Say she is left on the streets with her hands and feet bound. How will anyone know whether she's Hindu or Muslim? After all she has hands, feet, ears, and nose just like a Muslim, doesn't she?'

Side-stepping the subject Debabrata said, 'In Zia-ur Rahman's regime, there was a long march to the border to settle the Farakka dispute. Khaleda's regime will start in 1993 with a communal long march to reconstruct the Babri Masjid. Just as the Farakka march was not really for the sake of water, so too the march to rebuild the Babri Masjid will not be for the sake of the Babri Masjid. Actually all this hue and cry about the Babri Masjid is to communalise politics and thereby boost their flagging fortunes. At the same time, it is meant to divert attention from the anti-Gholam Azam campaign. Also, one can't help noticing the government's complete silence on the rioting and destruction. There are calamitous happenings every day and the government continues to say that there is communal harmony in this country!'

At this point, Pulok entered the room, and said, 'How come you are sitting with your door wide open?'

'The door is open, we are shouting, screaming and drinking . . . . There's really nothing to fear. We'll die if we have to! How come you have ventured out?'

'The situation has calmed down considerably. That is why I've had the courage to come out.'

'And you'll lock yourself in once again, if the situation goes back to being unpredictable, right?' Suranjan bellowed with laughter.

Pulok was shocked to see Suranjan in this drunken state. To think he had actually mustered up the courage to ride through the tense city on his scooter, while Suranjan who was always up and about and politically active was doing nothing more than getting drunk at home! He couldn't believe his eyes. What had gone wrong? Why had his friend changed so dramatically?

Suranjan took a sip from his glass and said, 'Gholam Azam, Gholam Azam, Gholam Azam . . . . so what's that got to do with me? What will I gain if Gholam Azam is punished? Why should I campaign against him. And Maya . . . Maya is disgusted by the name. She feels like vomiting when she hears it. Did you know that during the war of independence, two of my uncles from Baba's side, and three uncles from Ma's were shot and killed by the Pakistanis. I still don't understand why they spared my father's life. Perhaps they wanted him to enjoy the fruits of independence. And now, isn't he enjoying himself? Isn't Dr Sudhamoy Dutta basking in the glory of independence with his wife, son and daughter?'

Suranjan was sitting with his legs outstretched on the floor. Pulok sat by him. The room was coated with dust. Books and papers were strewn all over the place, broken furniture scattered here and there. Cigarette stubs and ash added to the general disorder in the room. In the corner of the room was a broken almirah. Pulok thought that Suranjan had destroyed the furniture in a rage. When there was no one talking, the house was so quiet that it seemed deserted.

Pulok said: 'Ekram Hussain visited Bhola. According to him, the police, administration and BNP at Bhola maintain that the events were a natural reaction to the demolition of the Babri Masjid. The looting and carnage were a spontaneous fallout. In the process of uprooting Hindus, village after village was burnt to ashes. The air was filled with the stench of burning matter. Hay stacks, granaries,. in fact, everything was ruined beyond recognition. Clothes, shoes and even broomsticks for that matter were dragged out of houses, doused with kerosene and set on fire. Paddy fields and coconut groves were ruthlessly burnt down. Little boys were stripped of their lungis, girls and women were picked up at random and raped. The women were also robbed of their saris and jewellery. Some Hindus went and hid in the paddy fields. It was there that they found Nikunja Dutta, a teacher of the Sambhupur Khaserhaat School. They beat him up and demanded all his money. Nikunja Dutta might succumb to his injuries. At Bhola, they have been telling the Hindus that if they want to live, they must leave the country. They threatened to hack the Hindus into little bits and feed the pieces to the crows, if they didn't leave immediately. The rich Hindus were no better off. Everything has been burnt. They are now drinking water out of coconut shells and eating food on banana leaves. What is more, they depend on charity for the rice that they eat. Once a day, they somehow manage to cook some wild plants or roots for themselves. Wives are being raped in front of husbands, daughters in front of fathers, and sisters in front of brothers. There have even been cases of mothers and daughters being jointly raped. A number of people have openly declared, "We'll beg for a living if we have to, but we won't stay here." The organizations that offered to help were clearly told by the local

Hindus, that they had no need for charity. But there is no doubt that they could do with some help to get out of the place . . .Shambupur and Golokpur were attacked by M.A. Bachet and Shiraz Patwari who were leaders in Jamaat Shibeer earlier, but subsequently became members of the BNP. Each and every Hindu home that belonged to Lord Hardinge has been burnt. The house of Priyalaal-babu, who was a freedom fighter, was plundered and burned to the ground. His village was attacked by Abdul Kadir and Vilayet Hussain. Three power tillers belonging to Babul Das were destroyed. When Ekram asked him what he planned to do, he broke down, and said, he would leave the place as soon as he could . . . ' Pulok would have carried on but Suranjan stopped him with a shout. 'Shut up . . . !' he said, 'If you say one more word, I'll thrash you.'

Pulok was so shocked he stopped in mid-sentence. Why was Suranjan behaving so strangely? Was it too much booze? Perhaps. He smiled dryly at Debabrata.

For a long time no one uttered a word. Suranjan kept gulping down his drink. He was not used to alcohol. Once in a while he drank at social gatherings, and that too in small amounts, but now he drank with a vengeance. An unnatural calm had descended on the room since Pulok had been asked to shut up. In the midst of this silence Suranjan shocked everyone by suddenly bursting into tears. He rested his head on Pulok's shoulder and cried and cried until his head flopped down on the floor. The others in the room were now stiff with apprehension, it was all getting a bit too much for them. The dimly lit room filled with the stench of stale alcohol and echoed with the anguished wailing of Suranjan. Suranjan had not changed nor had he bathed or eaten. He rolled on the filthy floor in anguish and his dirty clothes became even more grimy. Finally, he sobbed: 'They took Maya away last night.'

'What did you say?' Pulok looked aghast. Debabrata, Nayan and Birupaksha were equally shocked.

Suranjan's body continued to be racked by agonized sobs. As he thrashed about, he tipped over the half-filled glasses of whisky and the liquor added to the filth on the floor. But no one paid any attention. Everything paled into insignificance before the news that Maya had been abducted. Stunned, no one could think of anything to say. What words of consolation would help in such a situation?

Belal entered the room at this moment. He looked around quickly and noticed Suranjan lying on the floor. He went over to him and asked, 'Suranjan, have they really made off with Maya?'

Suranjan did not raise his head.

'Have you made a GD* entry?'

Suranjan still did not respond. Belal looked at the others as though expecting an answer. But none of them had anything to say.

'Have you tried to find out who could have taken her?'

Suranjan continued to remain silent.

Belal sat on the bed and lit a cigarette. He said, 'I really don't know what is happening all around us. The crooks and thugs are having a field day. Meanwhile, in India, they are continuously killing us.'

'What do you mean, "us"?' Birupaksha asked.

'Muslims. The BJP is hacking us to pieces.'

'Oh, I see.'

'When they get such news from India, these people naturally lose their heads. Whom can you blame? We are dying there, and you here. What was the point in breaking up the mosque? Such an ancient mosque at that. The Indians have dug up a mosque in order to find out the birthplace of Rama, an epic character! Some days later, they might say Hanuman was born at the Taj Mahal. So why not break the Taj Mahal too? And they are supposed to practice secularism in India! Why has Maya been taken away? The heroes to ask are people like Advani and Joshi. I believe the situation at Metiaburuz in Calcutta is quite serious.'

Suranjan still lay unmoving like an unclaimed corpse. From the other room the persistent wailing of Kironmoyee and the indistinct groans of Sudhamoy reduced Belal's tales of woe to nothing.

'I'm sure Maya will come back. Surely they are not going to eat her up. Ask Kakima to be patient. And why are you crying like a woman? Are tears going to solve your problem? And why are you all just sitting around? Aren't you going to find out what happened to the girl?'

---

* The GD entry or General Diary entry is a term used in Bangladesh for a formal complaint registered with the police.

Birupaksha said, 'We have only just got to know about this. And since when has it been possible to simply go and retrieve someone who has been taken away? And where should we start to look for her?'

'I am sure they are drug addicts. Ganja and heroin junkies. They have to be local boys. Noticed a good looking girl, got a clear chance . . . and simply picked her up. Decent people don't do such things. The youngsters of today have really gone to the dogs, and the main reason for this is economic instability. Do you understand?'

Birupaksha sat with his head lowered. None of them knew Belal. Belal was getting rather excited. He fished out a Benson & Hedges and a lighter from his pocket. He did not light the cigarette and began speaking once more. 'Is alcohol going to solve problems? You tell me, will it? Has there ever been a major riot in this country? You can't really call this a riot. Children long to eat sweets and they naturally raid sweetshops. In India, until the present time there have been at least six thousand riots. Thousands of Muslims have died in the process. Tell me, how many Hindus have died here? In every Hindu locality, truckloads of police have been stationed to maintain the peace.'

Nobody spoke. Not even Suranjan. He did not feel like talking at all. The liquor had begun taking effect and he felt extremely sleepy. Belal did not light his cigarette. He said he had some work to do and left. One by one, the others left as well.

Day Nine

They had looted Gopal's house. It was the house next to Suranjan's. Gopal's younger sister, a small girl of about twelve, had come to visit them. She came in and surveyed the damage inside the house. Suranjan, who was still on the floor, watched her as she moved about. She was like a little cat. Despite her age, the magnitude of the disaster that had taken place seemed to register on her. She came up to Suranjan's room, stood at the door and stared wide-eyed at the wreckage within. Looking at the sunlit veranda, he realized that it was quite late already. He beckoned the little girl over and asked her name.

'Madol . . .' she said.

'Which school do you go to?'

'Shere Bangla Balika Bidyalaya.'

The school had earlier been called Nari Shiksha Mandir and had been founded by Leela Naag. But where was Leela Naag's name today? A pioneering educationist at a time when girls were not allowed any education, she had gone from home to home to encourage women to study. In Dhaka city, she had fought to set up a good school for women. The school still existed, but its name had been changed, for how could Leela Naag's name be allowed to exist? The name Nari Shiksha Mandir, too, wouldn't do for it stood for something that the present dispensation did not encourage. The name, therefore, had been changed just as in the case of B.M. College, or M.C. College. In short, the obvious reason behind this exercise was to make sure that Hindus did not in any way whatsoever gain a place in the sun in a Muslim country. In 1971, there had been a drive to change the names of roads in Dhaka. The Pakistanis had Islamized the names of more than 240 roads. Lalmohon Poddar Road became Abdul Karim Ghaznavi Street. Shankari Nagar Lane was converted to Gul Badan Street. Nobin

Chand Goswami Road would henceforth be known as Bakhtiar Khilji Road. Kalicharan Shaha Road was called Ghazi Salahuddin Road. Roy Bazaar was changed to Sultangunj. Shashibhushan Chatterjee Lane was changed to Syed Salim Street and Indira Road became Anar Kali Road.

'Why are you lying on the floor?' the girl asked him.

'Because I love the ground.'

'I do too. We used to have a courtyard in our house. Now we'll be moving into a new house where there is no courtyard.'

'Then you won't be able to play.'

The girl came and sat beside Suranjan, leaning against the bed. She was enjoying her conversation with Suranjan, and he on his part imagined her to be the child Maya, his long lost sister, with whom he had spent hours talking about school, about football games, and God knows, so many other things . . . . Oh how long it had been since he had sat and chatted with Maya!

When they were small children, Suranjan and Maya would make small clay huts on the banks of the river during the day. At night, the tide would come in and wash away their huts . . . . Other memories flooded in. He remembered how they would gorge themselves on sweets that would turn their tongues red . . . . Or that time when they had run away from home to play among the reeds.

Suranjan reached out to touch the girl. Her hands were soft, like Maya's. Who were the people holding Maya's hands now? They must have rough, crude and cruel hands. Was Maya desperate to escape? But try as she would, maybe she could not break their grip. Suranjan's body shuddered with the pain of this realization. He did not let go of Madol's hand . . . . it was so much like Maya's. If he let her go, someone might come and take her away too. They might tie her up with strong rope . . . .

Madol suddenly said, 'Why are your hands trembling?'

'Are they? Actually I am feeling very sorry that you will be going away.'

'Well, we aren't going to India. We're only going to Mirpur. Subol and his people are going away to India.'

'When they entered your house, what were you doing?'

'I was standing in the veranda and crying. I was very afraid. They have taken away our television set, and all the jewellery from our almirah. They have also taken away all the money that Baba had.'

'Did they say anything to you?'

'Before they left, they slapped me hard on the cheek and said: "Shut up and stop crying."'

'Is that all? They did not want to take you away?'

'No. They must be beating up Maya-di, too, isn't that so? They hit my brother on the head. He bled a lot.'

Suranjan thought that if Maya had been the same age as Madol perhaps they would've spared her. They wouldn't have dragged her away. How many of them were raping her at the same time? Five or seven? Or even more? Was Maya bleeding profusely?

'Ma asked me to visit Mashima,' the little girl said, 'because Mashima has been crying so much.'

'Will you come out for a walk with me, Madol?'

'Ma will be worried.'

'We'll tell your mother before going.'

Maya often used to say, 'Dada, will you take me to Cox's Bazaar? We could also go to the Madhupur jungle, and how about the Sundarbans? I'd love to go there too.' Or when she read Jibanananda's poetry, she would want to go to Natore. Suranjan had always made fun of her whims. He would scold her and say, 'Go to the slums of Tejgaon instead and see how people live there. That will be more worthwhile than to look at trees and plants.' Maya's enthusiasm would deflate instantly. Today Suranjan wondered what they had gained by looking at *life*. What was the point in wishing for the good of all men? Movements for the workers and the farmers, the rise of the proletariat, the progress of socialism . . . . all these were ideals he had nurtured from childhood. But what was the point of it all? Despite the conviction of people like him socialism had failed and the statue of Lenin had been pulled to the ground. Wasn't it the height of irony that the spirit of humanity was molested in the home of its greatest patron?

Madol got up slowly; she drew away her soft hands, hands so like Maya's, from Suranjan's grasp . . . .

Haider had not turned up today either. He must have got cold feet, although his excuse was that he did not want to get involved. By now, Suranjan had also begun to realize that there was no point in looking for Maya. Even if she did come back, would she return like the six-year-old Maya had, many years ago? Suranjan felt utterly lost and dispirited. When Maya had gone to Parul's house, the house had been silent and quiet but it had not been like this, it had not felt so cold and lifeless. The three of them had known that Maya would return. The silence now was the silence of a graveyard. It really seemed as though someone had died. Looking at the whisky bottles strewn all over the room and the empty glasses that were lying here and there, Suranjan's empty heart filled with tears. Strangely enough, the tears that should have been in his eyes were bottled up in his heart.

This time around his friends, Kamal and Rabiul, had not even bothered to enquire after him. Perhaps they thought that it would be best for everyone to look after their own interests. He thought about what Belal had been repeating over and over again. Something like 'Why did you break our Babri Masjid.' Suranjan wondered why the Babri Masjid should be Belal's. After all, it was in India and the property of the Indians. And could anyone say that Suranjan had broken the mosque? He had never even been to India. Was Belal looking at the Hindus in India and those in Bangladesh in the same light? Just because the Hindus had brought down the mosque, did it necessarily follow that Suranjan had destroyed it? Was Suranjan to be identified with the Hindu fundamentalists in Ayodhya? Wasn't he like Belal, Kamal and Haider? Or was his only identity that of a Hindu? How strange that he, Suranjan, should be held responsible for the demolition of a mosque in India. Did religion supersede nation and nationality? Perhaps the illiterate masses needed to cling on to the comfort and security that religion provided, but Belal? Belal was a highly educated freedom fighter. Why should he be buried in the slush and swamp of religion? There were no answers to these questions.

Suranjan found two biscuits and a banana lying on his table. Kironmoyee must have left them for him. Rather than eat the food, Suranjan felt like drinking the remaining whisky. Last night he had passed out cold. As he lay in that state, Maya had come to visit him, making him feel even more wretched and guilty. When his eyes were open he would see her smile and when he shut his eyes all he could see was a pack of killer dogs.

It was evident that Haider had not bothered to find out what had happened to Maya. It was because he knew the terrorists of the area so well that Suranjan had gone to him for help. If it had not been so, Suranjan would have gone looking for Maya on his own. But, he mused, things had got so bad that the thugs no longer had to be secretive about their activities. It was not necessary anymore to look for alleys in which to rape Hindus, they could now rape women openly just as they could loot and burn openly. This was possible because of the indirect support of the government. It was not after all the government of a secular State. In fact, it was the interests of the fundamentalists that were being espoused. Sheikh Hasina had said that in order to safeguard the lives and property of the 140 million Muslims in India, it was necessary to maintain communal harmony. Why did Sheikh Hasina have to think of the safety of the Muslims in India? As citizens of this country didn't the Hindus of Bangladesh have the right to expect an atmosphere of communal harmony? Why was it necessary to show more sympathy towards the lives and properties of the Muslims of India, rather than towards one's own citizens? Should it then be taken for granted that the Awami League was feeding the public the same stuff as the Jamaatis—in other words, anti-India and pro-Islam?

The government had got it completely wrong, he thought. What was important was not the interest of the Muslims in India. The most fundamental and logical reason to maintain peace and harmony was to preserve the rights guaranteed by the constitution. The Hindus in this country had the right, as free citizens, to preserve and protect their lives and property along with their own ideals and religion. It was not because of the compassion of any other religion, or any political party, or any particular person's pity, that the Hindus were allowed to live in this country. It was because the nation's code of conduct allowed them to live just like any other citizen, that the Hindus were living in Bangladesh. Why then should Suranjan seek the sympathy or the refuge of Kamal, Belal or Haider?

In Mirsarai, Chittagong, the Students Union leader Kamal Bhowmick's house was set on fire, as a result of which he lost his aunt. In the Hindu colony of Qutabdia, three children died when hooligans set fire to the place. In Shaatkania Nathpara, Surjomohon died as a result of burn injuries. Bashudeb of Mirsarai was asked who had carried out the attacks and he had replied, 'Those who kill by the night, are the very same people who come in the morning to sympathize effusively with the disasters that have taken place.' When Jatramohon Nath of Khajuria was asked the same question, he had said 'I'd rather you killed me.' Meanwhile, within six days of the increase of life-threatening communalism, the non-communal political parties of Bangladesh, the national integration parties, and Union of Cultural Committees had formed a joint committee of communal harmony. This committee was formed when communal riots had somewhat abated. Until the present time, this committee had succeeded in organizing only one peace march, and one public gathering. There was a general feeling that the Jamaat Shibeër Freedom Party's political ideas should be banned if an atmosphere of peace and communal harmony was ever to come about, but it was yet to be seen how much importance the peace and harmony committee would give to this demand. However, Suranjan knew that even if the government failed to ban the Jamaat's political ideas and the harmony committee protested this inaction on its part, the leaders of the country would take no notice of it. Some members of the committee had spoken about punishing those who had been looting and plundering Hindu homes and temples. However, one person who was a victim of the plundering at the Shoni gymnasium, said, 'I know the people who have committed all these atrocities. But I don't think it will be wise to take them to court, because the parties who failed to protect us when we were attacked, will surely not provide us with any security after litigation.' As a matter of fact, this was exactly how every victim could be expected to react when faced with the prospect of initiating legal action. Suranjan felt the call for litigation was clearly a political stunt.

Democracy was clearly not strong enough to arrest the spread of communalism. On the other hand, the communal groups had much more strength, and were working towards the fulfilment of their goals with great conviction. What then was the purpose of these committees for the maintenance of communal peace and harmony? What satisfaction did the republican political parties gain from the constitution of such an all-party committee? Many in the intelligentsia believed that communal riots in Bangladesh were far fewer than those in India and Pakistan. What they didn't realize was that in Bangladesh the whole thing was one-sided. In

India, the Muslims retaliated, but in Bangladesh the Hindus did not.

In the three major countries of the subcontinent, the evils of fundamentalism and fascism had been indirectly encouraged by the respective governments for their own political gains. And the fundamentalists were trying to gain in strength all over the world; in India, Pakistan, Tadjikistan, Afghanistan, Algeria, Egypt, Iran and Serbia. Their only aim was to maim the spirit of democracy. In Germany, two fascist parties had been banned because they had torched three Turkish women. In India, too, the fundamentalists had been banned, but then it was anyone's guess how long this order would remain in force. In Algeria, such parties had been banned too. The Egyptian government had dealt a strong blow to these groups, while in Tadjikistan, the fundamentalists and the communists were at war with each other. But had the Bangladesh government ever thought of restraining fundamentalist and fascist groups in the country? Suranjan thought with great regret, that in his country, at least, politics would never be free from the clutches of religion.

In aid of the hard-core communal parties in India, the BNP, presently in power in Bangladesh, had taken on the Gholam Azam case as a pretext to forward the interests of the communalists. On this issue, the Jamaat Shibeer Freedom Party and other communal groups had zealously supported the government. Much of the tension caused by the Gholam Azam case was thus successfully averted by diverting the interests elsewhere.

At an Integrated Cultural Party meet, a slogan was raised: 'Bangladesh will stop the activities of the communal rioters.' Oh how thoughtful of Bangladesh! Suranjan thought as he smoked a cigarette, 'Bloody bastards . . . bloody swine . . . that's Bangladesh for me.' He repeated the lines of invective over and over again, deriving immense pleasure from doing so. Then he laughed aloud, his laughter hard and bitter.

*

Madol snuggled up against Kironmoyee. She said, 'Mashima, we're going away to Mirpur. Those ruffians will not be able to come there.'

'Why not?'

'Because Mirpur is very far away . . .'

To the little girl, thugs were to be found only in Tikatuli. Since Mirpur was far from Tikatuli, she would be safe from their depredations. But Kironmoyee wondered if it was that simple. If the people who looted and burnt Hindu homes or ran off with the Mayas were simply ruffians they wouldn't stop to distinguish between Hindus and Muslims, would they? For those who consciously chose to attack in the name of religion, the names ruffian or hooligan or thug were really too mild.

Sudhamoy was lying down. There was nothing he could do but lie down. What was the point in living this paralyzed life? He was just an unnecessary nuisance for Kironmoyee. Kironmoyee's powers of patience and endurance were really incredible. She never seemed to be tired. All night long she would cry miserably, and then at the break of day she would be at work in the kitchen, whether or not she wanted to. The needs of the stomach always triumphed above every other.

Their lives had really taken a turn for the worse. Suranjan had almost given up bathing and eating, Kironmoyee had done the same, admittedly to a far lesser extent. Sudhamoy, too, did not feel like eating. And the worst thing that had happened to them was that Maya had not yet returned. Had she gone forever? If only he could get back Maya at the cost of his own life! Suppose he stood in the middle of the road and shouted out, 'Maya must be returned. I have the right to demand Maya's return. Right?' The word had no meaning at this time, thought Sudhamoy. He remembered a time in 1946. He had been quite young, and after eating sweets at a shop he had asked the shopkeeper for some water. The word he had used was *paani*, not the word he would have normally used, *jal*, for at that time hostilities between the Hindus and Muslims had been high.

The British had understood all too well, that if they wanted to perpetuate their presence in the subcontinent, it would be necessary to further enflame the existing feelings of ill-will between Hindus and Muslims. It was from this shrewd perception that the policy of divide and rule was born.

Sudhamoy wondered that the conflict could originate from the basic discrepancy. (In a country where ninety per cent of the farmers were Muslims, ninety per cent of the land was owned by Hindus). It was from the land that the Chinese and the Russians had risen in revolt, and, similarly, it was from land that the conflict between Hindus and Muslims had begun. A problem that was initially land-oriented had become religion-oriented. In 1906, it was thanks to the British that the Muslim League had been founded on communal principles. It was this party that was responsible for vitiating the social and political atmosphere with the poison of communalism. But then the Congress could not escape blame either.

After 1947, for twenty-four years, the Pakistani rulers who promoted the ideas of imperialism, clamoured for the propagation of Islam, the denunciation of India and the perpetuation of communalism, thereby depriving the citizens of Bangladesh of their democratic rights. In 1971, when Sudhamoy had acquired this right, he had breathed a sigh of relief. After the attainment of independence, amongst four clauses, a clause that enshrined secularism was included in the Constitution of Bangladesh. This was an invincible weapon against the possible resurrection of communalism. But after 15 August 1975, communalism was reborn. Along with it came the forces of fundamentalism, fanaticism, malice and despotism. In order to make communal thought socially acceptable, it was necessary to give it the veneer of idealism. Even before Pakistan was created, this was given the name 'two-nation theory', and after the creation of Bangladesh in 1971, it was dubbed 'Bangladeshi nationalism'. The heritage of the Bengalis, which was more than a thousand years old, had been wiped out in favour of what was known as the Bangladeshi spirit. Like cows, donkeys, paddy and jute, man, too, came to be identified as Bangladeshi. After the 8th Amendment in 1988, the Constitution of Bangladesh acquired the following insertion: 'The State religion of the Republic is Islam, but other religions may be practised in peace and harmony in the Republic.' Why were the words 'may be' used? Why not 'shall be'? Where fundamental rights were concerned, the Constitution declared, 'No citizen shall, on grounds only of religion, race, caste, sex or place of birth, be subjected to any disability, liability, restriction or condition with regard to access to any place of public entertainment or resort, or admission to any educational institution.' But all this talk about 'non-discrimination' must merely be a facade for if it were not so,

why was Maya abducted? Why were they abused as 'low castes?'
Was this the sort of invective common hoodlums and thugs used?
No, the current violence and destruction could not be passed off as
mere hooliganism.

The most obvious indicator of the current trend in Bangladesh
was the rate at which schools were being converted to madrasas,
mosques were increasing and Islamic functions were burgeoning.
The sounds of the azaan were now deafening as for every three
houses in a neighbourhood there was now a mosque equipped
with loudspeakers. And underlining the current mood was the fact
that the use of microphones was restricted during the Hindu pujas.
If mikes were to be allowed, then why should the Muslims be
allowed to use it more than the Hindus? According to the 28th
clause of the United Nations Human Rights Community
Declaration, 'Everyone has the right to think, feel and practice his
or her religions independently. Should anyone wish to change his
or her religion or beliefs, link up or separate oneself from any
particular religion, openly or secretly educate, profess, or practice
one's religion independently it should be considered well within
his rights.' If this were true why should Hindu temples be broken
down? It was not that Sudhamoy had any faith in temples, but his
objection was simple: When it came to demolishing something,
why should only temples be singled out? And would any justice
be meted out to those who were responsible for the mass
destruction of temples? According to the Penal Code, for such
offences the punishment was a jail sentence for one year,
sometimes two, and at the most three.

Sudhamoy seemed to forget his own ailments in the face of the
country's indisposition. The country was gradually failing in
health. After many years of struggle, Bangladesh had freed itself
from the grips of Pakistan, and a new constitution had been
framed: 'We, the people of Bangladesh, having proclaimed our
Independence on the 26th day of March 1971 and through a historic
struggle for national liberation, established the independent,
sovereign People's Republic of Bangladesh.

'Pledging that the high ideals of nationalism, socialism,
democracy and secularism, which inspired our heroic people to
dedicate themselves to, and our brave martyrs to sacrifice their
lives in, the national liberation struggle, shall be the fundamental
principle of the constitution.'

'Struggle for national liberation' was changed in 1978 to 'a historic war for national independence.' An addition was also made (to struggle for national liberation) . . . 'high ideals of absolute trust and faith in the Almighty Allah, nationalism, democracy and socialism meaning economic social justice . . .' Moreover, 'liberation struggle' became 'independence'.

In 1978, the commencement of the constitution of 1972 was changed to *'Bismillahir Rahmanir Rahim'* (In the Name of God, the Compassionate, the Merciful). The 12th clause of the Constitution was completely done away with. The clause read as follows: *Secularism and freedom of religion.*

12. The principle of secularism shall be realised by the elimination of
   a. communalism in all its forms.
   b. the granting by the State of political status in favour of any religion.
   c. the abuse of religion for political purposes.
   d. any discrimination against, or persecution of persons practising a particular religion.

The word 'secularism' was removed and clause 25(2) now read, 'The State shall endeavour to consolidate, preserve and strengthen fraternal relations among Muslim countries based on Islamic solidarity.'

In 1972, clause 6 had read thus: 'The citizenship of Bangladesh shall be determined and regulated by law; citizens of Bangladesh shall be known as Bangalees.' Zia-ur Rahman had changed this to 'The citizens of Bangladesh shall be known as Bangladeshis.'

Sudhamoy saw darkness all around him. It was still afternoon . . . why should it be dark already? Was his eyesight failing him? Or was it because his spectacles had not been changed for a long time? Maybe it was because of the growth of cataracts . . . . Or was it just tears that were blurring his eyesight?

Even Suranjan was changing. Not once had he come to sit beside him. Ever since Maya had been taken away, he did not even step into this room. Sudhamoy could hear what was going on in his son's room, including the loud discussions that accompanied the drinking. Was the boy becoming immoral? He had never known Suranjan to drink inside the house. Perhaps he did not care for anyone anymore. Had he actually forgotten Maya in two days' time! Sudhamoy could not bring himself to believe this. His son's transformation added to the heavy burden Sudhamoy already carried. Was Suranjan going to the dogs?

*

Suranjan had no intention of leaving the house. He had realized that it was futile to look for Maya. Instead it was better to stay at home and avoid meeting people on the streets who might shout obscenities like: 'Here comes one of those bastards responsible for breaking the Babri Masjid! These buggers should be kicked out of the country to India!' Suranjan was sick and tired of hearing these things. He no longer had any faith in the Socialist Party or in any communist leader. He'd even heard many leftist leaders swearing when Hindus were referred to. 'Bloody swine,' they'd say. Even Hindus in the Communist Party were bowing to the current mood. Krishna Binod Roy was now Kabir Bhai and Barin Dutta had had his name changed to Abdus Salaam. If even in the Communist Party such things happened, then whom could one trust? Or should he enrol himself in the Jamaat-i-Islami party? He would have to go straight to Nizami and say,'Huzoor, Assalaam Aleikum!' and the very next day the newspaper headlines would scream, 'Hindu joins the Jamaat-i-Islami.' Even in Jagannath Hall, which was an exclusive hostel for Hindu boys, you could get a Jamaat-i-Islami vote; and the reason was money. If someone was given five thousand takas a month, why should he not vote for the Jamaat? Suranjan wanted to take his revenge on the leftist groups, those parties who had stolen his hopes rather than fulfil them. In fact, these very party people had relinquished their memberships one by one, and had joined other parties. They would say one thing today, and sing a different tune altogether the next. When comrade Farhad passed away, a Quran Khani and Milad Mehfil were organized by the CPB office. Later, he was buried with great pomp and grandeur. But why? Why did communists have to take shelter under the Islamic flag? Because they wanted to escape the misplaced accusations of the public, that they were non-believers, wasn't that so? But did they get any redemption because of this? Suranjan did not blame the public, he blamed the so-called leftist leaders, who were themselves completely bewildered and lost.

The number of madrasas were increasing in the country. This plan was an excellent one to cripple the economy of the country. Perhaps, not known to anyone, it had been Sheikh Mujib who had gone from village to village in an effort to popularize madrasas. The disaster that had befallen this country had to be seen to be believed. It was incredible that these things could happen in a country where people had participated in the Language Movement, and had fought for and achieved independence in 1971. Where were all those feelings of Bengali nationalism now? All those cries of common Bengalihood among the Hindus, Buddhists, Christians and Muslims . . . where had they disappeared to? Suranjan wasn't sure of anything anymore, all his points of reference had been wiped out. It was as though he was not a human being any more, not a Bengali, but just a two-footed creature called a Hindu. Suranjan felt like a foreigner in his own country.

In this country, there was a ministry called the Religious Affairs Ministry. Over the years, religion had been awarded a pretty sizeable budget. Indeed, a major portion of the national development budget was used to help religion and religious institutions. The Islamic Foundation, Dhaka, was granted, 1,500,000 takas. The Waqf Proshashak Grant was given 800,000 takas. Other religious foundations were granted 26,000,000 takas. The Zakat fund Proshashak was awarded 220,000 takas. The Islamic Mission Establishment Fund walked away with 25,000,000 takas. The minorities got 250,000 takas. 12,000,000 takas were granted for the free supply of electricity to all the mosques. The mosques got 5,000,000 takas for free water supply. The Dhaka Tara Masjid was granted 300,000 takas. Altogether, 84,570,000 takas were granted to religious institutions. For the supervision and care of the Baitul Mokarram Masjid, 1,500,000 takas were spent. Once again, only 250,000 takas were granted for the minority treasury. Towards training and production-oriented programmes, inclusive of ad hoc grant, a total development fund of 109,338,000 takas was instituted . . . . There were twenty-five million people belonging to religious minority groups in the country. It was ridiculous that for these twenty-five million people only twenty-five million takas had been granted.

The development budget of the Ministry for Religious Affairs was 2,000,000 takas. The compilation and publication of the *World Treasury of Islam* gobbled up 20,000 takas. The new cultural centre of the Islamic Foundation was estimated to cost 19,000,000. The programme for the publication and translation of books and research for the Islamic Foundation was given 16,875,000 takas. The Imam training project and the development of Islamic Foundation library was given 1,500,000 takas. The Masjid Library project got 2,500,000 takas. The expansion of Islamic cultural centres in the new districts and a training academy swallowed 15,000,000 takas. The total amounted to 56,895,000 takas. Furthermore, 260,000 takas were subdivided towards Islamic religious functions/ other festivities, as also an additional amount of 500,000. Based on work programmes of Islamic religious organizations 2,860,000 takas were granted.

The renovation, repair and relocation of different masjids through the approval of the honourable Members of Parliament got 20,000,000. For religious groups coming in and going out of the country—1,000,000. Donation to religious organizations—640,000. Rehabilitation of needy Muslims—1,000,000. Altogether this amounted to 26,000,000 takas. It was observed that for the year 1991–92, the budget for development of religious activities was 16,621,3000. The budget for the rehabilitation of neo-Muslims was strange. One million takas were sanctioned for this purpose, while there was no provision at all for the development of minorities! It was indeed a shame that in a poor country inhabited by people of various religions and castes, only the dissemination of one religion was favoured.

The country had no economic backbone. Suranjan thought: Have we ever considered our per capita income, our foreign debt? How can we spend so much on Islamic matters when the economy is completely crippled? It is because of the skewed budgetary allocation that national harmony has no chance at all. Does no one give this any thought? Suranjan was musing on all this, when his door opened and Kajal Debnath walked in.

'What is the matter, Suranjan, why are you lying down at such an odd hour?'

'I have no specific hours for anything!' Suranjan moved up on the bed and made space for him to sit down.

'Has Maya returned?'

'No . . . . ' Suranjan heaved a long sigh.

'What do you think we can do? Really, I think we should do something about it.'

'What will you do?'

Kajal Debnath had greying hair. He was over forty years old. His forehead wrinkled into a frown, as he took out a packet of cigarettes and offered one to Suranjan.

Suranjan reached out and accepted the cigarette. It had been long since he had bought a cigarette.There was no money to buy any and he dared not ask Kironmoyee for financial help. He was ashamed of even going into their room, as though the shame of Maya's abduction was entirely his responsibility. Perhaps it was, for after all it had been he, more than anyone else, who had wanted to think of this country as non-communal. Naturally it was his shame more than anyone else's. He could not go and show his face to his honest and idealistic father.

Suranjan smoked on an empty stomach. Had Maya seen him, she would have protested: 'Dada, you're not being fair to yourself at all! If you smoke on an empty stomach, you'll die of cancer, don't you know that?'

If only Suranjan had cancer, it wouldn't be bad. He could have been lying in bed waiting for death. At least, he would not have had to wait for the fulfilment of any hopes.

Kajal Debnath did not know what to do. He said, 'Today they have taken your sister, tomorrow they'll take my daughter. Yes, of course, they will. Today, it is Goutam who's been bashed on the head, tomorrow it may be you or me.'

'Tell me one thing,' said Suranjan, 'are we humans first, or Hindus?'

Kajal looked around the room and asked, 'They came to this room too, didn't they?'

'Yes.'

'What was Maya doing at that time?'

'They say she was mixing the rice to feed Baba.'

'Couldn't they beat up the bastards?'

'How could they? They had heavy rods in their hands. And, in any case, Hindus don't have the right to touch Muslims, do they? In India, the Muslim minorities have the right to retaliate. When two opposing groups clash, only then can you call it a riot. And to think people talk of riots in this country! What is happening in this country is nothing short of communal terrorism. You could even call it torture, oppression or persecution. One group arbitrarily thrashing another.'

'Do you think Maya will come back?'

'I don't know,' said Suranjan.

Every time he spoke of Maya, Suranjan felt his voice choke and sensed an emptiness in his heart.

'Kajal-da, what else has been happening in the country?' Suranjan asked, in order to get away from Maya as a topic.

Kajal Debnath looked up at the ceiling, blew out some cigarette smoke and said, '28,000 houses, 2,700 commercial establishments, and 3,600 temples have been damaged or destroyed and twelve people have died. There has been damage worth two billion takas! Village after village has been destroyed. Forty-three districts have been affected. Two thousand six hundred women have been molested. Among those temples that have been damaged beyond repair is the Gouranga Mahaprabhu temple, more than five hundred years old, in the southern part of Sylhet. An ancient Kalibari, many hundred of years old, was destroyed in Baniachong. Also damaged were Kaibolyadhaam and Tulsidhaam in Chittagong, the Madanmohon gym at Bhola and the Ramakrishna Missions at Sunamgunj and Faridpur respectively.'

Suranjan asked, 'Hasn't the government offered any help?'

'No. Not only has the government not helped, they have not allowed other organizations to help either. However, there are a few private organizations that have offered help. Thousands and thousands of people have been rendered homeless, and are out in the open without food or hardly any clothes. The girls who were raped have either become so traumatized that they cannot even speak or there is no trace of them. Businessmen have lost everything. Despite that they are being squeezed for whatever little they have left. In Barisal, 750 million takas worth of property was destroyed; in Chittagong 200 million, a 100 million in Dhaka, while in Khulna and Rajshahi the damages were worth ten million each. Altogether there has been 1,070 billion takas worth of losses. If commercial establishments are included, a further 220 million takas have gone down the drain. The destruction of mandirs alone has cost us 570 million takas.'

'Oh I can't bear it anymore, I just can't.'

'You know, the worst thing is that a mass exodus from the country has begun. There seems to be no way to stop it. The government always says that the Hindus are not leaving the country, but this is not true. Maybe you've read about it in the *Desh* magazine published in Calcutta. Apparently at least 150,000 Bangladeshis have infiltrated into Indian territory, and the majority of this number have not returned. In the last two decades more than half-a-million people belonging to minority communities have been forced to leave the country. Note what has been said in six census reports. In 1941, the Muslims were 70.3 per cent of the population, while the Hindus were 28.3 per cent. In 1951, the Muslims were 76.9 per cent and Hindus were 22.0 per cent. In 1961, the Muslims constituted 80.4 per cent, Hindus 18.5 per cent. In 1974, there were 85.4 per cent Muslims and 12.1 per cent Hindus. In 1991, the Muslims were 87.4 per cent, and the Hindus approximately 12.6 per cent. What do we understand from this? That every year the number of Muslims is increasing, while that of the Hindus is decreasing. What is happening to the Hindus? Where are they going? If the government insists that they are not migrating, then how will they explain away the figures of the census? Do you know the latest about the new census? Apparently Hindus and Muslims will not be counted separately.'

'Why not?'

'Because, the Hindus are dwindling so rapidly they may as well be clubbed with the Muslims, instead of being considered a separate entity,' Kajal Debnath said sarcastically.

'This government is very shrewd, what do you say, Kajal-da?' Suranjan said.

Kajal Debnath didn't comment. Instead, he looked around for an ashtray to stub out his first cigarette in order to light a new one.

'Do you have an ashtray?' he asked Suranjan.

'You could use the entire room as an ashtray.'

'I would like to meet your parents, but I really have no words of consolation for them!' Kajal Debnath said, and hung his head in shame; he looked so ashamed it was as if it had been his own brother who had picked up Maya, and gone off with her.

Maya again! The old anger surged up in Suranjan like lava from a volcano. Before he blew, he quickly changed the topic.

'Kajal-da,' he said, 'didn't Jinnah promise that we would all be Pakistanis, not Hindus or Muslims. Didn't that stop the Hindus from migrating?'

'Jinnah was an Ismaili Khoja. Even though his community was Muslim, they followed the Hindu rights of succession. His surname actually was Khojani. His name was Jhinabhai Khojani. He kept the Jhina part of the name, and did away with the rest. Yes, it is true, that Jinnah had made such a promise, but despite that, the Hindus were victims of discrimination. If that were not so, why would eleven million Hindus leave East Pakistan by June 1948 for India? In India, unfortunately, they came to be identified as refugees.'

'Many Muslims left West Bengal and came to this city during the riots, didn't they?'

'Yes, people did arrive in large numbers from Assam and West Bengal. At that time, the Indian and Pakistan governments came up with the 'Nehru-Liaquat Pact'. According to the treaty, "In both countries, the minorities will be allowed to enjoy the same rights as every other citizen, irrespective of his religion." The right to live, have one's own property, and to follow one's own culture, was granted to all the minority communities. At the same time, they were given the right to express their own opinions and to profess their own religion. On the basis of these conditions a number of people went back to India, but those people who had gone away from East Pakistan did not think of coming back. But, in 1951, the Pakistan Legislative Assembly passed two particular laws, the East Bengal Evacuee Property Act of 1951 and the East Bengal Evacuee Act of 1951. Because of this, the number of evacuees went up to three-and-a-half million. Your father will be able to tell you more about all this.'

'He never speaks to me about anything of this nature. Every time the topic of leaving the country arises, he fumes. He simply won't have anything to do with leaving the country.'

'Do you think we want to leave the country? But those who have left, have done so secretly. How will you bring them back? After all, you have to give them some assurance. Otherwise why should anyone want to leave his motherland? You know, we have a saying, that the person who lives on his own soil is the happiest. Muslims are used to travelling from one place to another for the purpose of Haj, but a Hindu would any day prefer to live on his own land for all practical and religious purposes.'

At this point, Kajal Debnath, who had been getting increasingly emotional, went out onto the veranda, presumably to calm himself down.

He came back to the room and said, 'I really feel like a cup of tea. Come, let's go to some tea shop . . .'

Suranjan's clothes were filthy as he hadn't changed them in a long while. He had not bathed for days, and hadn't had a proper meal either in some time, so when Kajal proposed tea, he jumped up, and said, 'Let's go. The body is becoming rusted, just lying around like this.'

Suranjan did not shut the door when he left the house. Why should he close the door? The worst mishap that could have taken place had already happened. As they walked, Kajal Debnath asked him, 'Are you eating anything at home?'

'Ma leaves the food in my room every day. Sometimes I eat, sometimes I don't. Actually I don't feel like eating.' Suranjan ran his fingers through his hair, to comb it out. His purpose was not so much to set his hair, as it was to ease the pain inside him.

Suranjan went back to the old subject. 'In 1969 and 1970, I think the number of Hindus that migrated was comparatively less, Kajal-da.'

'In 1966, the six-point movement for self-rule had started. In 1969, there was a popular uprising. In 1970, between the elections and independence, the number of Hindus who migrated had indeed gone down. From 1955 to 1960, many Hindus had left. Between 1960 and 1965, one million people left. When the war started, almost ten million people took refuge in India, and of them eighty per cent were Hindus. After the war, when the Hindus returned to this country, most of them found that their land and property had been confiscated. As a result, many of them left again though some stayed behind, hoping that an independent country would give them social security. Then, of course, you know, even in 1974, the Mujib government only changed the names of the enemy property. Zia-ur Rahman put his faith in the anti-independence, communal rabble. The ideal of secularism was removed from the constitution. Ershad came after this, and revived Islamization. On 22 December 1982, Ershad declared that Islam and the principles of the Quran would be the basis for reframing the constitution. Who would have thought that religion would stage a comeback with full honours after twenty-four years of continuous absorption in the political atmosphere of the country!'

They stopped at a tea shop. Kajal Debnath looked at Suranjan thoughtfully and said, 'You seem very distracted. You've been asking questions to which you know the answers. I know that you are very disturbed but you must pull yourself together. A talented person like you should not lose hope so easily.'

They sat facing each other across a little table in the shop. Kajal asked him, 'Will you have something to eat with your tea?'

Suranjan nodded. He ate two singaras. Kajal also had a singara. After they finished eating, he asked the boy who was serving them, 'Can we have some *paani*?'

Suranjan was surprised to hear Kajal use the word *paani*. At home, he always used the word *jal*, but today he had said *paani*. Did he always use this word in public? Or was he afraid? It was suddenly very important for Suranjan to know. He was about to ask, but stopped himself. He had the feeling that a number of eyes were watching them. He quickly took a sip of tea. Was he scared, too? What had made him so scared? He burnt his tongue for the tea was very hot. The young man who appeared to be keeping him under observation from the next table, sported a beard and a knitted cap on his head. He seemed to be around twenty years old. Suranjan felt that he must be one of the men who had taken Maya. Otherwise, why should he be looking so intently at them? He also thought the young man was smirking at them. Was he smirking because he was projecting the message, 'How does it feel? We've had a grand time with your sister . . . ' He suddenly couldn't take it any longer. Getting up quickly, he said, 'Come on, Kajal-da, let's go. I don't like this place.'

'Leave? Already . . . ?'

'Yes, I can't stand it here.'

Day Ten

In the country's General Assembly in 1954, there were 309 members. Of these seventy-two belonged to the various minority communities. In 1970, out of 300, the minorities numbered only eleven. In 1973, there were twelve out of 315, in 1979, it had gone down to eight out of 330. In 1986, there were seven out of 330, in 1988, there were only four and in 1991 it had gone up slightly to twelve out of 330 . . . . The situation was as bleak in the army and in the administrative services. In all government, semi-government and self-governing bodies, there were not more than five per cent minority community appointees in the ranks of first class and second class officers. In the police, the minorities numbered 2,000 out of 80,000. Also, as far as officers were concerned, they numbered fifty-three out of 870. Where excise and customs officers were concerned, there was only one person of the minority community among 152 officers. In the Income tax department there were only eight persons belonging to the minority community out of 450 officers. In the national industrial organizations there was only one per cent of minorities at the officer level, 3–4 per cent among the workers and less than one per cent among the labourers. And that was not all. In the Bangladesh Bank or any other banks for that matter, there were no Hindus at the Director, Chairman or MD level. Nor were there any posts for Hindus in any of the branches of commercial banks.

Suranjan had tossed and turned all night, his depression driving away sleep. Kironmoyee had come once to his room in the morning. Perhaps she had wanted to ask if he had any news of Maya. Would they live the rest of their lives without Maya? In the past few days, Kironmoyee had become more and more listless. There were dark circles under her eyes, her face was drawn, she never seemed to speak or smile. Suranjan had pretended to be asleep.

All through these terrible days, he had not let Kironmoyee see how much he was suffering inside. Kironmoyee would silently leave food for him on his table every day. At times, her silence would infuriate Suranjan. Did she have nothing to say about her sick husband, about her son who was only present in body, so to speak, or her daughter who was lost? Was she made of stone that she did not react to anything at all? Did she have nothing to oppose? How strange she was—unresponsive, unrelenting and as unemotional as a corpse.

Suranjan decided to sleep the whole day. He needed sleep, because he had not slept well for a long time. But every time he shut his eyes, a huge paw seemed to stretch out towards him . . . with the intention of strangling him. Not one . . . many such paws seemed to rush towards him. He simply could not get a moment's peace . . . .

*

Nonigopal, a distant relative of Sudhamoy's was visiting from Manikgunj with his wife, son and daughter. He did not evince any surprise at the wrecked condition of Sudhamoy's house, but merely said, 'So they did not spare your house either?'

Nonigopal's wife, Lolita, had wiped the sindur from her parting. She had also pulled down her sari over her face to cover it as much as possible. She hugged Kironmoyee and wept loudly. Lolita's daughter stood watching awkwardly. Sudhamoy could not recall her name. She was probably Maya's age, maybe somewhat younger. He stared at the girl and as he did so his eyes filled with tears. Maya was no more. He couldn't come to terms with this incredible fact. He wanted to believe that Maya was next door, or that she was out taking tuitions and would be back in the evening. In fact, it was probably true to say that everyone in the house nursed the hope that the tortured, raped and brutalized Maya would return one day.

'Dada, I don't think it will be possible to stay in this country anymore. Our daughter has come of age, and that makes things all the more frightening . . .' said Nonigopal.

Sudhamoy took his eyes away from the girl and turned to him. 'Don't say anything about going away, I don't want to hear it. I believe Goutam's family next door is also going away. What do you think you are up to? Aren't there any hooligans in the place you plan to escape to? Isn't there any cause for fear in those places? Young girls are insecure everywhere. Don't you know, the grass always seems more lush across the other man's fence? That is your problem.' Nonigopal had stubble on his face, and he wore a kurta and pajamas. There was nothing he could say to Sudhamoy's outburst so he sat quietly, his head lowered.

Lolita suddenly began to cry once more. Kironmoyee made no move to comfort her or to talk to her guests. She could not even bring herself to say that Maya had been abducted.

Nonigopal was a timber merchant. They had burnt down the godown where he stored his timber. But even this had not scared him as much as the fear that one day his daughter, Anjali, might be kidnapped. He said, 'Dada, Lolita had a relative in Feni, Chandpur. They took him away, stole all his property and later killed him. In Pingail, Jaidebpur, Ashwini Kumar Chandra's fourteen-year-old daughter, Miko, was abducted and raped. Didn't you know about this? The girl died. In Vedgraam, Gopalgunj, Harendra Heera's daughter, Nandita, was taken away. In Banchharampur, Kshitish Chandra Debnath's daughter, Karunabala, was carried away by the Muslim boys of the village and raped. In Bhola, Kalinath Bazaar, Shovarani's daughter, Tandrarani, was kidnapped and raped. In Tangail, Adalatpara, Sudhir Chandra Das' daughter, Mukti Rani Ghosh, was abducted by a Muslim businessman. In Bhaluka, Purna Chandra Barman's daughter was taken away by force. In Rangpur, Taragunj, Tinkori Shaha's daughter, Jayanti Rani Shaha, was abducted. Haven't you heard of all this?'

'When did all this happen?' Sudhamoy asked weakly.

'1989,' said Nonigopal.

'All this happened so long ago, yet you remember everything perfectly?'

'How can one forget such things?'

'Don't you keep track of what is happening to Paribanu, Anwara, Monowara, Sufia, Sultana? Don't they also get carried away and raped?'

Once again, Nonigopal bowed his head. After a while he said, 'I heard about your illness. In fact I had been planning to come and see you for quite some time, but I had to make sure things were safe for my family. Before leaving, I decided to come and see you at least once. We are leaving tonight for Benapole, across the border. We couldn't sell our home and property so I have asked a cousin of Lolita's to sell it whenever he can.'

Sudhamoy realized that there was no point in trying to dissuade Nonigopal from leaving. All the same, he still could not understand what people hoped to gain by going away. If the total number of Hindus in the country decreased any further, they would only be persecuted the more. In fact, it was a no-win situation in which those who remained and those who left both lost. It was a loss for the poor, a loss for the minorities. Sudhamoy wondered exactly how many more Hindus in this country must suffer and die, to pay for the sins of the Hindus in India, both past and present. If he knew, perhaps he could have committed suicide, so that by doing so some measure of peace could accrue to the Hindus.

*

In the evening, Shafiq Ahmed's wife, Aleya Begum, came to visit them. Earlier, she used to drop in almost every day but lately many frequent visitors had stopped coming. Even Haider's parents had not come over for quite some time. Sudhamoy realized how lonely Kironmoyee had become. When she opened the door, she looked surprised at the sight of Aleya Begum, as though she hadn't been expecting anybody to visit them any more. And why should they? Their house had become a deserted waste, not fit for human habitation. Looking at Aleya Begum's smiling face, shining clothes, and sparkling jewellery, Sudhamoy wondered whether Kironmoyee felt diminished in her presence. As he did often, Sudhamoy fell to wondering whether he had been unfair to Kironmoyee. He had brought a girl from a well-to-do, educated, cultured family into an insolvent, hopeless family. Over and above that, he had deprived her of the needs of the body for the past twenty-one years. Always, it had been his own interest that had mattered more, otherwise why had he not insisted that Kironmoyee marry again. But would Kironmoyee have gone if he had asked her to? Didn't she secretly yearn for a life like Aleya

Begum's? Full of sparkle and vigour? After all she was human, and it would not have surprised him had she left. And, he supposed, that it was because of this lurking fear that he had always kept her close. He had even stopped inviting his friends over. As a result, he had become practically friendless. Not that that worried him, because what would have been worse, from his point of view, was the possibility of Kironmoyee being attracted to any one of his 'able', male friends. He tried to compensate for his shortcomings by loving her as fiercely as he could to convince her that she must not leave such love for the pleasures of the flesh. But was it possible to satisfy a person's feelings with love alone? After all these years, Sudhamoy realized that something more than love was probably required.

Aleya Begum took in the destruction in the room and Sudhamoy's semi-paralyzed condition, heard of Maya's abduction, and expressed her sympathy and her concern. At one point, she asked Kironmoyee, 'Boudi, don't you have relatives in India?'

'Yes, we do. Almost all our relatives are there.'

'Then why are you stuck here?'

'Because this is my own country.'

Aleya Begum could not conceal her surprise at Kironmoyee's answer. After all, how could Kironmoyee say as confidently as Aleya herself that this was her country? Sudhamoy understood at that moment that Kironmoyee and Aleya, despite being women and citizens of the same country, could never be regarded in the same light. Somewhere, a fine line of distinction had been drawn.

Day Eleven

It was Victory Day, the day on which Bangladesh had finally attained independence. The word independence seemed to sting Suranjan like a poisonous ant. The whole country was charged with excitement as it prepared to celebrate the momentous occasion. Military parades thronged the streets and the crowds were happy and full of good cheer. In the past, Suranjan would leave the house early in the morning on Victory Day and attend functions all over town, in between riding atop a truck singing patriotic songs. Today, he felt it had been a complete waste of time. What had he gained from the independence of the country? What independence did he have?

'Joi Bangla, Bangla'r Joi' and all sorts of encomiums showered on Bangladesh by a galaxy of poets headed by the Nobel Laureate, Rabindranath Tagore, Nazrul and Jibanananda, came to Suranjan's mind. Much as he desired to break into these songs, Suranjan did not. The enthusiasm with which Suranjan had always been charged on this occasion tried to raise its head, but he chose to crush it this time.

As he lay in bed all day, a certain desire was born in Suranjan. He nursed this secret desire with tender care and did his best to keep it alive . . . so alive that it would eventually take wing and fly. All day long he nourished his desire, watering it and tending it carefully. He watched it grow and blossom, till he was able to breathe in its fragrance. Having nourished his desire throughout the day, Suranjan finally left the house at about eight in the evening. He told the rickshaw puller to go wherever he pleased. He took Suranjan to Topkhana, Bijoy Nagar, Kakrail, over to Mogh Bazaar and finally to Romona. Suranjan glanced at the illuminated city decorations. Did the brightly lit streets know that he was a Hindu? If they got to know this, perhaps the tarred roads would split apart in protest. Today the desire that was burning in every cell and tissue of his body, had to be fulfilled somehow. Fulfilling this hunger of his might not really solve anything, but it would give him immense satisfaction. Moreover, by succumbing to it he would, at least to a certain extent, alleviate his anger, regret and suffering.

Suranjan stopped the rickshaw in front of the Bar Council and lit a cigarette. He had almost given up hope where Maya was concerned and decided to tell his parents not to expect her return. It would be easier for them if they tried to think that she had died in a road accident . . . . His mind wheeled and plunged into despair once again. Only the other day, Sudhamoy was healthy and capable of normal activities; and now he had been reduced to such a pitiful state that Suranjan could not bear to look at him. All day long, the man groaned with the pain and suffering of being deprived of his Maya. They must be tearing Maya apart, just like vultures tore carcasses apart. They must be feasting on her, he thought. Were they enjoying her flesh just as cannibals did? These thoughts stirred up a terrible pain within Suranjan. It was as though he himself was being devoured by a pack of seven hyaenas. He had not yet finished smoking his cigarette when a girl came up to the rickshaw. Her face shone in the glow of the neon lights. She appeared to have smeared her face with pancake make-up. She was around nineteen or twenty years old.

Suranjan threw away his cigarette and said to the girl, 'Come here!'

The girl pressed herself against the rickshaw. She twirled her sari about her and smiled.

Suranjan asked her, 'What is your name?'

The girl giggled and said, 'Pinky.'

'Tell me your full name?'

'Shamima Begum.'

'Your father's name?'

'Abdul Jalil.'

'Where do you stay?'

'Rangpur.'

'What's your name once again?'

'Shamima.'

The girl was suspicious now. Nobody had ever asked her what

her father's name was, or had wanted to know where she lived. What a strange customer this was! Suranjan looked sharply at the girl. Was she lying? Maybe not.

'Okay. Get into the rickshaw.'

Shamima got into the rickshaw. Suranjan asked the rickshaw puller to go to Tikatuli. On the way, he stared coldly ahead, and did not speak or look at the girl. She seemed not to notice but snuggled close to him, and chattered incessantly. Sometimes she broke into song on other occasions she would laugh wildly. But he did not react and only moved to light cigarette after cigarette. The rickshawwallah seemed to enjoy the ride. He turned to his passengers more than once and even broke into song now and again, tunelessly singing Hindi film songs. The whole city had decked itself up tonight and red and blue lights lit up the whole scene. Only Suranjan took no part in the gaiety. He was cold sober tonight, and he had planned his every action before he had set out.

He had locked his room from the outside. He had decided not to knock on the main door and disturb anyone. Silently, they walked into his room. As soon as they entered, Shamima said, 'We haven't discussed rates even once . . . .'

Suranjan motioned her to be silent, saying, 'Keep quiet . . .absolutely quiet.'

The room was still a mess. The bedsheet on his bed hung half-way to the floor. There was no sound from the room next door. In all probability, they had fallen asleep. Suranjan strained his ears to hear and heard Sudhamoy groaning. Did he know that his dear son, a brilliant student, had actually brought home a whore! Suranjan, however, did not look upon Shamima as a whore. To him, she was a girl who belonged to the majority community. He was longing to rape one of them, in revenge for what they had done to his sister. He turned off the lights in the room. He threw the girl on the floor and stripped her of all her clothes. Suranjan took quick, deep breaths, as he dug his nails into the girl's flesh. He bit her breasts, one part of his mind understanding that what he was doing was certainly not love. Relentlessly he pulled her hair, bit her on the cheek, neck and breasts. He scratched her waist, her stomach, her buttocks and her thighs with his sharp nails. The girl was only a prostitute, after all! As Suranjan attacked her naked body, the girl moaned with pain, screaming occasionally, 'O my God! I am dying of pain . . . .' Suranjan laughed with savage satisfaction. He continued to hurt her till he could do no more and then he raped her. As he moved above her, the girl thought fearfully that this must be the worst, most savage customer she had ever encountered. Just as the deer tries to escape the tiger, she somehow pulled herself away from Suranjan, grabbed hold of her sari and ran to the door.

Suranjan had cooled down now and a heavy weight had been lifted from him. The desire that had burnt in him all day was finally extinguished. Now, all he needed to do to be truly happy was to kick the girl out of the house. As the tension began to pour back into his body, his breathing grew heavier. Should he kick the girl out of the house? Naked and shivering with fright, the girl stood by the door. She dared not ask any questions, since she had been told not to talk.

Where was Maya? Had they tied up her hands and legs to rape her? Were all seven of them raping her together? Poor Maya . . . . she must have been in great pain, she must have screamed out aloud too. Once, when Maya was fifteen or sixteen, she had yelled out 'Dada . . . Dada . . .' in her sleep. Suranjan had run to her and found her shaking all over. 'Maya, what is it? Why are you trembling?' he had asked. Even after she had woken up, Maya had continued to shiver, for the nightmare hadn't loosened its hold. 'You and I had gone to a beautiful village. We were walking through lush green paddy fields, talking to each other. There were some other people too, and they would talk to us once in a while. All of a sudden there were no paddy fields. In its place was a wilderness. You were not there, and some men were coming to get hold of me. I was very scared and I kept running for my life, screaming for you . . .' Poor, dear Maya . . . . Suranjan thought of his lost sister, and his breathing quickened once again. Maya must be inside a locked room somewhere, screaming for help but no one could hear her. She must be crying, but there was no one to hear her. She was probably inside a locked room begging, pleading and crying in front of a pack of wild animals. Where was Maya? This was such a small town, and yet he did not know where his beloved sister was. Was she in a garbage bin or in a whorehouse, or had she been thrown into the Buriganga? Where, oh where, was Maya? All he wanted to do now was catch hold of the girl standing by the door and throw her out.

The girl was terrified by the way Suranjan was behaving. She put on her clothes as fast as she could and said, 'Give me my money.'

'Shut up . . . . ' Suranjan said. 'Get out, I am warning you. Get out immediately!'

Shamima opened the door, put one foot outside, hesitated, and then turned back to Suranjan with a pitiful look. Blood trickled down her cheeks as she said, 'Even if it's ten takas, please give it to me.'

Suranjan's body shook with anger. But the look in the girl's eyes softened him somewhat. She was a poor girl after all . . . selling her body to feed herself. She was a victim of a callous social system that had ignored whatever talent she may have had, and pushed her into the gutter. She could use today's money to have a meal. Suranjan wondered how often she had to skip meals. Suranjan took ten takas from his pocket and gave it to the girl and said, 'You're a Muslim, aren't you?'

'Yes.'

'You people are in the habit of changing names. Have you gone and changed yours too?'

'No.'

'Okay. You can go.'

Shamima left. Suranjan relaxed. He had promised himself he would not feel sorry for himself today. Today was Victory Day. Everyone was enjoying the fruits of an independence that was won twenty-one years ago. Today, another milestone had been achieved as well. Shamima Begum had come to Suranjan Dutta's house and had been conquered. Suranjan wanted to snap his fingers and sing a familiar patriotic song, that went, 'Bangladesh is my first and last love . . . . I'll live for Bangladesh and die for her too . . . .'

He had not mentioned his own name to Shamima. He should have told her that he was Suranjan Dutta. She would then have known that the man who had bitten her and made her bleed was a Hindu. Yes, Hindus also knew how to rape. They, too, had hands, feet and a head full of ideas. Their teeth were sharp and their nails could scratch like claws . . . . Shamima had been a mild, gentle girl . . .but a Muslim all the same. If he had been able to so much as slap a Muslim, it would have made him happy.

Suranjan tossed and turned restlessly for the rest of the night. He seemed to be in a trance, but sleep eluded him. All through the night, he was alone in the company of silence, stillness, and a terrible sense of insecurity. Today, he had wanted to take a small revenge, but had failed. He was not capable of taking revenge. All night he was tortured by vivid recollections of Shamima's face. He felt terribly sorry for her. He should have felt angry and empowered but he did not. In that case, what kind of revenge had he taken? One could even say that this was a kind of defeat for him. Was Suranjan in fact defeated? Yes, of, course, he was a loser, because he had not succeeded in tricking Shamima. As it was she was tricked by her social status. To her there was no difference between sexual intercourse and rape. Suranjan cringed in his bed, as he realized this truth. He suffered as his shame swamped him.

It was so late in the night . . . . why then was Suranjan awake? Was his whole system rotting away? It seemed as though everything inside him had been breaking down gradually, ever since the demolition of the Babri Masjid. He was actually feeling sorry for the girl whom he had torn apart with his manhood, bitten and caused to bleed profusely! If only he could have wiped away the blood from her cheeks before she left. Would he ever meet the girl again? He resolved that if he ever saw her again he would ask her forgiveness. He was hot, despite the cold weather. He threw off his quilt. The bedsheet lay near his feet in a messy roll. He put his head between his knees, like a dog.

Early in the morning he wanted to urinate, but he did not feel like getting out of his bed. As usual, Kironmoyee came and left him tea but he was in no mood to drink it. He felt like puking, and more than anything else he wanted to bathe in hot water. But where could he get hot water? In the house at Brahmapalli, there was a pond in which he used to bathe on cold winter mornings. He would have loved to bathe in the luxury of a pond . . .but where would he find one? He hated to bathe with an allotted amount of water in the bathroom. Why did life have to be so measured, so incremental?

Day Twelve

Suranjan got out of bed at ten the next morning. He was standing on the veranda brushing his teeth when he heard Khadim Ali's son, Ashraf, say to Kironmoyee, 'Mashima, you know Putu was saying last evening that a girl who looked like Maya was seen floating under the Gendaria bridge.'

Suranjan's grip stiffened on the toothbrush. A swift shudder passed through his body and he felt terribly, awfully alone. He could hear nothing from the other parts of the house, no crying, nothing. The whole house was still, unnaturally still. It was as though the slightest conversation would echo against the wall of silence that stretched through the house. No one, it seemed, but Suranjan had been living in this house for the last thousand years. All around him the city lay quiet—it had not woken up after the celebrations of Victory Day last night. He was still standing with his toothbrush in his hand, when Haider walked by. Because their eyes had met, decency called for an exchange of greetings. Haider stopped. 'How are you?' he asked Suranjan; Suranjan smiled and said, 'Fine.'

It was expected that their conversation would come around to Maya, but it did not. Haider leaned against the railing of the veranda and said, 'Yesterday, at the Rajshahi University, after the celebrations, the people from the Jamaat Camp desecrated the mass graves.'

Suranjan spat some toothpaste out on to the floor and said, 'What do you mean, mass graves?'

'You don't know the meaning of mass graves?' Haider looked at Suranjan in surprise.

Suranjan shook his head.

Haider's face darkened with annoyance. How could Suranjan, who had been at the centre of activity during the war of

204

independence, not know the meaning of mass graves. As far as Suranjan was concerned, if the people at the camp had broken the epitaphs on the mass graves, they were welcome to. They had weapons in their hands, and if they had found something to use them on who could stop them? In time they would even break the invincible Bangla, the self-acquired independence of the country and the grand country itself along with all those who had fought for her. Who could stop them? A few processions and meetings would be organized. Some slogans such as 'Jamaat Shibeer Youth Command Politics should be put to an end' would be chanted. And that would be about all. Nothing much would change because of these protests.

After his flash of annoyance, Haider had fallen silent. He appeared to want to say something. After some minutes, he spoke, 'Have you heard? Parveen is here these days. She's divorced.'

Suranjan made no comment. He was not in the least sorry that Parveen was divorced. On the contrary he was quite pleased about it. They had insisted on marrying her off to a Muslim instead of a Hindu and see where that had led them! Suranjan had already sexually abused Parveen in his mind. This early in the morning, especially while one was brushing his teeth, sexual abuse held no attraction whatsoever. But in this case, as it was all in the mind, it still had its attractions.

After a while, Haider said, 'I'll see you,' and left. Suranjan did not say anything at all.

Sudhamoy was now able to sit up. Sitting up with a pillow supporting his back, he listened to the silence that haunted the house. Sudhamoy thought that in this house the only one who had really wanted to live was Maya. If he had not fallen ill, Maya would not have had to come away from Parul's house, nor would she have been abducted in this manner. It was said that someone had seen her body under a bridge. Who would go and identify the dead body? Sudhamoy knew no one in his family would because everyone wanted to believe that Maya would return one day. If they were able to identify the body as Maya's, then the hope that she would come back in a day or two, maybe a month or two, or maybe even longer, would be shattered once and for all. There are

some kinds of hope which help keep us alive. There was so little in
life that made it really worth living, that there was no sense in
letting go of such hopes that kept life ticking over.

He called Suranjan to his room. It had been a long time since
he had done that. He asked him to sit beside him. He said in a
broken voice, 'It makes me feel ashamed to sit behind locked doors
and windows.'

'You feel ashamed? Well, I feel angry.'

'I feel very worried for you too.' Sudhamoy said.

'Why?'

'You return home so late. Haripada had come over yesterday.
The situation in Bhola has got worse. Thousands of people have
lost their homes, and many women are being raped.'

'So all this is news to you?'

'Yes, of course, it's news. That is why I am so worried about
you, Suranjan.'

'You are worried about me? Why? Aren't you worried for
yourself and Ma? Aren't you Hindus?'

'What will they do to us?'

'They will chop off your heads and fling them into the
Buriganga. Haven't you still understood the nature of the people
in this country? They'll make a snack out of a Hindu, if they find
one. And they won't distinguish between young and old, I can
assure you.'

Sudhamoy's forehead wrinkled with frowns of irritation.
'Aren't you one of "the people of this country?"'

'No, I can't think of myself as part of this country anymore. I
am trying very hard, but without any success. Earlier when
Kajal-da talked of partiality towards Muslims, I used to be upset.
I used to tell him, "Let's not waste our time estimating how much
Hindus have lost and how they have been deprived. There is much
to do in this country, we should think of all that instead." Now I've
come to realize that he was right. I am changing. It should not have
been like this, Baba . . . ' Suranjan's voice faltered.

Sudhamoy patted his son reassuringly and said, 'People are
already talking about it, protesting too. The newspapers are
publishing reports of all this; intellectuals are giving their opinions
too.'

'All this is stuff and nonsense.' Suranjan was annoyed now.

'One group has stormed the battlefield with knives and axes while the other group is replying with raised voices, and sometimes with their empty hands. This will not do. An axe has to be met with an axe. It's foolish to confront a weapon with bare hands.'

'Are you suggesting that we give up our ideals?'

'What ideals are you talking about? All that is nonsense.'

In the past few days, Sudhamoy's hair had turned even more grey. He had become a shadow of his former self, yet his mind remained firm about his convictions. He said, 'Don't forget that people are at least protesting against injustice. In how many countries are you allowed to do that?'

Suranjan did not say anything. It was his guess that the name 'People's Republic of Bangladesh' would soon be changed to 'Islamic Republic of Bangladesh'. Islamic doctrines would guide the country's way of life. Women would walk in the streets with burkhas on, and the number of men in caps and beards would also increase. Instead of schools and colleges, there would be numerous mosques and madrasas. And slowly but surely the Hindus would be slaughtered. The very thought of it sent shivers down Suranjan's spine. And, if one were to live, one would have to stay at home like an anti-social or shy person. If he saw a procession going down a street protesting something or the other, he would be expected to stay indoors because of the risk involved as far as he was concerned. Muslims could protest without the slightest hesitation, but Hindus would not be able to. Not that the present was any better. That the Hindus were being persecuted could be better said by a Muslim, rather than a Hindu himself. This was because there wasn't much of an alternative. If a Hindu chose to protest aloud, he ran the risk of having his throat slit in the middle of the night for having done so. If Ahmad Sharif committed a crime, they'd declare him guilty, but keep him alive nonetheless. On the contrary if Sudhamoy so much as said something that he should not have, they might come and murder him in the middle of the night. If the Hindus went on the warpath, not only would the fanatics react, but the modern progressive Muslims would do so as well. Suranjan laughed at the irony of it all. Progressive people actually defining themselves as Hindus and Muslims! Suranjan thought of himself as a modern man. Now he was beginning to feel like a Hindu. Once again the thought occurred to him. Was he rotting inside? He was almost convinced that he was. Sudhamoy asked Suranjan to come closer to him. He asked in a broken voice, 'Will Maya not be found at all?'

'I don't know.'

'Kiron has not slept a night since the attack. And she's worried about you too. Should anything happen to you . . . .'

'If I have to die, I'll die. A lot of people are dying anyway.'

'Now I am able to sit up. Kiron helps me to the bathroom. But unless I am completely fit, I won't be in a position to examine patients. The house rent for the past two months has not been paid. Perhaps if you got some job . . . .'

'I am not going to work for strangers . . .'

'Actually, our family . . . I mean we don't have our zamindari any more. A granary full of paddy, a pond full of fish, a farm full of milking cows . . . yes I've had a taste of all that. You have not seen anything like that and I am truly sorry about it. I have even sold all the land that we had in the village. If some of that land was still ours, we could have built a small house and somehow spent the rest of our old age there.'

Suranjan was beside himself with anger. He shouted at his father. 'Don't talk like a fool. Could you have survived in the village? Don't you realize that the village chiefs would have come with their rods and smashed your head in, just to take away all your property?'

'You should not suspect everyone. Surely there are some good people left?'

'No . . . there aren't any.'

'You are being unnecessarily pessimistic.'

'Not unnecessarily.'

'What about your friends? All these days you studied communism, joined movements and discussed these subjects with like minded people . . . . Aren't they good people?'

'No, none of them are. They are all communal.'

'Are you becoming communal yourself?'

'I am. This country is making me communal. I am not to be blamed.'

'This country is making you communal?' Sudhamoy sounded incredulous.

'Yes this *country* is.'

Suranjan stressed the word *country*. Sudhamoy fell silent. Suranjan looked at the broken things in the room. Bits and pieces of glass were still lying on the floor. Wouldn't these shards pierce their feet? They had pierced their hearts already.

Suranjan stayed in bed all day. He did not feel like going anywhere, nor did he feel like talking to anyone. Should he go and take just one quick look at the body that been found under the bridge? Should he look at the soggy, bloated form of Maya, if, in fact, it was her body? No. He decided he would not go anywhere today.

Late in the afternoon, he got out of bed and began pacing around in the courtyard. Suddenly, he decided there was something he had to do. He went into the house and brought out all his books and scattered them on the ground. From inside the house Kironmoyee thought he must be sunning the books to drive out the silverfish. *Das Kapital*; the thoughts of Lenin, Engels, Marx and Morgan; Gorky; Dostoevsky; Tolstoy; Jean Paul Sartre, Pavlov, Rabindranath, Manik Bandyopadhyaya, Nehru; Azad; books on sociology, economics, politics and history, books the size of bricks and those much smaller . . . . When he had gathered them all in the courtyard, he began tearing the pages from them and scattering them on the ground. When he was done, he lit a matchstick, and set fire to the whole bunch. Just as fundamentalist Muslims flare up the moment they see Hindus, so did the fire when it found the paper. The courtyard was filled with black smoke. The smell of burning paper brought Kironmoyee out of her room. Suranjan smiled and said, 'Do you want to warm yourself by the fire? Why don't you come along?'

In a weary voice, Kironmoyee asked, 'Have you gone mad?'

'Yes, Ma. All these days, I was a good boy. Now, I've decided to become a madman. Unless one is mad, there is no satisfaction.'

Kironmoyee stood at the door and watched Suranjan's flames of sacrifice. That she should rush to the bathroom and fetch water to douse the flames, did not occur to Kironmoyee. Against the thick dark flames, Suranjan's body could hardly be seen. It looked, Kironmoyee thought, as though Suranjan himself was on fire.

Inside the house, it dawned on Sudhamoy that his brilliant, studious son, who until now had provided the antidote for poison, was now devouring the poison himself. All those long hours of lying in bed, having heated arguments with his friends, abusing Muslims and now burning books . . . . Sudhamoy realized how wounded and full of pain Suranjan was. He had been hurt by his family, society and above all his country, and today he was burning himself in the flames of an inferiority complex.

Suranjan was delighted by the blaze. All over the country, this was how they were burning Hindu homes. But was it only homes and temples they had burnt? Hadn't they burnt the hearts and minds of the Hindus as well? Suranjan was determined not to cling to Sudhamoy's idealism anymore. Sudhamoy was a believer in the ideology of the left and Suranjan had grown up on his dogma. But not anymore. Why, he had heard leftists abuse Hindus as bastards! Suranjan's eyes, stung by the smoke, filled with tears. Were these tears of sorrow, or were they merely because of the smoke?

He was glad when the flames died down and nothing was left of his books but ashes. In the recent past his books had irritated him a great deal with their spurious ideas and principles. He was sick and tired of these principles. If at all, he would love to kick these principles with all his strength. Why should he alone stick to such beliefs? Most people sipped from the cup of knowledge, they never drank from it. Why should he alone stupidly drink deep from the well of knowledge?

At the end of the sacrifice, Suranjan longed to sleep. Try as he might, he could not sleep. He kept thinking of Ratna. He had not met her for a long time and wondered how she was. He thought Ratna's deep dark eyes were so expressive that there was no need for her to say anything. She must be hoping that one of these days Suranjan would knock on her door. Together they would sit and talk about their lives over cups of tea. As he lay in bed, Suranjan decided to call on her that evening. He would tell her, 'Why should it be only me who comes to do the visiting? Don't others feel like doing the same?'

Suranjan had the strange feeling that one depressing evening, Ratna would suddenly come to him and say, 'I felt very odd, Suranjan, so I thought I would come and see you.' It had been a long time since anyone had kissed Suranjan. Parveen used to kiss him. She would hold him tight and say, 'You are mine, only mine. Today I'll kiss you a hundred times.' If Kironmoyee entered the room unexpectedly they would quickly move away from each other. But, despite all this, Parveen had ultimately chosen to marry a Muslim, in the hope that all sorts of problems would be avoided. With Ratna there was no complication of caste or creed. It was at her feet that he would lay his unhappy life. He must call on her this evening, he resolved. He would wash all the dust and grime from his body, put on a freshly washed shirt, and go to Ratna's house. Just then there was a knock on the door. He opened it to find Ratna on the doorstep. She looked beautiful; she wore a dazzling sari, and her hands were bedecked with bangles that tinkled as she moved them. She smiled and he was filled with wonder at her beauty and her softness. 'Come in, please come in . . . ' Even as Suranjan ushered her in, he noticed a handsome young man standing behind her.

Where could he ask her to sit down? The room was in such a wretched state. All the same he gave her a broken chair to sit on. Ratna smiled and said, 'Guess who I've brought with me?'

Suranjan had not met Ratna's brother and wondered if he was the young man. Ratna's voice tinkled like the bangles she wore as she said, 'This is Humayun, my husband.'

A turbulent hurricane swept across his heart. The last tree that he had hoped to cling to for survival had been uprooted right in front of him. He had been hoping to make up for his wasted life by settling down with Ratna and here she was with a Muslim husband! Suranjan's face darkened with anger. How could she have done this to him! And to think she had the gall to bring her husband over. He was certainly not going to sit around with Ratna and her handsome, perhaps even rich, husband and make small talk in his poor, damaged room. Nor did he want to shake hands with them and ask them to visit again. To hell with these social niceties. Brusquely, he turned to his guests and said, 'I am afraid I have to go out on some urgent work. I don't have the time to talk to you.' Surprise and outrage showed on their faces; quickly apologizing for the intrusion they left. Suranjan banged the door shut and stood with his back to it. He stood motionless for a long time and only stirred when Kironmoyee came into his room and asked, 'Have you returned the money that you had taken on loan?' The word 'loan' seemed to have a poisonous edge to it. He glared at Kironmoyee's face without replying her.

Suranjan felt suffocated. His room seemed to be like an iron box, out of which there was no means of escape. He walked on the veranda for a while, but nothing could prevent the sadness that deluged him like the monsoon rain. Kironmoyee came in with a cup of tea, which she put down on his table silently, as was her usual practice. She left. Suranjan made no attempt to help himself to the tea. He lay in bed for a while and then got up again. Should he go to the bridge and check on the body? The thought of it was intensely disturbing. Suddenly an image of the body floating in the drain outside the house rose before his eyes. The whole house was as silent as an ancient pool. Just as water insects skate above the still waters of such pools, the three members of this house padded about the decrepit premises, never colliding, never communicating.

Without warning Kironmoyee rent the silence of the house. She wailed and the sound of her crying seemed to rise from the depths of the earth. So intense and unbearable was the sound of her wailing that Sudhamoy sat up in shock and Suranjan came running. He found her standing with her head against the wall, and crying uncontrollably. Suranjan knew that these were not tears that could be stopped. These were tears that had to be released. For days and nights together she had kept these tears in check but the dam had burst and the only thing they could do was wait for the waters to drain away. Sudhamoy sat still with his head bowed. Her wild lament had pierced his heart and left him helpless. She sobbed and she sobbed but nobody asked her why she cried, there was no need to ask, and nobody consoled her because nobody could.

Suranjan had been standing at the door of the room. Now, he walked in silently, lest his footsteps disturb Kironmoyee's tears. The house of his dreams had fallen to pieces, it had been burnt to cinders. Just as Kironmoyee had shocked them all with her sudden wailing, so too did Suranjan as an anguished wail burst forth from him. 'Baba . . . .'

Sudhamoy looked at him, utterly shocked. Suranjan grasped his father's hands in his and said imploringly, 'Baba, I've been thinking of only one thing all last night. I know you will not accept my suggestion but I'm begging you to. Please, Baba . . . please. Come, let's go away.'

Sudhamoy asked, 'Where?'

'India.'

'India?' Sudhamoy looked disgusted. He looked as though his son had abused him, as though he had not expected him to even mouth such a word.

Kironmoyee's tears slowly abated. Her body shook convulsively, and she slumped to the floor. Sudhamoy continued to look disgusted. 'Is India your father's home or your grandfather's? From your family, who the hell stays in India? Do you want to run away from your own homeland . . . doesn't it make you feel ashamed?'

'What homeland are you talking about, Baba? What has this country given you? What is it giving you? What has this country of yours given Maya? Why does my mother have to cry? Why do you groan all night? Why don't I get any sleep?'

'Riots break out in all countries. Aren't there riots in India? Aren't people dying there? Have you kept track of the number of people who've died?'

'If it were riots I'd understand, Baba. These aren't riots. It is simply a case of Muslims killing Hindus.'

'So you call yourself a Hindu?' Very agitated, Sudhamoy tried to get out of bed. Suranjan pushed him back and continued to plead with his father, 'However much we call ourselves athiests, however much we call ourselves humanists, those people out there will call us Hindus. They'll call us bastards. The more we love this country, the more we think of it as our own, the more we'll be forced into a corner. The more we love the people of this country, the more they will isolate us. We cannot trust them, Baba. You have treated so many of them free of cost, but how many of them have come and stood by you in your time of distress? Sooner or later all of us will be shoved under a bridge to die. Baba, please let's go . . . let us go . . .'

'Maya will come back.'

'Maya will not come back, Baba. Maya won't come back.' Suranjan's voice was thick with grief.

Sudhamoy fell back on his bed. His body went limp and he

muttered weakly, 'If I could not protect Maya, whom then will I protect?'

'Ourselves. Do we have to stay back only to mourn the loss of what we have already lost? And that too in the midst of such troubled times? We have no security, nothing, please let's go away from this place.'

'What will we do there?'

'Anything. What are we doing here? Are we very well off? Are we very happy?'

'It will be a rootless existence . . .'

'What will you do with your roots, Baba? If your roots are so powerful then why are you hiding behind locked doors and windows? Will you stay this way all your life? It has become a habit with them to break into our houses, or to kill us. I feel ashamed to live like a rat, Baba. It tears me apart, but my hands are tied. When I am angry am I able to burn down a couple of their houses? Why should we just sit and watch ourselves being humiliated and devastated? If a Muslim slaps me, why don't I have the right to slap him back? No, Baba . . . let's get out of here, please let's.'

'The situation is cooling down somewhat. Why are you so worried? You cannot let yourself be carried away by your emotions.'

'Cooling down? All that's completely misleading. Deep down the cruelty and the maliciousness will always remain. They wait for us with bared nails and teeth, with traps that we'd never suspect. Why have you forsaken your dhuti for pajamas? Why don't you have the independence to wear your dhuti? Come, let's go away . . . .'

Sudhamoy roared in anger. 'No, I will not go,' he said. 'You go if you want to.'

'You won't come?'

'No . . .' Sudhamoy turned his head away in disgust.

'I am asking you again, Baba . . . . Please let us go away,' implored Suranjan.

Sudhamoy repeated firmly: 'No.'

The word 'No' fell like an iron rod on Suranjan's back.

Suranjan had known all along that his efforts would be thwarted. Sudhamoy was so stubborn, so strong in his convictions, that there was no way in which you could shake him. He could be kicked and battered, but he would not uproot himself from the soil of his homeland. The snakes and scorpions of that soil might bite him, but he'd still fall back on it.

Kironmoyee had stopped crying and was now gazing raptly at the picture of Radha-Krishna in a corner of the room. She seemed to be praying to Lord Krishna, for a life free from worries and anxieties, insecurity, torture and death.

Suranjan seemed doomed to swim alone up the stream of hopelessness. Night set in. Late in the night a crushing wave of loneliness broke over him. He could call nobody his own. There was absolutely no one to depend upon. He was an alien in his own country. His own understanding, insights and sense of the world were dwindling to nothing. It seemed as though he had almost come to the end of his road ...

It was as though everyone was waiting for some awful end to their lives. Now it was no longer for Maya, but for his own future that his heart quaked with fear and apprehension. They were all alone, so alone. Sure, acquaintances and Muslim friends visited them once in a while, but no one could give them the reassurance that it was safe to live in this country. Nobody could say: 'You need not worry. Don't cringe with fear. You can walk about safely, work fearlessly, laugh heartily and sleep peacefully.'

All through the night Suranjan tossed and turned in his bed.

Day Thirteen

Suranjan finally slept in the last hours of the night. In his sleep he had a strange dream. He was walking all by himself beside a river. As he walked, a wild wave came and swept him into the depths. He was caught in a whirlpool and kept sinking gradually. He wanted to live, but there was no one to pull him to the shore. As he kept sinking into the fathomless waters, Suranjan found he was sweating.

Just at that moment a gentle hand touched him and woke him up. Desperate and terrified as he drowned in the whirlpool with no one to hear him, he had, at the very last moment, discovered a hand that was reaching out to rescue him. He gripped it with all his strength. And as he came fully awake, he discovered that what he was holding onto was the strong hand of Sudhamoy.

With his wife's help, Sudhamoy had walked upto Suranjan's bed, where his son screamed in the grip of a nightmare. Now, as he sat holding his son, his eyes glowed with a new light.

'Baba?'

A mute question thumped inside Suranjan's heart. It was almost dawn and through the cracks in the window, sunlight streamed in. Sudhamoy said, 'Come, let us go away.'

Suranjan could not conceal his surprise. 'Where will we go, Baba?' he asked.

Sudhamoy said, 'India.'

And his voice cracked as the shame swept over him. But he had said it, he had forced it out, he had compelled himself to say that they would go; and he had realized that that was the way it would have to be because the strong mountain that he had built within himself was crumbling day by day.

216

MORE ABOUT PENGUINS

In every corner of the world, on every subject under the sun, Penguin represents quality and variety—the very best in publishing today.

For complete information about books available from Penguin—including Pelicans, Puffins, Peregrines, and Penguin Classics—and how to order them, write to us at the appropriate address below. Please note that for copyright reasons the selection of books varies from country to country.

In India: For a complete list of books available from Penguin, please write to *Penguin Books India (P) Ltd., 706 Eros Apartments, 56 Nehru Place, New Delhi, 110019.*

In the United Kingdom: For a complete list of books available from Penguin in the U.K., please write to *Dept E.P., Penguin Books Ltd. Harmondsworth, Middlesex, UB7 0DA.*

In the United States: For a complete list of books available from Penguin in the U.S., please write to *Dept BA, Penguin,* Box 120, Bergenfield, New Jersey 07621-0120.

In Canada: For a complete list of books available from Penguin in Canada, please write to *Penguin Books Ltd, 2801 John Street, Markham, Ontario L3R 1B4.*

In Australia: For a complete list of books available from Penguin in Australia, please write to the *Marketing Department, Penguin Books Ltd, P.O. Box 257, Ringwood, Victoria 3134.*

In New Zealand: For a complete list of books available from Penguin in New Zealand, please write to the *Marketing Department, Penguin Books (NZ) Ltd, Private Bag, Takapuna, Auckland 9.*

In Holland: For a complete list of books available from Penguin in Holland, please write to *Penguin Books Nederland B.V., Postbus 195, NL-1380AD Weesp, Netherlands.*

In Germany : For a complete list of books available from Penguin, please write to *Penguin Books Ltd. Friedrichstrasse 10-12, D-6000 Frankfurt Main 1, Federal Republic of Germany.*

In Spain: For a complete list of books available from Penguin in Spain, please write to *Longman, Penguin España, Calle San Nicolas 15, E-28013 Madrid, Spain.*

In Japan: For a complete list of books available from Penguin in Japan, please write to *Longman Penguin Japan Co Ltd. Yamaguchi Building, 2-12-9 Kanda Jimbocho, Chiyoda-Ku, Tokyo 101, Japan.*